## The diver came from the far side of the rig

Like an astronaut on the moon, he advanced in a series of slow-motion bounces. He carried an underwater knife, razor-sharp on one edge, saw-toothed on the other. Blinkered by the mask, the Executioner didn't see him until he was almost within striking distance.

For an instant they stared at each other. Then Bolan kicked his flippers against the ocean floor, raising a cloud of sand that boiled up between them, allowing him to move backward, his speargun coming up just as a desperate lunge with the blade split the front of his wet suit.

But the warrior had his distance, and the speargun's powerful spring recoil jolted his arm. The diver vanished behind a cloud of inky blood, dropping his knife.

Bolan dived to retrieve it. It was then that the second man attacked. Strong fingers wrenched at his breathing tube and the concertina rubber tore away, dragging the life-giving tube and mask back over Bolan's head.

# MACK BOLAN®
## The Executioner

| | |
|---|---|
| #106 Run to Ground | Stony Man Doctrine |
| #107 American Nightmare | Terminal Velocity |
| #108 Time to Kill | Resurrection Day |
| #109 Hong Kong Hit List | Dirty War |
| #110 Trojan Horse | Flight 741 |
| #111 The Fiery Cross | Dead Easy |
| #112 Blood of the Lion | Sudden Death |
| #113 Vietnam Fallout | Rogue Force |
| #114 Cold Judgment | Tropic Heat |
| #115 Circle of Steel | Fire in the Sky |
| #116 The Killing Urge | Anvil of Hell |
| #117 Vendetta in Venice | Flash Point |
| #118 Warrior's Revenge | Flesh and Blood |
| #119 Line of Fire | Moving Target |
| #120 Border Sweep | Tightrope |
| #121 Twisted Path | Blowout |
| #122 Desert Strike | Blood Fever |
| #123 War Born | Knockdown |
| #124 Night Kill | Assault |
| #125 Dead Man's Tale | |
| #126 Death Wind | |
| #127 Kill Zone | |
| #128 Sudan Slaughter | |
| #129 Haitian Hit | |
| #130 Dead Line | |
| #131 Ice Wolf | |
| #132 The Big Kill | |
| #133 Blood Run | |
| #134 White Line War | |
| #135 Devil Force | |
| #136 Down and Dirty | |
| #137 Battle Lines | |

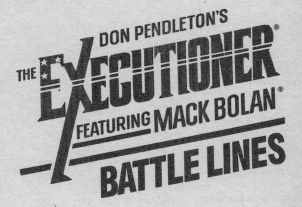

DON PENDLETON'S
THE **EXECUTIONER**®
FEATURING MACK BOLAN®

BATTLE LINES

A GOLD EAGLE BOOK FROM
**WORLDWIDE**.

TORONTO · NEW YORK · LONDON · PARIS
AMSTERDAM · STOCKHOLM · HAMBURG
ATHENS · MILAN · TOKYO · SYDNEY

First edition May 1990

ISBN 0-373-61137-4

Special thanks and acknowledgment to
Peter Leslie for his contribution to this work.

Printed in U.S.A.

Wars may cease, but the need for heroism shall not depart from the earth, while man remains man and evil exists to be redressed.

—Mahan: *Life of Nelson*, 1897

Few men are born brave; many become so through training and force of discipline.

—Vegetius: *De Re Militari*, iii, 378

I simply do what has to be done, no matter the circumstances. If that is bravery or courage, then so be it.

—Mack Bolan

# THE
# MACK BOLAN®
## LEGEND

Nothing less than a war could have fashioned the destiny of the man called Mack Bolan. Bolan earned the Executioner title in the jungle hell of Vietnam.

But this soldier also wore another name—Sergeant Mercy. He was so tagged because of the compassion he showed to wounded comrades-in-arms and Vietnamese civilians.

Mack Bolan's second tour of duty ended prematurely when he was given emergency leave to return home and bury his family, victims of the Mob. Then he declared a one-man war against the Mafia.

He confronted the Families head-on from coast to coast, and soon a hope of victory began to appear. But Bolan had broken society's every rule. That same society started gunning for this elusive warrior—to no avail.

So Bolan was offered amnesty to work within the system against terrorism. This time, as an employee of Uncle Sam, Bolan became Colonel John Phoenix. With a command center at Stony Man Farm in Virginia, he and his new allies—Able Team and Phoenix Force—waged relentless war on a new adversary: the KGB.

But when his one true love, April Rose, died at the hands of the Soviet terror machine, Bolan severed all ties with Establishment authority.

Now, after a lengthy lone-wolf struggle and much soul-searching, the Executioner has agreed to enter an "arm's-length" alliance with his government once more, reserving the right to pursue personal missions in his Everlasting War.

## 1

Flames streaked from the jetliner's starboard engine pod ten minutes after the plane leveled out at twenty-six thousand feet.

None of the passengers noticed at first. They were flying through thick cloud. And a twenty-man trade delegation, relieved to be free of the no-liquor restrictions in fundamentalist Tehran was celebrating its return home by hitting the duty-free vodka and slivovitz as though there was no tomorrow. The cabin-crew girls, good-humoredly fending off the tipsy delegates, were trying to distribute the shrink-wrapped, prepacked lunch trays from a couple of trolleys in the center aisle. Most of the other travelers—there were fewer than fifty of them, businessmen, minor diplomatic officials, a couple of families—watched with tolerant amusement.

Suddenly the plane lurched violently to the right. A woman passenger glanced out the double-glazed port and gave a cry of alarm. At the same time, a heavy shuddering shook the fuselage, a plastic glass full of red wine tipped over on one of the pull-down tables, splashing its contents into the gangway, and smoke billowed into the cabin around the door leading to the flight deck.

They already knew about the flames up there.

The jet engine slung beneath its backswept delta wing was a long way behind their field of vision, but the General Warning lights above the console separating the captain from his copilot had blazed red five minutes before. Almost at once the Engine Fire Alert warning on the starboard side of the console flickered and then steadied into a menacing amber glow.

The copilot swore, ramming the starboard engine fire-extinguishing lever fully open. But the warning lights remained bright, and now they could see, reflected on the underside of the cloud fragments whipping past the Plexiglas windows, a pulsating crimson radiance that grew more brilliant every moment.

The captain was calling up air traffic control at Ankara, reporting engine failure and asking if there was a field nearer than the Turkish capital to set down the crippled jet. His eyes, wide with anxiety, scanned the needles trembling across the dials and gauges arrayed on the panel in front of him as he listened to the controller's reply. "It'll have to be on one," he said. "I'm getting zero reaction from the extinguisher activity.... We have some kind of flame-out, and I'm going to have to shut down on that side." He turned his head to call over his shoulder to the navigator. "Go through into the cabin and take a visual. Try to stop them from going out of their skulls. Feed them a line about fuel starvation."

The navigator nodded and pushed himself to his feet as he fanned the smoke sucked in through the air circulation pressure system away from his face. He coughed, shoving open the door to the passenger cabin.

There was panic in there now.

The cabin crew milled up and down the gangway, snatching back the lunch trays they had put out and stowing them in their trolleys. The members of the trade delegation, suddenly sober, fought to regain their seats. Somewhere in back a woman was screaming hysterically, and a senior stewardess, her voice high-pitched with fear, called out instructions for passengers to fasten their safety belts and remain calm. "There is no cause for alarm," she lied, "but we have a problem with one engine, and although the plane is designed to fly safely on a single engine, we may have to make an emergency landing."

"You can say that again, baby!" the navigator muttered to himself, edging into an unoccupied row of seats and peering through the window of an emergency exit. The whole airframe was shuddering uncontrollably as the damaged engine spit streamers of fire alternating with vivid flashes of violet light. The muffled whine of the portside jet was drowned by the roaring, thumping racket hammering from the pod below the starboard wing.

The navigator pressed his forehead to the cold glass and stared down. Through a gap in the cloud cover he could see, five miles below, the iron-hard, craggy contours of a barren mountain range. "Sweet Jesus!" he muttered.

He shook his head, exchanged a despairing look with the chief stewardess and returned to the flight deck. "She'll stay up in the air on one," he said to the pilot, "but you're not going to find a level space big enough to put her down in fifty miles. Wouldn't it be better to nurse her along and try to make Ankara?"

The pilot gestured helplessly at the instruments. Some of the needles were swinging wildly across the dials. "I can't understand," he began, "why the damned—"

A series of sudden, sharp detonations shivered through the flight deck. Pieces of incandescent metal flew past the cabin windows. One large fragment scythed through the stressed skin of the fuselage near the jetliner's tail, and the scream of the doomed engine was lost in a blast of decompression. A stewardess and several passengers, shredded on the sharp edges of the breach, were sucked out into the void.

The pilot's hand was still closed over the knuckle grip of the starboard power lever, cutting off the fuel supply to the engine, when the plane's right wing dipped earthward, the nose dropped and the jet stalled out.

From his cockpit five thousand feet higher in the sky, the pilot of a Chinese-built F-7 Airguard pursuit plane watched the jetliner drop like a stone through the clouds, spewing fiery debris.

From that altitude, the explosion when it hit the bare rock of the mountainside looked no more impressive than a spark struck from a steel. "I would be surprised," the pilot of the Mach-2 fighter reported via his radio, "if there were any survivors."

## 2

"There were no survivors," Brognola said tightly. "The plane was a short-haul twin-engined Ilyushin, on the milk-run from Tehran to Sofia, in Bulgaria, with a thirty-minute stopover in Ankara to land passengers with no Eastern bloc visas."

"And the carrier?" Mack Bolan asked.

"Local. Pan-Caucasus Airlines. They link Tehran and Damascus with Sofia, Bucharest and a handful of cities in the southern part of the Soviet Union."

"They serve Beirut?"

"I guess so." Brognola's eyebrow lifted. "Why?"

Bolan shrugged. "Just that Beirut's a likely center if there's any bad news involved."

The two men were sitting outside a waterfront café in Istanbul—Hal Brognola, the troubleshooting Fed who bossed the NSC's Sensitive Operations Group, and Bolan, the crusading loner whose life was dedicated to the pursuit of terrorists and criminals, both domestic and international. Across the dark water of the Golden Horn, the lights of pleasure boats shone brilliantly through the dusk. "Is there bad news involved?" Bolan queried after a moment.

Brognola poured coffee from a miniature pan with a long copper handle. The jacket of his cream seersucker suit was as creased and rumpled as the features wrapped around his unlit cigar. He had arrived in the city only that morning, and he was still suffering from jet lag. "Could be," he replied.

"Yeah, if the plane was sabotaged. Maybe, if it crashed on account of engine failure."

"Maybe?"

"It's a complex story, Striker. We'll know more when the aviation inspectors have finished examining the wreckage."

"Fill me in on the story so far."

"PanCal's Ilyushins are powered by turbofan engines that are a design steal from the CFM-56s used on some of the later Boeing 737s," Brognola said. "The blueprints for the fan air-exhaust ducts, the thrust reverser cascades and the tail cone could be carbon copies of the Boeing motor."

"This technical detail must tie in somehow—otherwise you wouldn't be giving me the specs, right?"

"Just so you realize why we think there may be parallels between this crash and one that totaled a Midland Airways 737 in Britain at the beginning of '89."

Bolan nodded. "Forty-four dead. I remember. And if I don't see the connection, you're gonna tell me."

"The Brits' plane stalled out on approach," the big Fed explained. "One engine on fire, the other unaccountably screwed up. According to the experts, the odds against both engines failing at the same time were millions to one. Yet it happened."

The Executioner looked up assessingly. "And the investigators?"

"They found that there's been a fuckup in maintenance. The wiring on the alarm circuits was crossed, so the warnings alerted the pilot to a fire in the wrong engine. In fact he killed the good one, and there wasn't enough power left in the burning unit to keep the plane in the air."

"You figure that's what happened here?"

"It's a possibility. Among others. But why was one of the engines on fire in the first place?"

"You tell me."

"There could be two reasons, neither of them necessarily sinister," the Fed went on, answering his own question. "Flame-out for one, flood-out for another. In each case there's a risk of fire when the pilot attempts to reignite after the engine has cut out.''

"Flame-out I know," Bolan said, "but not flood-out."

"A danger in this particular type of turbofan. It can be produced by a combination of low temperature, heavy precipitation and a dense overcast. When the Ilyushin took off from Tehran, the conditions were 8° Celsius, persistent rain, and cloud cover from two thousand to ten thousand feet. Prime conditions, the experts tell me, for building up a possible cutout later in the flight.''

"Okay," Bolan said. "Optimum weather conditions and crossed wires. Tough for passengers and crew. What else?''

"Tough enough if it's an unfortunate coincidence. Tougher still if one of those conditions has been, shall we say... organized.''

"Or both?''

"Or both.''

"You can't sabotage the weather," Bolan objected.

"No, but you can cross wires. And there are other ways of provoking a fire in a jet engine.''

"For instance?''

"Weaken a titanium turbine blade so that it shears sometime during the flight. A wildcat blade lost under full power could run amok and disintegrate the fan. Then, if the protective cowling was unable to contain the damage, you'd wind up with fire among the fuel lines. A rogue blade would explain the flashes and shuddering the pilot reported to Ankara control.''

"Look, Hal," Bolan said, "you didn't bring me here to explain the intricacies of modern jets. What's really on your mind, guy?''

The café terrace was on a deck that extended over the water. Brognola tossed the unlit stogie into the wavelets swilling against the wooden piles from the wash of a passing pleasure boat. He settled his bulky frame more comfortably in the rattan chair. "We had a man aboard," he said briefly.

"Ah!" Bolan's interest quickened at once. He leaned his muscular forearms on the table. "A spook?"

"Not exactly. Nothing to do with the Company, either. More of an industrial investigator—an oil engineer, name of Shapiro."

The warrior looked surprised. "No other sensitive material on the passenger list?"

"Uh-uh. A Bulgarian trade delegation. Businessmen, sales reps, family stuff. Arab embassy guys from a couple of small states on the Gulf."

"No military attachés? What was the trade delegation aiming to move?"

"Agricultural hardware. No, Shapiro was the target . . . *if* there was a target."

"According to whether it was sabotage or an accident, okay. So, what was Shapiro into?"

Brognola sighed. "That's what fazes me, Striker. It was routine stuff, a simple checkup. It's just that the Administration likes to keep tabs—especially as the whole damned world revolves around the oil situation today."

"Go on."

"Okay, we're into economics. Romania, for starters. With the Ploesti oilfield and the Danube refinery ports of Galati and Braila, the country chalks up, next to the Arabs, one of the world's most important petrochemical industries. The Russkies have Baku, over on the Caspian Sea, which is almost as big. But Bulgaria ain't so lucky. Place was almost entirely agricultural until after World War II. All she has now, oilwise, is one small site at the southern end of the coastline. You read me?"

"Loud and clear so far," Bolan said.

The big Fed allowed himself a grin. "There *is* a message!" he promised. He fished another cigar from his breast pocket and bit off the end. Music from one of the brightly lighted launches blared across the water from the far side of the Golden Horn. Reflections shivered and broke up on the dark waters as a police patrol boat chugged past. "Given the situation," Brognola continued, "nobody was surprised when the Central Committee in Sofia, following reports of a huge underwater find three hundred miles out in the Black Sea, ordered the construction of a giant oil rig out there."

"I'm not surprised. All these communist-ruled countries have had their economy crippled, and now there's a scramble to recover," Bolan said. "There is more?"

"Shapiro had been asked to check out the type of platform, the probable yield and stuff like that. End of story."

"Yeah," the warrior said thoughtfully. "End of story. For Mr. Shapiro, anyway. You figure . . . ?" He left the sentence unfinished.

"It comes down to the investigators' report, when we get it," Brognola said. "They reckon the crack-up was a genuine accident, and it's flowers to Mrs. Shapiro and our sincere condolences to the widow's family."

"And if they don't?"

"If they don't, if someone thinks it worth the loss of an eight-million-dollar aircraft and the death of seventy-five innocent people just to stop Shapiro making his report . . . then in that case—" Brognola paused significantly "—there must be something very special indeed about that oil rig."

**3**

Mack Bolan wasn't in the sniper's sights long enough for the first shot to score.

He was climbing up from the business quarter near St. Sophia to an Arab enclave on higher ground not far from the famous Topkapi Museum when the rifleman made his play. Bolan's contact lived in one of the bazaars beneath the cypresses surrounding that huge complex, and the route led through a network of narrow streets, past the Haseki Hamami Baths and the sixteenth-century Mosque of Sokullu Mehmed Pasha and finally across a small public garden where the ground was dusty and the leaves of unwatered lemon trees hung limp in the heavy evening air.

The killer fired from behind a stone trough that was still used for watering mules and donkeys loaded with produce for the stallholders in the bazaar. The trough was at the far end of a fifty-yard alley, and although it was well suited for a quick getaway, it was badly chosen from a tactical point of view, since the target, striding past the mouth of the alley, was only in view long enough for that one shot.

Bolan heard the echoed whip-crack in the very instant when a shower of stone chips stung his cheek. The gunner had delayed one-tenth of a second too long before he squeezed the trigger, and his slug furrowed the corner of the wall.

A heartbeat later the Executioner was prone beneath the nearest lemon tree, an automatic pistol clenched in his right hand. The gun was a Beretta 93-R, which had been tucked into the waistband of his Levi's beneath his loose sweat-shirt: in the close, humid atmosphere of the city, garments that would conceal a shoulder rig or a holster for the heavier caliber weapons he favored were not practical.

A street lamp supported on an iron bracket cast a pool of light over the cobblestones at the nearer end of the alley. Bolan aimed carefully and shot it out.

Another lamp illuminated the far end of the lane and the trough the gunman had used as cover. Bolan wasn't sure if the sniper was still crouched down behind it—and he couldn't risk using the shadowy patch now ahead of him to flush the killer out while that second light still burned. Raising himself on both elbows, he drew a two-handed bead and coaxed the autoloader's trigger toward him.

It took two slugs from the 9 mm gun's magazine to kill the second street lamp.

Bolan was on his feet and running while shattered glass from the reflector was still tinkling to the ground. An orange flash, followed by another, printed the image of the stone trough against the dark as rifle shots echoed again. One flew high and wide, but the second was near enough to fan the rivulet of blood congealing on the Executioner's cheek. He raced another twenty feet and flung himself flat beside the wall of the alley before a fourth shot zipped over his head and screamed off the ironwork hinging a shutter somewhere above. The killer was still behind the trough, all right!

But no longer in business after that last round. Bolan had blasted off a fourth shot himself as he fell, not expecting to score but hoping that he might rattle the rifleman enough to make him run for it. The ruse paid off. The warrior heard a scraping, shuffling sound, the graze of leather on stone and then a quick patter of receding footsteps. The man had crawled out from behind the trough, made it to an adjoining lane and taken off. The Executioner scrambled to his feet. Like an avenging shadow, he plunged in pursuit.

A wider lane ran left and right on each side of the trough. Ten yards along the right-hand branch, there was an arch with a flight of steps curving down behind it. A shadow, splashed against the wall bordering the stairway, showed the way the killer had gone.

Bolan ran through the arch and took the steps three at a time.

His hunch that the man gunning for him was inexperienced had paid off. In a pursuit situation such as this—one man with a handgun chasing another toting a rifle down a narrow alley—all the odds are on the pursuer. By the time the man in front has stopped, swung around and brought the barrel of his long weapon to bear on his adversary, a pistol on semiauto will have choked out half a magazine. Bolan knew that he was in no danger; he could risk closing up until his quarry found cover again.

The alley, punctuated by steps every few yards, continued to twist downhill. Bolan closed up until he could see the killer—a slight figure wearing a red tarboosh and a striped shift over jeans and leather-soled sandals. The gun looked like a Kalashnikov, probably one of the older AKs churned out on a production line in Moscow or Prague and sold in millions all over the Middle East.

The man was running desperately, weaving from side to side as he heard the pounding footsteps behind him. Bolan tried a ranging shot, firing on the move. The tarboosh spun off the killer's head, hit the wall and rolled down the next flight of steps. He gave a yelp of alarm and leaped out of sight through an open gateway.

Lights had come on behind the shutters of some of the flat-roofed houses sprawled over the hillside on either side of the lane. A window was thrown up, and an angry voice called something unintelligible into the night. Bolan stopped, flattened himself against the wall, then sidled through the gateway.

Yet another flight of stone stairs, short, wide and shallow, led to the covered section of the Arab market. The place was dark and deserted—a chaos of stalls and bivouacs and counters and empty barrows roofed over with a glass canopy supported on cast-iron pillars. Somewhere among them, the killer was hiding.

Bolan lowered his body to a squatting position, sat on the top step and began easing himself down stair by stair. The nearest street lamp was fifty yards up the lane, so he reckoned there'd be no silhouette for the marksman to aim at. But he couldn't move entirely without noise.

The flash and the blast, when it came, was much nearer than he expected. The concussion, thunderclapping his ears from no more than fifteen or twenty feet away, galvanized him into action. Full-length, he rolled, barreling down to the market entrance as the ricochet whined skyward.

He lay flat behind a stack of empty crates, breathing in the odor of rotting fruit while his heavy lungs steadied to a normal rhythm. Above and behind him, the twanging quarter-tones of Arab music filtered from the upper story of a house overlooking the lane.

Beneath the glass roof of the bazaar, the silence was gradually invaded by everyday sounds. Bolan heard the ticking of his watch, the faint rasp of his breath, a drip from a leaking faucet somewhere in the distance. Among the girders supporting the roof, a bird rattled its wings.

He tensed, aware of a different noise, a new one. In the darkness ahead, the feeblest rustling scrape. Supporting himself on his elbows, he extended his right arm, the wrist cocked so that the barrel of his gun was free to range right or left. He heard the sound again, louder this time, but still barely above the threshold of hearing. Was it a rat, a prowling cat? Or the whisper of cloth against wood or stone as a hunter, oriented already in the Executioner's direction, positioned himself for the kill?

Bolan felt around him with his left hand. Squashed fruit and limp vegetable leaves littered the slick cobbles. His fingers slid over tomato skins, touched a rubbery pepper that was slimy at one end, sank through the rind of an overripe melon. Farther away he encountered a curve of hardwood, rimmed with iron. The wheel of a handcart. Now that his eyes were accustomed to the darkness, he could dimly make out its silhouette where it sat, parked in the aisle between two rows of stalls, with its shaft resting on the ground.

Swiftly he ran over the options. The killer had fired five times, but there was no percentage in tempting him to exhaust his magazine and rush him while he reloaded; if the Kalashnikov's curved magazine was fully charged, there'd still be twenty-five rounds in there. Bolan figured on a different kind of ploy—have the hitter give his location away.

Holding his breath, moving only a half-inch at a time, he edged toward the handcart. When he could touch the shaft, he raised it experimentally a fraction. The cart moved easily on its wheels. The music of the Arab strings above the lane had now been replaced by a group of reedy wind instruments accompanying a female singer with a high, keening voice.

Bolan relocated the melon, dug in his fingers and a thumb hard enough to give him a good grip, and drew back his arm. Then he flung the overripe fruit high and wide in the direction of the rustling noise he heard.

The melon splatted against something hard and then dropped, falling with a loud metallic clatter among what could have been the stock of a tinsmith's stall. Involuntarily, almost as a reflex, the rifleman blazed off two shots in quick succession.

The warrior had what he wanted—now he knew approximately where the gunman was holed up. As the rifle shots cracked out, he hurled himself across the aisle, to end up kneeling on the far side of the cart. He raised the shaft as high as he could and shoved hard.

The aisle ran down a very slight incline, but it was enough to allow the cart to get under way. The shaft dropped to the stone floor, the wheels grated on the cobbles and the cart rumbled for a good ten yards before it slowed and stopped.

The killer had to assume that the cart served as a cover, and he pumped four shots into the woodwork while it was still moving.

That was all Bolan needed. He stood in the center of the aisle with the Beretta in 3-shot mode and pounded a trio of 9 mm fleshshredders in below the muzzle-flashes of the rifle.

A sudden cry, choked off short, a stumbling fall, and the bazaar was silent again except for an angry fluttering up among the girders.

The Executioner approached warily. The killer's body was a darker blur sprawled across the dark lane between the stalls. When he was certain there was no movement, Bolan switched on a penlight that had been clipped in his hip pocket. He saw a mop of black hair, brown eyes staring sightlessly at the glass roof and, a mouth open in a soundless scream above the bloodied ruin of the rifleman's chest. The man couldn't have been more than twenty-two, twenty-three years old.

Bolan thrust the Beretta back in his waistband and picked up the assassin's gun. It was a Kalashnikov, all right. There was no bayonet lug, no cleaning rod, and the furniture was laminated wood. Bolan whistled softly to himself.

Bulgarian manufacture.

He looked over his shoulder. He heard voices. Folks from the neighboring houses, alerted by the shooting, had gathered in a nervous bunch at the top of the short flight of steps leading down to the bazaar. Bolan still had a ten-minute walk in front of him before he made the house where he was to meet his contact. He got out of there.

The fact that the rifle was the Bulgarian model intrigued him. Sure, he'd been in Bulgaria when he got Brognola's coded request for a meet in Istanbul, and the frontier between the two countries was less than one hundred miles away. But he'd made damned certain he was clean when he crossed it. In any case his investigations in Bulgaria hadn't progressed enough for anyone to consider eliminating him.

In the shadowy reaches of the international underworld where Bolan was forced to stalk his prey, Bulgaria was known as a kind of spaghetti junction where clandestine arms shipments, dope deliveries and the active members of terrorist cells, whatever their political color, were permitted freely to pass from East to West—and vice versa if the pace became too hot. This was because Bulgaria remained the most hard-line, the most Stalinist of all the Eastern bloc states, and anything that was likely to destabilize Western society was good news to the Bulgarian bosses. *Glasnost* and *perestroika* were still dirty words in Sofia.

It was the Bulgarians who organized the failed attempt on the life of Pope John-Paul II in Rome, the Bulgarians who poisoned the sharp tip of an umbrella in order to murder an emigré broadcasting anti-Communist propaganda from London.

And it was the Bulgarians who signed an end-user certificate for a shipment of deadly chemicals originating in North Korea via a mysterious armament company known as Kwang Jin Trading.

It was this consignment that concerned the Executioner.

The chemical was Methyl Phosphonyl Difluoride, or MPD, the basic ingredient of Sarin, a nerve gas developed by Nazi scientists in World War II, which provoked death within minutes of contamination.

Before the chemical warfare treaty was signed and a ban on manufacture imposed in 1983, forty thousand pounds of MPD refined at Britain's Porton Down research station had been sold to Iran. One-tenth of that amount had been sold to Iraq, who was alleged to have used it in the Gulf War. But there was still one hell of a lot of it around someplace.

Bolan was trying to trace the portion that had found its way to North Korea and from there back to the Balkans.

So far the shipment seemed to have vanished—which was odd, because the stuff was so dangerous that it couldn't be moved without the most stringent, and therefore noticeable, safety precautions.

The illegal transfer even of a small amount of such a deadly substance would certainly be important enough to the consignees to warrant the removal of any snooper threatening to reveal the secret. But Bolan's researches so far had never raised the question of MPD, of chemical weapons or even the Kwang Jin Trading company. The few dissident contacts he had in Bulgaria had merely been requested to check out arms transfers in general. So, why the assassination attempt on Bolan?

The man he was to meet tonight, Suleiman Ben Yassir, was in fact the first prospect who might conceivably know something about MPD and the fate of that twenty-ton delivery made six years before to Iran.

Ben Yassir was a technician who had worked for the Atomic Energy Organization at a secret research center near Esfahān, in central Iran. He had also put in a year at the Amirabad nuclear complex near Tehran, where the Iranian authorities were secretly attempting to reassemble a plutonium reprocessing plant built during the last days of the Shah and partially destroyed in the revolution that brought Khomeini to power.

Like most of the scientists working on the project, Ben Yassir, who was himself a Palestinian, had fled the country once the fundamentalist nature of the regime became evident. But Bolan figured he was more likely than anyone to give him a lead on the missing chemicals.

How it would all dovetail with anything Hal Brognola wanted followed up, he had no idea. He had left the big Fed with a promise to rdv again at noon the following day, when the air-accident investigators would have turned in more Intel on the Ilyushin disaster.

If the plane crash was what the insurance assessors called an act of God, and the presence on board of Brognola's operative no more than a tough coincidence, then the file could be closed on that one. On the other hand, if it was sabotage . . . well, then it became a matter of priorities.

Bolan was not an official member of Brognola's team. He had once headed an undercover operations group secretly funded by the U.S. Administration, but now he was strictly a loner, keeping authority at arm's length, with the free-

dom to accept or reject any unofficial request for his help—
and with the knowledge that he would instantly be dis-
owned if anything went wrong.

But Brognola, apart from being the only link between
Bolan, the Sensitive Operations Group and the White
House, was also a friend. There could be, therefore, a con-
flict between the Executioner's duty to his buddy and his
commitment to the antiterrorist crusade that occupied all his
waking hours.

The hell with it. He'd attend to that when the crunch
came . . . and somehow he had a hunch, a gut reaction that
there might *be* a crunch. For the moment though, it was wait
and see: wait until the investigators reported; see what Suleiman Ben Yassir had to say.

The Palestinian's house was at the far end of a passage-
way that led to a small paved courtyard where a fountain
played. He was a short, neat man with bright eyes and a
fringe of black beard outlining his jaw. Bolan reckoned he
was maybe fifty years old.

"It is kind of you to come and see me," he said formally
after the warrior had presented his letter of introduction,
"but I fear that I may not be able to be of much help. As a
chemical engineer, I was employed mainly on the redesign-
ing of the Amirabad plutonium plant and in the research
section at Esfahān. And your MPD, so far as I know, was
stocked at Būshehr, on the Gulf."

"On the contrary," Bolan said equally politely, "it is
good of you to receive me. But look, as a chemical engineer
you must at least have heard gossip about this lethal material. Anything you can tell me, anything at all, would help.
Even an unconfirmed rumor might give me a lead. Did you
hear, for example, whether or not the MPD had been pro-
cessed yet into Sarin gas?"

Ben Yassir poured coffee and pushed a silver filigree bowl
containing honey cakes toward the warrior. They were
squatting in the oriental fashion on cushions, on opposite
sides of a low table, in a small tiled room hung with Ispa-

han rugs. "You have to understand," the scientist said, "that the old men running the country today are religious maniacs, intellectually blocked back in the sixth century, when The Prophet was around. They don't really understand today."

"Sure," Bolan said, "but they don't mind taking advantage of—"

"Modern technology? No, of course not. But in some ways they're scared of it. The Shah commissioned a study, for example, with the idea of building twenty nuclear power plants. Khomeini killed the project because there was nothing about nuclear power in the Koran. Then they heard during the Gulf War that Iraq had the bomb. Pakistan had the bomb. And all of a sudden nuclear energy was in favor. Iranian engineers were sent to train in Pakistan. Abdel Qader Kahn, Pakistan's top nuclear scientist, was sent to Iran to advise on the Būshehr plant. Top-quality uranium ore was imported from South Africa. All this, naturally, just for industrial use."

"Yeah," Bolan said. "It's no more than a coincidence that the by-products can be used for nuclear weapons."

"Indeed." Ben Yassir drained his coffee and set down the cup. "Like my colleagues, I have been asked to go back. A great deal of money was offered. We all refused—the situation seemed too unstable to risk a long-term commitment. But Feridun Fesharaki, one of the Shah's scientific advisers, remembers Khomeini telling him: 'It is your duty to build this bomb. Our civilization is in danger, and we have to do it.'"

"Okay," Bolan said. "Now, about the MPD—"

"What I say," the Palestinian cut in, "is not really so much of a digression. Because part of the Pakistan deal, I heard, was to set aside a secret fund that would be used to finance the purchase of specially designed five-hundred-pound bombs at a cost of fifteen thousand dollars each, and—"

A wooden shutter closing off a small window set high up in the wall burst inward with a splintering crash. Glass shattered and fell. The perforated snout of a submachine gun poked through the wreckage and belched flame.

Bolan's shouted warning was drowned in the appalling clamor of the stuttergun. His fighter's reaction, honed in half a lifetime of combat situations, hurled him sideways as the SMG spit fire.

Suleiman Ben Yassir wasn't so lucky. The down-slanting deathstream smashed the coffee cups, split the marble table, and then, angling upward, flailed across his spare frame. Bludgeoned off his feet by the impact of a dozen .45-caliber hollowpoints, he thudded against the wall and dropped. A rug, dislodged by his hurtling body, folded forward and fell, mercifully covering the gory pulp where his chest and throat had been.

Bolan was out the door, down the passage and running for the entrance, the Beretta in his hand. But when he made it to the lamplit courtyard, he saw it was hopeless: the only way out was into the street, and he would have to race around the entire block to get to the alley behind the house from which the killer had fired. And by then he'd be long gone.

So far as the scientist was concerned, that was a shut-end situation. Bolan had seen enough dead men to know when there was no point trying to help. There was already a babble of voices from the surrounding buildings. He shoved the autoloader back into his waistband and kept up a relentless pace.

**4**

A couple of murder attempts within one hour, one failed and the other successful. Two assailants, using different guns.

Did they also have different targets?

Or were both assassins supposed to ice Bolan himself, with Ben Yassir cast as the fall guy who happened to get in the way?

Uh-uh, Bolan thought. The SMG had been specifically targeted on Ben Yassir; once the Palestinian had fallen, the gunman had taken off, although he could easily have sprayed the rest of the room with a longer burst and wasted the Executioner.

Ben Yassir, then, had been killed to stop him talking.

Bolan considered why he hadn't been killed at the same time to stop him listening. Was it because the second gunman thought the first would already have attended to that, and he wouldn't have known the warrior by sight?

Hell, no, that made no sense at all. Could the two murder attempts, in that case, be unrelated?

A possibility perhaps, but why would anyone want Bolan out of the way at this time and in this place when he himself hadn't known twenty-four hours earlier that he was going to be there? How come any organization, however efficient, could be that wise to his plans, could stake out a killer—even an inexperienced one—to ambush him?

The rawness of the young rifleman Bolan had killed could be explained if he was the only talent on hand at the time.

But that still left far too many questions and not enough answers, the Executioner thought the next morning, waiting for Brognola at the waterfront café.

The Fed was late arriving. Wrestling with the problems while he waited, Bolan gazed idly at the floating traffic choking the sunlit waters of the Golden Horn. Skiffs, launches, motorboats, ferries chugged past in each direction. Beyond the brightly colored small craft cramming the jetties, pleasure boats with glassed-in decks maneuvered to show sightseers the spires and domes and minarets of Istanbul's fifty-five mosques. Eastward, where the Golden Horn ran into the Bosphorus, a Soviet corvette lay at anchor on the far side of the Galata bridge.

When Brognola finally showed, he was accompanied by two men—a short, trim-looking man in a summerweight suit and a tall, shambling character with a bald head and a bristly mustache. They appeared from behind a line of red and yellow tourist buses and hurried down a broad flight of steps to the café.

Brognola handled the introductions. The short man was a Company spook specializing in sabotage situations, and the other was an officer from the accidents branch of the Turkish civil aviation authority. Bolan was presented as Mike Belasko, a newspaperman—an alias he frequently used.

"It doesn't look so good," Brognola said heavily when four beers had been ordered.

"Sabotage?"

"I would think. Mr. Mazuklav here—" he nodded at the Turkish official "—had a team out there within two hours of the crash. Flew them there from a military field on the far side of Ankara. And what do you think they found?"

"You tell me," Bolan said.

"Nothing! That is to say they found wreckage strewn over more than a square mile of mountainside. They found bodies. They found smashed-up elements from the cargo hold.

What they didn't find was what they were looking for. Both black boxes were missing.''

"Both?"

"The one recording movement of the controls, and the tapes of the conversation on the flight deck up until the moment of the crash."

"Couldn't they be hidden someplace? In a tree? Lodged in some crevice? Maybe they rolled a long way?"

"The slope is perfectly bare," Mazuklav said. "An enormous slant of bald rock, broken up here and there with patches of shale, but no vegetation, no ground cover, no hiding places at all."

"Someone had been there before them," said the CIA man, whose name was Zabriski. "Someone who paid no mind to all those broken bodies, who didn't waste time searching for survivors, who didn't even trouble to loot the burst-open baggage. Someone who wanted the black boxes and nothing else. There's mud at the foot of one of those shale patches. We found fresh tire tracks there. A big off-roader."

"Someone who was tracking the plane," Bolan said slowly, "or who knew at least roughly where it was expected to crash. Someone who figured there might be recorded evidence in the boxes that would prove the wreck was no accident."

"Right."

Bolan turned to Brognola. "This cross-wire routine, I guess that's being checked out?"

"They were crossed, all right.... Anyway, that's what the investigators' preliminary report says."

"Crossed wires on the pilot lights doesn't necessarily mean sabotage, of course," Mazuklav remarked. "It's happened before, more than once, with inexperienced or careless maintenance crews."

"Yeah, but when the black boxes are also missing...?"

"Exactly."

Bolan sipped his beer, staring across the Bosphorus at the suburb of Üsküdar. A jetliner was planing down above the sprawl of medieval houses and minarets and high-rise apartment blocks on the far side of the mile-wide waterway. "It seems," he said, "kind of a roundabout way to sabotage a jet. Complicated, too. And not even one hundred percent sure, since the pilot might have gotten wise to the fact that he'd activated the fire extinguishers on the wrong engine. Why not use a bomb? A wad of Semtex packed into a transistor radio, with a detonator operated by radio or atmospheric pressure. They could set it to go off at a certain height."

"The plane had reached its operational height some time before," Zabriski commented. "And a bomb leaves traces— fragments of charred material embedded in the bodies, that sort of thing. Also, even in a one-horse town like Tehran, it's easier these days to buy yourself a technician and have the dirty work done during a preflight checkup than trying to smuggle something through an airport security control, even if it's only Semtex, which doesn't show on the X-ray scanners."

The Turkish officer nodded. "Tehran and Sofia handle between four hundred and eight hundred outgoing flights a week," he said.

Zabriski had hoisted rimless shades to view a Romanian oil tanker steaming south through the straits. "There is one other thing," he said. "Air traffic control at Ankara told us there was an unidentified aircraft flying through the zone at the time of the crash. It was five thousand feet higher than PanCal's Flight PC803. No flight plan had been filed, and they couldn't raise the pilot on the radio. According to its radar signature, one of the guys there figured it might be an F-7M pursuit plane."

Bolan whistled. "An Airguard? The Chinese-built Mach-2 fighter? But that's the ship the Iranian air force hope to get. I heard they ordered fifty of them."

Zabriski inclined his head. "You got it," he said.

"What route was the F-7 taking?" Bolan asked. "Where did it go after the jetliner stalled out?"

"It was flying on a parallel course," Mazuklav replied. "After the crash, it banked and flew out over the Black Sea. Then it dived down below the radar screen, and they lost it."

"You can't organize a precise time for a turbine blade to shear," Brognola said. "For my money, that ship was shadowing PanCal's Ilyushin. Then, as soon as it hit the deck, the pilot reported the location and peeled off, leaving a ground crew to drive in and pick up the black boxes and any other damning evidence there was."

"Okay," Bolan said. "Ankara didn't hear any talk about turbine blades?"

"Uh-uh. Just the engine fire and the fact that it wasn't out."

Bolan turned to Mazuklav. "And the engine itself? Could your experts tell the difference between deliberate sabotage and the damage suffered by a piece of heavy machinery falling five miles and hitting solid rock at its terminal velocity?"

The Turk smiled. "But certainly. Shearing and compression leave quite different traces. But we won't know whether there *was* a broken blade in the turbine until tomorrow. The starboard engine had broken free and dug itself a grave in a patch of soft shale. It takes time, you understand, to disinter this kind of material, even with the most modern equipment. And it's wild country, a long way from anywhere."

"Yeah," Bolan said. "Where *did* the Ilyushin crash?"

"Over in the east. Not far from the Russian frontier and quite near our border with Iran. The area is...well, it's one of the foothills leading up to Mount Ararat."

The Executioner smiled wryly. "The Mount Ararat of Biblical fame. But I'll bet there was no olive branch in the beak of *that* bird!" he said.

Later, in the small hotel where Brognola was holed up, Bolan voiced his concern. "I don't know how you read this, Hal, but to me it doesn't add up. I mean, okay, it looks like we know how it happened, and we know, according to you, *why* it happened. But everything points to Iran, when logically, surely it should be the Bulgarians responsible?''

''Let's not oversimplify, Striker,'' Brognola said. ''Iran has been anti-Communist as well as anti-West recently. It's clear the Bulgarians don't want to get tagged with this— otherwise they wouldn't try to make it look like an accident. And I guess, if the accident label doesn't stick, it'd suit them well enough to have Iran blamed. If they wanted Shapiro killed for some reason, surely the Iranians would have organized it while he was in the country?''

''You could be right. Why *was* the guy in Iran, anyway?''

''Search me. Shapiro actually had contacts among the Ivans, believe it or not! My guess is that he had been checking out something to do with that rig among the Soviet oilmen at Baku, on the Caspian. The southern shore of the sea is only fifty miles from Tehran.''

Bolan was thinking of something else. The mention of Iran had switched his attention back to the even more puzzling events of the night before.

He thought of the sentence started by Suleiman Ben Yassir and so tragically cut short by the lethal blast of an automatic weapon. *Specially designed five-hundred-pound bombs at a cost of fifteen thousand dollars each.* Financed, the Palestinian had said, by a secret fund connected with a nuclear treaty between Iran and Pakistan.

But at that price, what kind of bombs could they be? It was hardly likely they would be nukes when there were missiles available to carry warheads any distance required. Bolan compiled a list of possibles: terrorist bombs, car bombs, bombs to be dropped in the old way from aircraft.

Or should he be thinking of bombs designed for chemical warfare?

Ben Yassir had been killed before he could say. But his revelation followed Bolan's attempt to steer him back to the subject of chemical warfare. The question was whether a connection existed between the mysterious bombs and the missing shipment of MPD.

If it did—and this was the most puzzling of all—how in hell did the parties responsible know that the warrior was interested and in what manner had they unearthed where he was going to be the previous night?

Bolan shook his head. He could answer none of those questions.

"Hey, Striker! You're not with me!" Brognola's husky voice broke into his reverie. "Something on your mind, huh?"

"You could say that."

"Fill me in."

Bolan had already briefed the Fed on the general outline of his investigation, but Brognola knew nothing of the dramatic events of the night before. Bolan quickly updated him.

"You know something," Brognola said when he had finished. "It sings loud and clear to me that you got yourself a mole in there someplace. Somewhere along the line, a body's turning you in."

"A mole?" Bolan frowned. "But I'm not working with anyone, Hal. The few people in Bulgaria that I contacted know nothing of the chemical angle. Nothing at all."

"Here's what we'll do," Brognola said after a moment. "You feed me every goddamned thing you know about this missing chemical—names, dates, places, people, the lot. Add details of the contacts you made who *don't* know anything on that side of the story, and I'll have a multiple trace run on the Stony Man computer...checking out every one of those elements against all the others. Shit, if that kind of cross-checking don't come up with something, nothing will!"

The command room at Stony Man Farm, in Virginia's Blue Ridge Mountains, from which Bolan himself had once directed covert antiterrorist operations, was keyed in to one of the world's most sophisticated data bank systems. But frankly he doubted, in this case, whether even that computer could provide the kind of Intel he wanted. But it was always worth a try. "Thanks, Hal, that'd be great," he said.

"In return for which," the Fed continued smoothly, "I'll ask a small favor from you."

Bolan gave him a level look. "Shoot!"

"I'd like you just to take a look—a simple outside check—at this damned oil rig," Brognola said. "As a personal favor."

"I'd considered doing just that, but right now I'm kind of tied up with this MPD deal," Bolan said.

"Your nerve gas can wait two, three days," the Fed interrupted. "You said yourself the stuff's already been floating around between Iran and Korea for who knows how long—and you ain't getting any place. You said so. I can fix a rented boat at Sinop, on Turkey's northern coast. All I want you to do is sail out there and take a look-see. If it seems ten on ten, we forget the whole thing and assume maybe Shapiro was out of his skull. Or maybe stumbled on some different slimebucket scheme. There's enough in Bulgaria."

"And if I think something smells?" Bolan asked.

"You make your report to me. If it looks scary in any way, I send in a penetration agent to make an on-the-spot analysis, and by that time you're back on your gas warfare deal. That's it—nothing more."

The Executioner nodded slowly. "Okay, you've convinced me."

"I'm grateful, Striker. And look, if it's a question of—"

Brognola broke off in midsentence as a bulky man in khaki uniform sprigged with gold strode into the bar where they were sitting. A heavy-caliber automatic was holstered at his waist. Two more men stood outside the entrance, cradling Uzi submachine guns.

The bulky man lifted the flap of his holster and approached the table. "Colonel Ecevlic," he announced, bowing stiffly. "Istanbul Police Department, crime investigation unit." He turned to the warrior. "Mr. Bolan, I believe? We are inquiring into two shootings last night in the Cagaloglu bazaar district. Each is being treated as a murder. A number of witnesses testify that you were seen, armed, in the area at the material times. I must ask you, therefore, to accompany me at once to the central police station."

"You're arresting me?" Bolan queried, astonished.

"Not yet," the colonel replied. "Let's just say there are certain questions we should like to put to you."

5

Mack Bolan knew a stacked deck when he saw one. He knew something about Turkish prisons, too. And this was a case where one and one made three; those two items of information at once suggested a third.

He knew he had to get out of there, fast.

Five people, one of them a woman of fifty, had picked him out of a lineup at the central police station. He had never seen any of them before, and he doubted if any of them had ever seen him before. But they had been well briefed, and probably well paid...although their task had been made easier by the fact that Bolan was the only man in the lineup to weigh over two hundred pounds, the only one with blue eyes and the only one a couple of inches over six feet tall.

The authorities, of course, would claim that the woman was among the group of neighbors huddled at the top of the stairway when he left the bazaar. But it was highly unlikely that she would genuinely have been able to single out a man briefly seen on a dark moonless night without some official help, but her testimony would shore up and lend respectability to the "evidence" supplied by the others—as shifty a group of rent-a-mob villains as Bolan had seen in a long time.

The murder weapon that had blown away Suleiman Ben Yassir had yet to be located, Colonel Ecevlic told the warrior, but the Kalashnikov found by the body of the young rifleman in the market was covered with his fingerprints.

Bolan doubted that very much, as he had drawn on a pair of thin cotton gloves before he'd handled the gun. But since the whole thing was a setup, it would have been easy enough to lift a set of prints from his hotel room, photograph them and introduce them together with sworn testimony that they had been discovered on the rifle.

It was true of course that he *had* wasted the kid with the AK. But he didn't aim to argue the legal definitions of self-defense in a Turkish courtroom. Nor did he wish to waste time dreaming up replies to whatever they threw at him on the Ben Yassir killing.

He was not sure whether Ecevlic and his men were in on the scam. There was a chance they were being fed the Intel from outside and really believed he had decked the Palestinian. But it wasn't a chance he would have laid money on . . . not when everything else smelled so much, not when it was becoming obvious that Brognola was right and there must be some kind of mole burrowing away somewhere.

No, with the cards dealt the way they were, there was only one way he could go.

Out.

But how to get out was . . . well, that was something else. Right now Bolan was in a nine-by-nine with seven other men, a bench covered by a filthy blanket and a cracked toilet that didn't flush.

He reckoned Brognola would be pulling strings like crazy—at the consulate, at the Turkish foreign office, in foreign newspaper bureaus. But so far he had heard nothing. And he wasn't so dumb as to believe that the accused had the right to call his lawyer or receive a visit after an arrest in this neck of the woods.

Most of the men in the cell were vagrants or petty thieves, but there was one very cool dude wearing high-profile threads who was in on some charge connected with prostitution, and an unshaven, tousle-headed dropout as grimy as the others but who spoke a language Bolan could recognize.

His name, he told the warrior, was O'Riley. He was an Australian who had lived most of his life in San Francisco. He had already been held for five weeks.

"On what charge?" Bolan asked.

O'Riley snorted with laughter. "Charge? That's a good one, mate, that is! They keep you here as long as they want, and one day, if you get lucky, they tell you what the sentence was. You're the week's lucky winner if you even get to see the inside of a fucking courtroom."

"You can't buy your way out?"

"Not even if you have money. Not if they want to keep you."

"And do they?"

The Australian shrugged. "Search me. Depends if they wanna show trial, to show how upright the administration is."

"So, what's your line, guy?"

"Smuggling," O'Riley said briefly. "I got busted running stuff ashore in the Turkish part of Cyprus."

Bolan went on full alert. "What did you move? Dope? Arms?"

"Hell, no. I wouldn't mess with that shit." The voice was scornful. "Each way there, you're helping stupid bastards to kill each other."

"So, what were you hitting?"

The smuggler grinned. "Kentucky sour mash aftershave!"

"Come again?"

"Alcohol in the form of liquor is forbidden in Moslem countries. You know that. But not in the form of perfumery. And plenty of Arab tycoons like to spoil their wives, even if they are in purdah. You dig?"

"There's a glimmer," Bolan said. "Go on."

"Cologne, toilet water, after-shave, you name it—most of the big houses market a maximum size to attract the oil sheikhs. Four-forty-five milliliters or fifteen ounces. That's near enough what you'd call a fifth, right? Well, after I've been the rounds, Caron, Givenchy, Chanel and the rest, they find they're running new brand names on the jumbo sizes. Like Jack Daniel's, Johnnie Walker, John Jameson. Homing now?''

"Off the ground and flying."

"Normally I'd hike the merchandise from Italy, land it in Cyprus and have the hired help run it through eastern Turkey to Iran. But I did it once too often, and the law caught a squeal."

"Tough break," Bolan said. "I have to get out of here. I'll need your help. Play it right and you'll be free, too. You in the game?"

"Right on, sport," the Australian said.

"I don't aim to waste cops who might, just might, be on the level. That's not my scene. But anything else is on. You read me?"

"Loud and clear. I said you can't buy your way out. What I didn't say, you can buy your way in. In a manner of speaking."

"I'm listening."

"What I mean, you can purchase a confrontation with what they call an examining magistrate..."

"Okay."

"Meaning you get a rundown on the evidence stacked against you. That gives you a chance to say you didn't do it. And after that they sling you back in here, and you start waiting again. But at least you get the fucking stink out of your nostrils for a half hour—and if you strike lucky, you can maybe bribe a guard and sink a cup of real coffee."

The last meal Bolan had was already barreling in the pit of his stomach at the fetid stench of the cell. "We'll do it," he said.

"There's one disadvantage."

"Name it."

"You need money."

"Money I have."

"Jesus! Don't say it so *loud!*" the Australian warned. "These sewer rats'd shred you if they thought there was a single dollar up your ass. The cops didn't take it off you when they brought you in?"

"They took my billfold, my ID and all the other papers, lifted a weapon I happened to be carrying—"

"Weapon?"

"The kind that packs 9 mm parabellums in a box magazine. But they didn't find my reserve supply of the folding stuff."

O'Riley's stubbled face expressed disbelief.

"Let's just say I am an illusionist," the warrior offered. In fact the money was stashed in the hollow heel of one shoe that could be slid outward to reveal the cavity. But he wasn't going to come across with the whole story until he knew more about the Australian. The guy was in poor shape; he smelled, his sleeveless denim jacket and jeans were filthy and he wore no shoes. But the eyes in his dirt-seamed face were bright and intelligent...and, hell, if he'd really been in that hellhole for five weeks . . . Bolan let it go. His instincts told him to trust the man. Okay, he was a smuggler, but he wasn't pushing the kind of garbage that destroys lives. And whichever way he played it, the soldier had to have backup. He didn't really have a choice. "You've bought this confrontation routine before?" he asked.

"That's affirmative."

"Okay. Now—the room they take you to, the stairways, the windows, the judge's desk, the number of guards—I want to know it all. So, give me the rundown."

O'Riley started talking.

"Can you fix it so that we *both* go before this magistrate at the same time?" Bolan asked a half hour later.

"I guess so. If the money's right."

"It will be."

"So, what did you have planned?"

Bolan told him what he had in mind. "It's long on risks and short on guarantees," he said when he had finished.

"There's no way to know if the plan will fly. But one way or another, headfirst or feetfirst, my nose tells me I have to leave here."

"Welcome to the club," O'Riley said.

"If you want to pack it in," Bolan pursued, "feel free to say so now, with no hurt feelings either side."

"You have to be joking," the smuggler concluded.

There was no guard to bribe until dawn the following day, when a battered aluminum pail of some watery stew would be handed into the cell. Bolan spent the most disagreeable night of his life leaning beside the Australian against a dank stone wall, surrounded by the muttered curses of the sweating, malodorous derelicts and the high-pitched, keening complaints of the pimp. Only the absence of immediate fear lifted the experience above his worst memories of the steaming hell of Vietnam.

While it was still dark, he maneuvered two hundred-dollar bills out of his shoe and passed them to O'Riley. "One to the guard for quick service," he murmured. "The other in reserve for the confrontation. After that, the plan as written—but mostly we'll be playing it by ear, okay?"

"Join the wrecking crew!" O'Riley replied in a whisper.

When daylight filtered into the cell through the barred window high up in the wall, the pimp was lying dead on the floor beside the cracked toilet bowl. Apparently he had been drowned. Most of the flashy threads adorned various members of the vagrant population.

"You see what I mean," was O'Riley's only response.

THE EXAMINING MAGISTRATE was a slender dark-skinned man of around sixty, with thinning hair and a pince-nez perched crookedly on his nose.

He sat behind a wide desk on which there were three different colored telephones and a single sheet of typescript. A uniformed screw stood behind him, and there were two guards, ordinary patrolmen drafted in for custodial duties, in back of Bolan and O'Riley. The prisoners' hands had been cuffed behind their backs before they left the cell.

"The case against each of you two men is damning," the magistrate said. "However—" he glanced down at the typescript "—if I must detail individually the counts on which you will be charged, and outline the evidence supporting them . . ."

The dry, husky voice droned on. Bolan took in the details of the room. The tall, narrow, shuttered windows. The two upright chairs between them and the desk. The Browning automatics carried by all three guards. The door behind the magistrate. The wider, heavier door they had come through, with another guard outside it, his Uzi SMG ready to fire.

It was almost dusk. They had had to wait all day for the soldier to collect. "We do it right at the beginning," Bolan had briefed the Australian, "and we do it hard. We hit them before they start expecting us to sing pity-poor-me, while the guy is still reciting his piece. Surprise is the name of the game."

"Got it," O'Riley said.

The office, as the smuggler had reported, was on the second floor. On the far side of the shutters there was a twenty-foot drop to a courtyard fronted by the police headquarters' administrative wing, a baroque pile with a pillared portico where crime prevention was a matter of computer software and steel filing cabinets.

And where chauffeurs waited by fat-tired limos to ferry home the chiefs who had been sticking pins in wall maps the whole hardworking day.

The courtyard was surrounded by formal gardens—the police chiefs were relieved to see the bright colors after eight hours' contact, even at second hand, with the seamier side of life—and one of the flower beds was immediately beneath the windows of the room where O'Riley and the Executioner were listening to a catalog of their supposed sins.

The magistrate had been talking for perhaps ninety seconds when Bolan uttered a quiet "Okay" from the side of his mouth.

He turned swiftly on his heel, took three quick steps, and exploded into action. Body twisting with the snap of an uncoiled spring, he flashed his left leg out and up in the *mawasha-geri* roundhouse kick favored by the masters of *Shotokan* karate. His foot slammed against the temple of the guard behind O'Riley with the force of every muscle in his body concentrated at the exact point of impact. The man dropped to the floor like a felled tree.

At the same time, the Australian had whirled around and dashed at Bolan's guard. Before the guy's hand could close over the butt of his holstered Browning, O'Riley's bullet-shaped head smashed into his face, butting the bridge of his nose with crushing power.

Half-stunned, the guard threw up his hands involuntarily as blood sprayed from his fractured nose and his eyes filled with tears.

Bolan took a running jump at the desk and hurtled over it feetfirst, spilling the magistrate out of his chair before he collided with the screw and brought him tumbling to the floor.

Cursing, the man struggled to his feet, clubbing the warrior with his left hand while he dragged the automatic free with his right.

But O'Riley had already pulled the gun from his gory victim's holster. The smuggler's body was contorted as he brought his manacled hands around above his right hip, but the Browning was grasped firmly between them and it was pointed straight at the screw. "Drop it," O'Riley grated.

The screw's gun thudded to the floor.

Bolan swooped on it. The magistrate, cowering in the kneehole of his desk, was shouting. The main door burst open, and the guard with the Uzi, alerted by the noise, stood there for a tenth of a second, the SMG nosing right and left, seeking a target.

The warrior hosed a couple of shots over the man's head by way of a counterargument, and he ducked out of sight, calling for help.

The Australian had run to the first guard Bolan knocked out and lifted the bunch of keys from his belt. Bolan raced over and took them. The square-shanked handcuff key was easy to identify. He freed O'Riley, passed him the key and reached out his own shackled wrists. The cuffs clicked open and fell.

A pounding of feet and a confused shouting outside the office signaled the approach of police reinforcements. Bolan jerked his head at the Australian, then picked up one of the upright chairs and leaped for the windows, smashing through glass and splintering wood before he dropped from sight.

The flower bed was immediately below. Automatic sprinklers, actuated at dusk, spiraled a fine spray over the plants, softening the earth. Even so, the impact, as he flattened geraniums and zinnias and snapped branches from an oleander, jarred the breath from his body. He rolled through the curtain of mist, sucking in air, and came up on a strip of damp grass separating the bed from the driveway. O'Riley, cursing volubly, was close behind.

The nearest limo, a black Toyota with a custom-built body, was parked fifty yards away with its motor idling. The chauffeur stood by the open driver's door. In back, a feather of smoke from the tailpipe brushed a red taillight glowing against the dark.

The fugitives raced toward the car.

Behind them, livid brilliance pulsed over the facade of the building as the guard with the SMG leaned out the shattered window and opened fire. Automatic pistols and single-shot revolvers joined the yammering chorus on either side. A hail of lead plowed into the turf and whined away off the stone-paved driveway.

Bolan fired two shots from the Browning over the limo's roof.

Cut by splinters of glass, his face was streaked with blood. The smuggler's bare arms, too, had been gashed, one of them deeply. Seeing the two scarecrow figures heading toward him with guns in their hands, the Toyota driver dived beneath the next car in the line.

Muzzle-flashes flickered again as another burst of gunfire erupted from the window of the magistrate's office. A dark-suited official treading down the flight of steps leading to the entrance of the admin building turned hastily and bolted back inside.

Bolan flung himself into the driver's seat of the Toyota and grabbed the wheel. He slammed the stick into first, flooring the gas pedal. The limo jolted into motion. With a screech of tires, it laid down rubber on the pavement, careering toward the courtyard gates with the open door swinging wildly. O'Riley was spread-eagled on the roof.

The officers guarding the gates leaped for their lives as the Toyota roared through and rocked on two wheels into the street. Shots cracked out. The rear window shattered. The windshield starred. Bolan punched a hole in it and raced for the lights at an intersection two hundred yards away.

Green blinked to red as he approached. He kept his foot down, swinging wide to pass a braking delivery truck, shooting the lights and snaking the limo through traffic released from the cross street in a blast of angry horns.

On the far side of the intersection, the street was deserted. The Toyota bucked to a halt. The driver's door had slammed shut when Bolan swung out of the gateway; now he fisted open the one on the passenger side so that O'Riley could slide from the roof and drop into the seat beside him.

"Oh, man," the Australian panted, "that was—"

"Later," Bolan snapped, sending the car rocketing forward. "This heap's going to be hotter than a Christmas chestnut. We've got to make it to a safe area and junk it, fast."

They sped past the twin minarets of the Sehzade mosque, turned right and shot through an arch beneath the remains of a Roman aqueduct. The traffic was heavier here, and already in the distance they could hear the blare of police sirens. When Bolan saw flashes of blue light reflected from the shopfronts half a mile ahead, he swung left off the broad avenue and maneuvered the Toyota through a network of narrow streets in the ancient Unkapani quarter. Finally they turned a corner and joined a stream of cars, buses and cabs moving swiftly along a riverside drive bordering the Golden Horn.

"The Abdülezel Paşa," O'Riley said. "A few hundred yards now, and you can turn onto the waterfront and make the parking lot by the Cabali landing stage."

Bolan nodded, following his directions. The limo bumped down a side street, turned into a wide asphalt lot and stopped. The warrior cut the lights, killed the engine and climbed out.

There were a few dozen cars ranged in the lot. An attendant hurried toward them from the far side. Strolling couples were already staring curiously at the Toyota's smashed screen and rear window. Bolan glanced quickly around him.

Below a wide flight of steps, passengers dismounting from a red and yellow tramway car flocked toward a crowd queued outside a pay kiosk by the landing stage. Beyond the press of small craft tied up along the waterfront, a ferry maneuvered alongside the wharf. "Time we split," the warrior decided. He nodded toward the Abdülezel Paşa. Blue light swept over the polished roofs of the traffic, advancing toward the landing stage.

"Too right, cobber," the Australian agreed. "But first I have to make it to the water, clean off some of this muck." He held up his lacerated arms. The blood had congealed, but in the state he was in, the smuggler wasn't going to pass unnoticed in a crowd.

"Me, too," Bolan said, fingering the scars of his face. "What say we make it that way?" He jerked his thumb to the right, where the eleven arches of the Ataturk bridge linked the riverside boulevard with the bright lights massed on the far side of the Golden Horn.

"Solid."

They moved away, starting down the steps. The parking attendant shouted something behind them. The patrol car with the blue light had turned into the side street. Bolan and O'Riley broke into a run.

Beyond the floodlit landing stage, upended boats strewed a concrete slipway, and on the far side of that the two men lost themselves among stacks of merchandise and forklift trucks outside a warehouse. A flight of stone steps led them eventually to the water's edge.

"For my money," Bolan said when they had cleaned up a little, "we'd best separate now. It was good to have you aboard, but . . ."

"Check," said the Australian. "They'll be looking for two guys, and I'm going to draw looks anyway, the way I am."

"It's not that. I have plans, and individually we'll have a better chance at this stage."

"No sweat. I'll make it across the bridge in a while. There's a boatman in Beyoglu who'll take me over the Bosphorus to Scutari—Üsküdar, I suppose we have to call it now—where I got contacts."

"Okay." The Executioner held out his hand. There was a hundred-dollar bill wadded in the palm. O'Riley shook his hand, glanced down, then looked up again and grinned. "Good on yer, mate," he said.

"Don't spend it all on perfume," Bolan said.

Upriver the crackle of police-radio voices sounded over the threshing of ferry screws. The bray of a siren groaned into silence as a second patrol car rolled into the parking lot. Men with flashlights moved among the boats on the slipway.

"I'm on my way," Bolan said. "Take care."

"Stay frosty."

The Executioner raised a hand. He vanished into the shadows beneath the bridge.

**6**

"I did everything I could," Brognola protested. "Jesus, I was around the goddamned Foreign Relations Department of the Interior Ministry so often the doorman began to think I was the new messenger boy! I was at the Embassy in Ankara three times in forty-eight hours. The Consulate here in Istanbul told me—"

"Okay," Bolan said. "Forget it, pal. It was just one of those things."

"It wouldn't have been so tough if I could've gotten more clout from Washington. But there are still guys there—even now Bush is at the White House—who wouldn't shed tears if you were to spend a few months in a Turkish jail. You know how it is."

The warrior knew how it was, all right. There were plenty of people—Administration lawyers, Company spooks, military men—who disapproved of the new, strictly unofficial relationship between the Executioner and the authorities. Guys who resented the fact that a one-off operator, a loner, could get away with stuff they were too scared, too inefficient or too hidebound to pull off. "Forget it," Bolan said again. "Let's reopen this oil rig inquiry, okay?"

"Whatever you say." Brognola spread a mariner's chart of the Black Sea on a table in his hotel room. Bolan had arrived there by way of a downspout, a perilous leap between two balconies and a forced window at two o'clock in the morning. Neither of the men had left the room since.

"You'll see," Brognola said, tracing with a forefinger the irregular outline of the inland sea, "that all around the littoral and clear across the northern half, the water's rarely deeper than fifty meters. That's a little more than one hundred sixty feet."

He tapped the center of the chart. "But here, in the south, the depth can go as much as six, seven thousand feet. Just the same, there's a series of one-hundred-meter, two-hundred-meter, three-hundred-meter zones offshore, before you make the deeps. And here—" another tap where the chart was colored dark blue "—there are a couple of islands under the surface where she shallows up to maybe one-fifty, two-fifty feet. The rig's built on the smaller one."

Bolan stared at the map. The deeps, roughly oval in shape, were surrounded by concentric rings of color, paling toward the coasts. The two "islands" of light blue that the Fed had indicated were, according to the scale, some eighty miles north of Samsun, on the Turkish coast.

"The exact position of the rig," Brognola told him, "is 36°15' East by 42°30' North, way outside Bulgarian territorial limits."

"It's more or less a straight line with Baku, on the Caspian, and Bulgaria's only oilfield at Burgas," Bolan observed. "I guess that figures. Strange nobody tumbled to it before, just the same."

"I ain't heavily into oil prospecting, to tell you the truth," Brognola said, "but if there's a series of geosynclines—that's like curves in the rocks underground, where the stuff gathers—then maybe this one was only revealed when the whole area was shaken during those Armenian earthquakes in '88?"

"Could be." The warrior dismissed the question. "You want me, anyway, to take a look-see. What did you have in mind, Hal? An overflight? Or, like you said before, are you still sold on a sea trip?"

"Negative on the overflight. We already have satellite photos, pictures taken by an SR-71 from eighty thousand feet, you name it. The thing looks like a fucking oil rig. To get anything extra, you'd have to go in real low, preferably with a bird, and that would not only tip them off that we're interested—they might pack defense equipment and shoot you into the sea."

"Does it matter if the Bulgarians know we're interested?"

"Bet your life—if things ain't what they used to be on oil rigs."

"I'll want something versatile then—fast, reliable, but not advertising it in neon."

"You got it."

"Tell me."

"A twenty-five-foot cabin cruiser, French-built, twin-screw, powered by two 170-hp Volvo AQ250 engines. They call it the Aruba Sport."

The Executioner grinned. "Story of my life!"

"Sometime after midnight," Brognola said, "we'll make like tourists, take a ferry across the Golden Horn, and hope to hell this guy Ecevlic doesn't have cops posted on every landing stage on the lookout for you."

"Has there been anything on the radio?"

The big Fed shook his head. "Not a peep. Loss of face, you see. Criminals don't escape from our friendly Turkish policemen. Lucky break for us."

"Say that again! And when we're safely across the Horn?"

"North of Beyoglu—that's the suburb on the far side of the water—there's a square mile of open country. The Yildiz Park. We're there at the right time, a chopper will fly in over the Sea of Marmara and pick us up."

"Swell. How do we fill in time until it's dark?"

"Drinking," Brognola said. He handed Bolan a glass of orange juice.

A COLD WIND from the Crimea scoured the waterfront at Sinop, crumbling the waves surging toward the wharf into dirty gray foam.

Everything about the town was gray—the steep-pitched roofs of the houses surrounding the harbor, the washed weatherboard facades, the fishing boats knocking the net-webbed gray stone seawall. The sky was gray, too, with scudding clouds streaming over the promontory sheltering Sinop to the north.

"Sounds fine," Bolan said.

"The Embassy rented it from some oil tycoon. Right now it's berthed at a small Turkish fishing port a couple miles south of the Cap Ince lighthouse. The coast veers north there, and it's only forty-five miles to the rig against eighty from Samsun."

"What's the name of the port?" Bolan was studying the chart. "Sinop? Is that it?" He placed a forefinger on the coast.

"Hole in one."

The warrior nodded, his finger tracing a course across the sea. "And the boat? What fuel? What's the tank capacity?"

"Gasoline. It's a three-hundred-liter tank. That gives you sixty-six gallons."

"Should be okay," Bolan said. "There's just one problem—how do I make it to the boat?"

Brognola rose to his feet. He poured the remains of a jug of orange juice, which had been brought to the room along with the breakfast coffee and rolls, into a tumbler. "We can't use the Consulate," he said. "H.E., making like an ostrich in Ankara, doesn't want to know. He won't have any part of us. We'll keep quiet, he told me, but you're on your own."

"That's the way I like it, Hal. You know that."

"Sure. But we have to get you out of here. The maid has to do the room. We can't very well operate that smuggling-you-out-in-a-laundry-basket routine. They don't have laundry baskets for a start. We're gonna be reduced to some kind of box-and-cox vaudeville, dodging in this door and out of that until we make it to the street after dark.''

Bolan was dressed in black.

Black trainers, black socks, a dark T-shirt beneath a black jogging suit with the bloused top loose enough to conceal a shoulder rig and the snub-nosed autoloader it supported.

Through mysterious contacts unconnected with the Embassy, Brognola had contrived to smuggle in via the diplomatic bag a replacement Beretta, the harness and several nonexplosive martial accessories the warrior did not like to be without. His famous formfitting blacksuit had been recovered from his hotel room and was rolled into a small canvas backpack along with shaving gear, a powerful flashlight and other necessities. The pack was strapped to the frame of a bicycle Bolan was using as transport.

Bike and rider had been offloaded from the chopper on a deserted stretch of moorland between two ranges of hills inland. "Embassy personnel sometimes drive up from Ankara to use the cruiser on weekends," Brognola had said, "but they're always in official limos. I could fix you a rental, but there's a chance it just might draw attention.''

"No sweat," Bolan replied. "A bike's . . . well, discreet. If we make it after dark, I could maybe get by without anyone noticing at all. In any case—" he grinned, punching the Fed's shoulder "—we can't very well fly the bird right onto the waterfront!''

It was fifteen miles to the coast from the dropping zone Brognola selected, most of it downhill. Bolan hit the outskirts of Sinop at dusk, and lights were already showing in some of the wood-frame cottages. Below the southbound clouds, the wind carried a hint of rain.

Bolan had coasted the bike to a halt on the wharf before the killers opened fire. If he hadn't leaned forward over the handlebars, swinging one leg across the saddle to dismount, the initial flaming burst would have blown him away.

As it was, one of the slugs aimed lethally at the upper part of his chest parted the hair on top of his head. Instinctively he threw himself to the cobbles, shoulder-rolling and then bounding up to leap sideways for the shelter of a stack of fish crates.

The gunners—he had realized there was more than one before he hit the deck—fired a second time as the bicycle clattered to the ground. Sparks flew and chips of granite danced between Bolan's feet.

Panting, he crouched behind the empty crates, the Beretta now in his right hand. The ambush site had been well chosen. He was fifty yards from the jetty where, according to his briefing, the cabin cruiser was moored. The hit men were firing from a narrow alley separating two shuttered buildings, in an area of near-darkness between the street lamps strung out along the quay. But the warrior himself would have made a perfect target, silhouetted against the light from a beacon at the end of a breakwater protecting the harbor entrance.

It hadn't registered in that first frantic moment, but the guns were silenced. He had heard no thundering clamor along with the blast of flame. Any noise they made had been lost in the suck and swash of waves against the wharf. So there would be no curious neighbors showing to see what the hell went on, no patrolling cop alerted by the sound of gunfire. It was a cold evening, and the fisherman had all gone home, so Bolan was on his own.

Wood split and splintered as a hail of bullets slammed into the stack. One of the crates on top fell to the ground.

The killers were firing SMGs or machine pistols. Bolan reckoned they had to be either Ingrams fitted with an MAC suppressor or Heckler & Koch MP-5s—the SD-3 subsonic version. Both of them had 30-round magazines, the H&K firing 9 mm parabellums, the Ingram .45-caliber ACPs.

The heavier gun firing 9 mm parabellums, the Ingram .45-caliber ACPs.

The heavier gun fired at a faster rate—more than 1,100 rounds per minute cyclic—but the MP-5 was more accurate on account of its closed bolt operation. It wasn't going to make a great deal of difference which one they used, Bolan thought grimly, if he was on the wrong side of the sights when they had a clear field of vision.

A couple more bursts like the last one and the crate stack would be no more than a collection of matchwood strewn across the wharf. Before that could happen, he had to find some other cover. He glanced swiftly around him.

The edge of the quay was ten yards away. But he'd be outlined against the pierhead light if he made a dash for it. And even if he succeeded, there might be no walkway below where the fishing boats were berthed; there were no steps leading down for as far as he could see in either direction.

There might be a chance if he dove into the water—unless they carried a flashlight, in which case he'd be a sitting duck.

Win, lose or draw, it had to be along the quayside, one way or the other. Between the fish stack and the jetty there was just a bare stretch of cobbles with a couple of crab pots by an iron cleat. Was the other side any better? Not much. An ancient flatbed truck with an equally old dinghy lashed topside down on it. A handcart piled high with nets and floats. A sandbin with a shovel clipped to its back, for use when the cobbled quay was iced over. Bolan's capsized bike.

Twenty-five yards, nineteen yards, twelve yards, six. Bullets burst through the flimsy rampart of wood. Several more boxes toppled over. One round ricocheted off the iron cleat.

Whether the cyclic rate of fire is five hundred, eight hundred or twelve hundred rounds per minute, an SMG on full-auto exhausts its magazine fairly fast. Thirty rounds can go in a matter of seconds. Yeah, Bolan thought, but if these guys were professionals, they'd be firing alternately—if the first burst failed to score, one man would hold enough back to continue shooting while his mate slammed in a fresh clip.

So, what was it the military theorists advised? The best method of defense is . . . attack!

Bolan sidled to the edge of the stack, ventured an arm, a shoulder and one eye around the corner, and choked out a trio of slugs in the general direction of the alley. The noise of the shots was deafening. Brognola had supplied the silencer Bolan was accustomed to, and the 93-R would have specially machined springs to chamber subsonic cartridges, but the silencer itself was in the pack on Bolan's bike.

The hell with stealth! Forget the flatbed and the cart. The moment the answering volley had been fired, the warrior rose to his feet and, using all his strength, spilled the entire stack over in front of him. The towers of flat, lightweight crates collapsed, bouncing off the cobbled quay, tumbling in chaos toward the ambushers in the alley.

Bolan ran with them, firing from the hip, high-stepping over the splintered wood.

Taken completely by surprise, the men with the silenced SMGs delayed their reaction a fraction of a second and then fired wild, overcompensating when they realized what was happening. Tongues of fire belched from the darkness, but the deathstream flew wide and high. A heavy-caliber slug twitched the sleeve of the warrior's jogging top, and another burned a red-hot channel through the lobe of his left ear. Then he was flattened against the wall of the building, on the side of the alley nearest the jetty where the cruiser was berthed.

If they wanted him in their sights now, they would have to emerge at least partially from the alley themselves in order to aim around the corner. He detached the half-used magazine from the Beretta and slammed in a fresh one.

Suddenly there was silence along the wharf.

In the distance waves cascaded against the outside of the breakwater. A shaft of light splashed across the cobbles somewhere beyond the jetty. Then, nervously, a murmur of questioning voices floated from the mouth of one of the narrow streets running down to the waterfront.

Still flattened against the weatherboard facade, Bolan edged stealthily away from the alley, the 93-R cocked and ready, his eyes focusing on the dark opening behind the litter of broken crates.

He saw nothing. But he heard something: over the muttering of voices and the faraway whisper of waves, a shuffling of footsteps, hurried, furtive, urgent—but definite.

It came from behind him, over the roofs. One of the gunners was circling the block. He glanced over his shoulder and saw that there was another lane leading to the dock.

The guy was cutting through on the far side of the building, so they could attack him from two sides at once.

Bolan tensed as he deliberated whether he could make it to the far side of the lane before the killer arrived.

It was highly unlikely. The footsteps were already nearing the wharf. In any case he would be silhouetted as he crossed the lane entrance.

Make it back to the dock edge then? Risk the water, after all?

No way.

Sidling toward the lane, he felt behind him with his free hand. The horizontal weatherboarding stopped, replaced by vertical planks. He was passing tall double doors leading from the wharf to the interior of the building.

Another glance over his shoulder. The doors were fastened with an old-fashioned iron hasp and staple. But the two were locked together with a large rusted padlock.

Beyond, right at the corner of the building, there was a single, smaller door. Bolan ran for it. There was a simple latch at one side of the weathered panels. He pressed it down, and the door swung open.

Reflected light from the street lamps showed him a steep flight of stairs leading up into the blackness. He eased the door shut and took the wooden stairs three at a time.

His nose told him where he was before the hip pocket penlight added visual proof. The place was a boat house: two dinghies shrouded in tarps lay just inside the double doors on the concrete floor below, and a broad-beamed craft that resembled a small whaler was shored up on wooden blocks in back. The stairs led to a fish loft that overlay three-fourths of the total area.

The building smelled of fish and weathered rope and tar. Bolan's shadow advanced and receded around the plank walls as he swung the penlight left and right over drying sails and oars and crawfish traps and still more crates. A complex arrangement of pulleys was slung from a hook in the raftered roof.

Abruptly the double doors shivered, splintered and swung half-open. Tiny shafts of light lanced the gloom below as a dozen bullet-holes appeared in the wood. One of the killers had blasted away the padlock and the staple it secured.

There was no railing at the edge of the fish loft. Bolan was prone just behind it. Raising his head, he saw a stocky figure shoulder its way past the savaged doors and raise the wicked muffler-covered barrel of an SMG hip high. At the same time he heard feet pounding on the stairway he had climbed less than a minute before. The killers had decided on a two-prong direct attack.

That could be dangerous, the warrior thought. For them.

He raised himself to a crouching position, offering himself as a target to the gunman below. The silenced SMG and the stinging snap of Bolan's Beretta spit flame at the same time, flickering on the walls with livid brilliance. Long slivers of wood as white as bone were gouged from the floor of the loft by Bolan's knee. His own single shot was more successful, coring the killer's left shoulder.

The guy sat down very suddenly, sprawling on his back between the two dinghies. The SMG fell from his nerveless grasp and skated away beneath the boat on the stocks.

The second man was at the top of the stairs.

Bolan had seen that the central pulley, supporting a counterweight with a large hook beneath it, hung just above the level of the loft floor, about eight feet away. With a silent prayer that he had worked out the mechanics of the hoist correctly, he launched himself into space.

The fingers of his left hand wrapped themselves around the cold steel curve of the hook as the guy at the top of the stairs opened fire.

Bolan's body dropped until he was hanging from the hook at the full stretch of his arm. The rope fed through the pulleys and he was lowered swiftly and smoothly to the floor below.

The hood with the wounded shoulder had produced a revolver. As the Executioner slid below the level of the loft, the thug fired a thunderous shot. But because of the position of his body, his uninjured arm was unstable, and the weapon climbed. The slug passed harmlessly over the Executioner's head. Then, before the man could improve his aim, the Beretta spit fire once more. This time the killer was slammed back and didn't move.

Bolan was behind one of the dinghies when the one up in the loft stammered out his second burst. Once more chips of wood flew. A strip of tarpaulin ripped free and fell across the warrior's wrist. He shook it free and pumped a 3-shot burst toward the roof.

The hood hadn't darted back far enough after his own volley, and the top of his head was still visible over the edge of the loft. A scarlet flower blossomed suddenly just below the hairline. He jerked half upright, fell forward onto his knees and pitched over the edge, falling with a loud crash across the whaler's center thwart.

Bolan rose cautiously to his feet. But it was obvious from the position of the guy's head and neck—even if it hadn't been for the blood dribbling out of his head wound—that there was nothing more to fear from that quarter.

The second man was dead, too. In the dim light that trickled in through the open doors, Bolan could see that they could just as well have been brothers: they were sturdy, swarthy, with thick dark hair, brown eyes and bushy mustache. Balkan types. They could have been Turkish, Romanian . . . or Bulgarian. He whipped out the penlight for a closer look.

No papers, no billfolds, no labels or laundry marks on the clothes. The one who had fallen from the loft wore a gold chain on his hairy wrist, but the oval ID tag was blank. Very professional.

Bolan had to make a hasty retreat from that place. He could hear a police siren in the distance, and there would certainly be folks from the nearby houses out in the street after that revolver shot and the fire from his own autoloader.

He dashed back to the fallen bicycle and whipped the rucksack from the frame. A group of people stood by a lifeboat house at the far end of the wharf, and blue light pulsed above the roofs of the waterfront buildings. He turned and sprinted toward the jetty.

Bolan thought fast as he ran. Nobody had seen him up close. He hadn't passed a soul, riding the bike. The police would find only a pile of splintered crates, a bullet-riddled door, the bike—and two stiffs in the boat house.

He couldn't risk involving the Embassy by making it to the cabin cruiser now. But if he could get clean away and lie low for a few hours, then there would be nothing to connect somebody who showed up to borrow the boat in the usual way with a shadowy gunman seen only briefly, and at a distance, the night before.

He halted, panting, raised the Beretta and shot out the nearest street lamp. Fifty yards farther on, at the top of a flight of steps that led down to the water, he killed another. A police car screeched to a stop at the far end of the wharf. He heard excited voices, questions, answers, a curt command. The car moved toward the boat house.

The warrior was opposite the jetty, invisible in the pool of darkness where the lamps had been. He turned and fled up a third lane that led toward the town's center.

Parked cars lined one side of the street. The nearest was a dark sedan. Like the others, it showed no lights; unlike them it stood with the engine quietly running.

A bulky figure emerged from behind the hood as Bolan drew abreast. He started back, automatically raising an arm in self-protection. The lead-cored nightstick smashed across his biceps, momentarily paralyzing the arm.

Inwardly Bolan cursed. He should have reckoned on the killers having backup. This thug must be their minder, waiting to make the quick getaway once the mark had been terminated.

He danced away, unwilling to bring the cops running with another shot from the Beretta. The hood was advancing again with the stick raised high.

Bolan went in low, spinning, his left arm muscles in trauma but the right reaching for the legs, unbalancing the man and then chopping a hand to the medulla, paralyzing the joint of the knee.

The minder staggered, uttering a grunt of pain. The stick swept up, then thudded across Bolan's back. But they were too close for the blow to be effective, and too close for foot blows. Bolan leaped in beneath a flailing fist, maneuvering for a bracket throw. His good hand chopping at the nape of the guy's neck to add force to his own momentum, Bolan drove his left knee up into his abdomen.

Bolan put the bracket on him as he folded, whisking him away in a flurry of *kizami-zuki* and *gyaku-zuki* punches from the straddle stance. The stick cannoned off the sedan's fender with a metallic clatter as the minder fell. He lay face upward with the whites of his eyes glimmering in the reflected light from a street lamp fifty yards inland.

Bolan hesitated, then decided it was best to leave him alive. For a while the law might figure the body to be the mysterious third man they'd dimly seen running from the wharf, but later they'd asked themselves, Okay, but who decked *him*? But by then the Executioner would be long gone.

He leaned in through the sedan's open window and cut the motor. Withdrawing to massage his numbed arm, he noticed irregular blotches, black in the dim light, staining the cobbles around the felled thug. At unequal intervals, more of them led back toward the entrance to the lane.

It was blood, his own blood! Dripping from the damaged lobe of his ear, his blood had left an unmistakable trail leading from the boat house to the parked sedan.

He'd turn it to his advantage. There was cotton waste in the backpack, included for use cleaning the gun. He unzippered the pack, ripped off a length and held it to the bleeding ear. Then he turned and hurried silently back to the quayside.

The trail of bloodstains led to the unconscious minder...and stopped there. Let them work that one out while Bolan split.

Two policemen with flashlights were already coming his way, the light beams swinging right and left as they followed the stains. He ran across the quay some way beyond the jetty, where the fishing boats were tied up side by side below the dock.

As he stared through the forest of masts and rigging toward the pierhead light, he counted six boats, maybe seven, between him and the cabin cruiser. He jumped lightly down onto the deck of the nearest. Then, climbing cautiously from gunwale to gunwale, he approached the jetty beneath the level of the quayside.

A tailored tarp was fastened over the well in the cruiser's stern. For a moment he thought of crawling under it. Then he recalled Hal Brognola's parting words: "Whatever you do, Striker, don't for God's sake involve the Embassy!" Okay. Best keep away until the panic was over.

The wooden decking of the jetty was supported on cast-iron piles with a network of girders beneath. He crawled across the cruiser's foredeck and swarmed in among the metal stays, finding a place in the angle between two girders where he could rest up comfortably enough. Above him he could hear footsteps, voices, the patrol car's motor, a crackle of instructions on a walkie-talkie. Below, water welled up between the piles and then subsided, rocking the boats on the swell.

Bolan touched his ear. The nick in the lobe was no longer bleeding. He dropped the pad of cotton into the water. His left arm was still numb; so he started rubbing the circulation back into it.

Unanswered questions chased through his mind about who had sent the killers to Sinop and how they had known to expect him. Was this second ambush, the third shooting in which he had been involved, connected with the first? If so, were the attacks designed to stop him from following up the chemical warfare lead or to discourage him carrying out the oil rig recon for Brognola?

Negative on that last one—he hadn't known himself that he'd be checking out the rig when the Istanbul attack was made.

The murder of Ben Yassir and the rifleman's ambush attempt must therefore relate to his private investigation of the missing chemicals, as he first thought.

How anyone could have known he was on that trail remained the leading question, but now there was another alongside it. Was it so important to stop that investigation that it was considered worthwhile to send a team all the way out to the Black Sea coast, rather than to wait for his return to the Bosphorus?

Affirmative. After all, that was exactly what they had done.

Unless the recent attackers were indeed unconnected with the Istanbul killers.

In which case Bolan could look forward to some interesting revelations when he finally checked out the oil rig.

## 7

Far away to the east, the ragged mass of the sixteen-thousand-foot ridge that separated the Black Sea from the Caspian appeared over the dawn horizon. Wind from the Crimea had blown away the clouds, leaving the air clear and cold. The sea was choppy, gray as a dead man's face beneath a sky the color of pewter.

Bolan had limited the Aruba Sport to eighteen or twenty knots throughout the dark hours to reduce the twin Volvos' thirst. Now the cruiser rocked on the swell with a sea anchor to keep her knife-blade bow facing the wind. Brognola's oil rig was a smudge ten miles to the northeast.

Before he went in any closer, Bolan checked over the gear he had asked for, which he'd stowed in the tiny cabin below the bridge.

Foam neoprene wet suit with helmet. Mask, faceplate and snorkel tube. Fins. Tank harness with instant-release buckle, lead belt, depth gauge, compass and diving knife. All present and correct.

Lying on one of the two bunks were two standard cylinders of compressed air with reserve mechanisms, nickel-plated interiors and a double-hose regulator. Each tank had a capacity of seventy-one cubic feet.

A powerful electric lamp and a speargun completed the outfit. Bolan was already wearing an underwater watch.

He hauled in the sea anchor, started the engines and climbed up behind the steeply raked windshield.

There was a railed chair in the stern, with a belt and harness lying ready, and a big rod with a Hardy reel socketed into the chair. The Aruba Sport was trolling two hundred yards of thirty-six thread with the drag screwed down and nothing on the end but a cork float. Bolan hoped the lookouts on the rig—for there would be lookouts—could be kidded into the belief that he was some Embassy freak on a fishing trip.

When he was a couple of miles from the rig, a small chopper took off from the helipad and circled the cruiser. Bolan was harnessed into the chair, pulling on the rod so that it arched against the weight of the line in the water. He turned around when the bird was directly overhead, shouting and gesticulating to the empty cabin, making a pretense that there were two aboard. The helicopter made a single pass and flew back to the rig.

The sun was half a dozen diameters above the Caucasus ridge when Bolan lowered the field glasses, fearful that a gleam reflected from the lenses might tip off the lookouts that the platform was under surveillance.

It looked innocent enough. A steel substructure of four splayed legs supporting two deck-levels spined with cranes, a derrick, various engine housings around the bore and living quarters on the upper deck. A flare pilot burned with a steady flame at the tip of a tall stackpipe.

The helipad was cantilevered out above the top deck. Bolan reckoned the stormwave gap—the distance between the lower deck and the surface of the sea—was around forty feet. Fifty was normal, but although the Black Sea could be rough, the landlocked waters never reached the wildness of the North Atlantic.

Back on the diminutive bridge, the Executioner swung the cruiser around and headed away from the rig on a zigzag course leading north and west in a pattern a fisherman might use if the big ones weren't biting. When the boat was almost invisible to the technicians on the rig, he cut the engines, put out the sea anchor again, made himself a meal from the food left in the galley and settled down to wait for darkness to fall.

At noon a small freighter flying the Bulgarian flag emerged from a haze veiling the sea to the west and passed within a mile of the Aruba Sport. From the cruiser's position, Bolan was only able to spot the upperworks when the ship approached the rig, but he thought it anchored a couple of hundred yards away—probably sending in a boat with supplies.

Later he watched a fleet of brown-sailed smacks maneuvering six or seven miles to the south. He supposed they were fishing the underwater shelf where the hundred-meter zone gave way to the deeps.

One hour after sunset he sailed slowly back toward the rig. When he was five miles away, he killed the engines and allowed the cabin cruiser to drift with the southeasterly current. The flare pilot still burned brightly above the platform's riding lights.

Bolan put out the sea anchor when he was approximately one mile from the rig.

The sky was still clear, the sea calmer, the wind veering east. He scrutinized the stars, unnaturally bright in the dark depths of sky—he might need them later if his compass needle went ape under the influence of the platform's metal pontoon legs.

Suiting up, he zipped the neoprene to his throat and started the preimmersion checks: tank pressure, valves, harness, buckles, backpack. He blew through the mouthpiece to clear the check valves, aligning the regulators with the butterfly bolts finger-tight. Now it was time to climb into the scuba gear.

It took him a while to get the harness buckled comfortably, because he didn't risk showing a light. When it was right, he memorized the exact configuration of the rig and its lights; if the structure sent the compass wild and clouds happened to blow up and obscure those stars, that image was the only thing he'd have left to guide him.

All he had to do now was activate the return beacon and check that the device clipped to the harness was receiving loud and clear.

All was well.

Bolan spit into the faceplate to minimize misting and put on the mask. He dragged the flippers onto his feet, picked up the lamp and harpoon gun and stole to the cabin cruiser's stern. He sat for a moment perched by the taffrail, then lowered himself silently into the sea.

The water was deathly cold at first, plastering the clammy wet suit to his skin.

Then, as he began swimming powerfully toward the rig, the body's natural central heating system took over. He moved in a silent, featureless world, the rhythmic inhalation and exhalation of his lungs, echoing cavernously inside his own head, his only contact with reality.

Time no longer had any meaning. Existence was measured by the bellowed pumping of his lungs, drawing air from the reservoirs on his back and then expelling it. Air that would not, could not, be replaced. He swam, using the gauge, at a depth of fifteen feet. His course, using the compass, led straight to the rig.

After twenty minutes he surfaced briefly to check his direction and demist the mask. Small waves slapped his face. In case the faceplate reflected a gleam of light from the illuminations on the rig, he turned his head away after that first comprehensive glance. The cabin cruiser was lost in the darkness behind him.

He guessed he was still perhaps a mile from the platform. Rather to his surprise, no sounds of activity floated across the water. Brognola had told him the installation had been operative for three months, with the crude already on steam. And if they were burning off residual lean gas at the flare pilot, Bolan knew, that meant the rig was running at production capacity. Which in turn suggested a twenty-four-hour shift system at the wellhead.

Yet there was no sound of machinery, and he could see no sign of life on either deck.

Bolan dived again and continued his swim. But this time the substructure was nearer, and the compass needle did swing wildly. Every few minutes, therefore, he was obliged to surface and check his position.

The configuration of the rig and its lights had altered; the current was carrying him too far south. He veered to the left and approached the nearest pontoon leg in a wide curve. Ten minutes later he surfaced again, removing the faceplate before he turned his head toward his target. This time he had overcorrected; he was swimming almost parallel with the rig.

Bolan cursed. He couldn't use the electric lamp until he was actually beneath the platform, in case a lookout spotted the glow under the surface of the water. Sea salt had seeped inside the neoprene helmet to stir up the pain from his wounded ear, and the lacerations on his face—legacy of his escape from the police in Istanbul—had been stinging ever since he left the cabin cruiser. To make matters worse, he was still a quarter of a mile from the rig.

It was with an impatience foreign to his nature that he plunged once more, deeper this time because the lookouts were relatively near. He was tired of hearing nothing but the hollow boom of his own breathing, the faint gurgle of expelled air escaping in the cold, dense, black silence of this undersea world.

He was two hundred yards away from the riding lights when his arm struck the steel cable. He allowed himself to eddy around, grasping the cable with his left hand. It was a little thicker than his thumb, moving gently back and forth with the current, plummeting down presumably as far as the seabed one hundred fifty feet below.

Naturally it also went up. Bolan began to hoist himself stealthily, hand over hand, toward whatever it was the steel hawser was attached to. He had moved up perhaps twice his own height, with his flippered legs floating out behind him, when the top of his head bumped against a hard projection.

He backed off, treading water, exploring with his hands.

He had hit some kind of metal horn, one inch and a quarter across and four inches long. It projected from a curved surface, also metallic. He continued his exploration. The faint hint of lightness that filtered through the water from the stars and the reflection of the riding lights could show him no more than an amorphous shape, a darker blur against the darkness.

His questing fingers found another horn, similar to the first. And then another... and a fourth. They were located at equal distances around the curvature of the main mass.

The main mass was the form of a sphere.

A sudden chill, colder than anything produced by the sea, shivered through the warrior, right down to the soles of his feet. He felt the hairs on his nape prickle against the rubber neck of the helmet.

The sphere was a floating mine, and the protrusions were soft copper detonation horns.

Bolan swallowed. If it had been one of the scuba tanks and not the top of his head that ran against that detonator...

He put the thought from his head. It hadn't been one of the tanks. The mine hadn't exploded. He was still alive and kicking.

He kicked away from the deadly sphere and began slowly to make a circuit of the rig. Tethered by its steel cable, the mine lay ten feet below the surface of the sea—a depth that would foul anything bigger than a sailboat or a small launch.

If they hit it.

There was a lot of sea around where they could move without hitting it. Put that another way: people didn't just lay a single mine, especially when it was of the old-fashioned nonmagnetic type.

Bolan continued his slow circuit, agonizingly aware of the amount of precious air he was consuming. But he had to find out; he had to know the strength of the target's defenses before he went in.

It took him another thirty minutes, in which time he found four other mines exactly like the first, each drifting a little with the current, swaying like deadly underwater flowers. There could have been a dozen more, two dozen more that he missed in the dark. There was no doubt about it—the oil rig was surrounded by a minefield.

Why the hell would they do that?

Anything in international waters was fair game, he supposed, but surely, even with the high barrel-price today, nobody was in business hijacking crude. Apart from Bulgarian supply ships and tankers—which would be able to run in close through a swept channel—what vessels would want to sail that close to a rig? Just who were the Bulgarians afraid of, and what kind of assault was this a protection against?

Not an isolated scuba diver carrying a harpoon gun, anyway.

There were simpler, less costly defenses against that kind of intrusion.

Bolan had dived in a long shallow curve down to one hundred ten feet, where the pressure was at four atmospheres and the water, directly beneath the platform, was still partly lit by some kind of floodlighting that percolated down from the lower deck. Twenty feet away through the milky, semiopaque depths, he could make out the massive, girdered pontoon leg where it slanted against the sandy bottom. Clumps of weed ballooned between the steel crisscross, and a shoal of small fish flicked silver bellies out of the sand as the flippers grounded and raised a small cloud above the floor.

The man came from the far side of the leg, advancing in a series of slow-motion bounces like a moonwalker. He carried a diver's knife, razor-sharp on one side, saw-toothed on the other, like Bolan's own. Blinkered by the mask, the Executioner didn't see him until he was almost within striking distance.

He was already too close for the harpoon gun to be effective, and in a flash Bolan took stock of the squat guy, a head shorter than himself, with malevolent slitted eyes behind the faceplate and the knife hilt down with the blade canted up at forty-five degrees.

Bolan was unprepared. He had unclipped the lamp from his harness, and the speargun hampered his other hand. If he reached for his own knife, the man's blade would have ripped into the belly of his wet suit before he could even draw it. It was no place, either, for the chops or blocks or kicks of the martial arts, since the resistance of the water at four atmospheres slowed down movements to a point where a close-quarters push was more effective than a swinging blow with the attacker's weight behind it.

For an instant they stared at each other. Then Bolan kicked his flippers against the sand, raising a sudden yellow cloud that boiled up between them, distracting the knife-man's attention long enough for Bolan to kick away backward, the gun coming up as the blade, desperately lunging, slit the front of his wet suit and let the water in.

Bolan lay back, streamlining away, moving fast while he could, because, once filled with water, the suit would slow him crucially. The attacker clawed for his breathing tube, striking out with the blade in a menacing arc. But Bolan already had his distance. The speargun's powerful spring recoil jolted his arm, almost dislocating the shoulder. The harpoon arrowed away to slam into the diver's body, penetrating just below the sternum to emerge between his shoulder blades. With his liver, pancreas and lung ripped apart by the wicked barbed head, the diver vanished behind a cloud of black blood, dropping his knife to the sandy floor.

Bolan dived to retrieve it. It was then that the second man attacked.

The first the warrior knew of it was a sudden force acting on him from behind. The crushing pressure of the man, added to the weight of the air tanks, flattened him to the sand. Harsh fingers wrenched at the breathing tube... This time the ribbed rubber tore away, and the life-giving tube, mask and faceplate were all dragged back over Bolan's head.

He rolled onto his back slowly, too slowly. The guy was bigger, heavier, but with the same slit eyes coldly evaluating the adversary. Steely hands grasped Bolan's arms, pinning him to the seabed. A stream of air bubbles feathered upward from his nose and mouth. Already he was consciously fighting to stop the autonomous nervous system instructing the muscles controlling the lungs to drag in more.

Bolan knew he had only seconds to live. Unless he could escape the attacker's grasp and float away—either to recover the tube and mask hanging somewhere behind his back or reach the surface—he would be unable to prevent his oxygen-starved lungs from drawing in water. The killer didn't have to use a weapon or resort to underwater unarmed combat tactics. He had only to maintain his hold and watched the Executioner drown.

Bolan's mind raced. There could be two opinions on that. But his instincts told him he didn't have much time.

The pinioning hands were around his upper arms. The attacker's arms were at full stretch, his body floating horizontally above Bolan's. But Bolan could move his forearms. He brought up the right arm, feeling for the man's knee, his thigh, anywhere on the top part of his leg, maneuvering for a nerve grip, finding it and exerting pressure.

The killer stiffened, shifted, slightly contorting as the pain flamed through his lower body. His right hand had slackened very slightly its grip as he strove to break the hold...slackened enough for Bolan to raise himself two inches from the sandy floor.

Enough for him to bring his left hand, the finger wrapped around the hilt of the knife dropped by the first man, out from under him.

The waves thundering inside his head, washing away the edges of his consciousness, were bloodred. The mind wandered. In slow, slow-motion he watched the hand holding the knife thrust upward.

His arm moved from the elbow only, but it was enough. The knife's point pricked the rubber suit, slit it, scratched the flesh beyond so that a thin thread of scarlet fanned out into the water. And then, as Bolan summoned his last reserves of strength to heave his torso away from the sand, the blade homed in on soft tissue, up to the hilt.

The killer stiffened again. His back arched. The fingers gripping Bolan slackened and fell away. A tide of red flowed through the rent in the wet suit and mushroomed out like an evil flower.

He floated away, turning over and over, trailing a spiral of his own blood.

Bolan was scrabbling for the life-giving tube, pulling it back over his head to bite on the mouthpiece, still fighting to counter a false euphoria due to nitrogen narcosis fed by the starved blood hammering at his chest.

He remembered to stay on his back, so that the mouthpiece would remain higher than the regulator, to exhale, to swallow, and at last, finally at glorious last, to breathe in the precious air from the tank.

When the mask was back in place, he turned over unhurriedly, moving gently, nothing energetic, allowing the organism to recover. The diver pays a high price for exertion, demanding more oxygen than the tube can supply, provoking a vacuum and a pressure lag at the regulator. Add near-drowning and nitrogen narcosis at four atmospheres, and the warrior's determination to take things really easy until the violent exertions of his heart quietened was no less than survival sense.

The speargun was gone, but he found the electric lamp where he had dropped it. He cleaned the killing blade in the sand and stuck it in his belt along with his own knife. Then, he reckoned, it was time to resurface.

He went up slowly, no faster than the bubbles streaming from beneath his face mask. His depth gauge registered thirty feet when he passed the body of the first killer, eddying with outflung arms in some pocket of tidal turbulence. The man was facedown, with the spearhead that protruded from his back trailing a skein of blood like a ship's pennant.

The neoprene helmet broke the surface near one of the platform's girdered legs. Immediately above, the underside of the storm deck, glistening with moisture, reflected the ripples welling below in the glow of a floodlight that illuminated a derrick. It was noisy this time—still no evidence of the pumping plant, but somewhere up there a generator was thumping. Bolan could hear, farther away, the hollow chatter of a riveter.

Steel ladders climbed two of the pontoon legs, and diagonally opposite, beyond the central bore, he saw a polished teak motorboat with three rows of cushioned seats and a V-shaped windshield.

Bolan leaned his arms on a metal stay that formed a crosspiece to one of the girders. He was still panting after the exertions of the struggles below. He removed his mask and breathing tube, lashing them, together with the tanks and scuba gear, to the girder with a nylon cord he had wound around his waist. They remained just below the surface, visible in the reflected floodlight if one knew where to look, but safe enough from anything but a detailed search. There was in any case no ladder on this pontoon leg.

Bolan wondered how soon the two divers he had bested would be expected to climb back aboard via one or the other of the legs that had ladders.

There was no way of telling. But he had to make that climb first himself. Because it was no longer a question of a perfunctory checkup, a simple look-around of the kind Hal Brognola had envisaged.

Clearly something was going on here that merited the Executioner's close professional attention. For what kind of an oil rig was it that posted murderous underwater sentries and surrounded itself with a lethal minefield?

**8**

A fake oil rig. That was the answer to the Executioner's unspoken question.

Soon after midnight he'd climbed the ladder that ran from the seabed to the lower deck, up the substructure leg where he had stashed the scuba gear. Catwalks ran inward from all four legs to a central ladder that served the drilling complex and gave access to the upper deck. Here on the lower level, Bolan saw four powered launches slung from davits, two pedestal cranes for loading supplies, some kind of control cabin beneath the floodlight he had seen from under the water and a row of louvered installations he figured for turbine housings.

The cabin windows were dark, the turbines silent and the catwalks deserted. Warily Bolan began to climb the central ladder.

Halfway up he rested with one hand hooked over an iron rung while he spilled the remainder of the sea water through the slit in his rubber suit. The generator he had heard below was no longer thumping, but from time to time he heard the stammer of the riveter. And sporadically, when the riveter wasn't working, the faint hollow boom of footsteps patrolling the deck above.

Very slowly Bolan raised his eyes above the upper deck's floor level. He saw another, larger control room, with the drilling rig complex beside it. Rig, derrick and cabin were again floodlit by a single arc. He saw what might be living accommodation, cabins that could have been lining the promenade deck of a liner, at the end of a wide corridor separating the rig from a series of powerhouses and winch gear.

And overhead the flame from the flare pilot burned the night sky.

Bolan pulled himself up and sped silently to an engine housing. He dropped down behind it, scanning every available angle with a practiced eye. The lookouts would be pacing the walkway that circled the platform, meeting at twelve o'clock and six o'clock on each circuit of the perimeter if—as he thought—there were just two of them. At this time of night, aside from unforeseen hazards, he should be safe from interference *inside* the perimeter. He stole toward the center of the platform.

It was, he reckoned, around four hundred feet long and two hundred fifty wide. Once past the living quarters, he saw that the riveters—there were three of them, with an overseer—were working on the helipad that was cantilevered out from the rig's longer side, the elevation farthest from his cabin cruiser. The chopper, illuminated by the portable electric lamps the men were using, was a four-seat recon ship of a type used by all the Eastern bloc armies. So far as he could see, it carried no insignia.

There was also work in progress on the far side of the drilling derrick: welding equipment and pneumatic rivet hammers lay strewn around a concrete mixer and a stack of metal sheets in a cleared site thirty feet across.

The rig's radio facilities were more sophisticated than Bolan would have expected. Two masts with microwave dishes projected from the upper deck, one each side of the helipad, and there was a third, fitted with a booster unit, among the forest of antennae above the control bunker.

But the big giveaway was on the far side of a block he identified as a communal mess hall.

The place was in darkness, but several of the cabin windows beyond showed lights, and the illumination from these and the central arc was enough to alert the warrior to the big deception.

Flame burned at the tip of the flare stack all right, but this was no lean-gas burnoff. The stack was fed from a huge cylindrical tank stocking commercial propane gas. What looked from the air like lean-gas coolers were in fact camouflaged naval guns.

The crude reservoirs on the far side of the false stack were flimsy structures of wood sprayed with metallic paint. They would have burst open the moment anything more than a trickle of oil was pumped into them. Bolan further confirmed that there was no wellhead, and the bore was as phony as the flare stack.

He squatted in the shadows behind the guns, his mind racing. What the hell was the point, spending millions of dollars on an elaborate fake that looked like an oil rig from the air but appeared to produce nothing?

There had to be a point, and a damned important one.

Important enough to warrant the massacre of a planeload of people in case Brognola's man Shapiro had tumbled to what Bolan knew now.

Important enough to call in more than one hit team to stop Bolan himself following through, and to command an organization smart enough to find out that he *was* following through.

The rig must be purpose built. For what?

He recalled that the mainland Chinese—back in the seventies, wasn't it?—had faked an offshore oil rig that was to be transformed into a missile base that could menace Hong Kong. They had lost out on that one. Were the Bulgarians now trying for a repeat?

That didn't seem to be the case here. There was no sign of heat shields or exhaust ducting, no sign of the alternative Polaris-style compressed gas launching installation.

Whatever, there had to be clues somewhere. Bolan's own plans were now zeroed. He had been intending to start the long swim back to the cruiser before dawn. But with the Intel he had, he reckoned he owed it to Brognola to stay in place until he had found out more. The Fed had been right, after all, to suspect that something smelled. The least the warrior could do was find out what it was.

Easy to say, yeah. Stick around under cover and keep listening. But those dead frogmen were going to be discovered anytime, and then the guys in charge of the rig would *know* there were strangers in town.

The underwater relief detail, two guys in black wet suits and flippers, emerged from the living quarters a few minutes before two o'clock. Bolan checked his luminous watch. He figured they would be working four-hour shifts. During this time they would probably check the minefield for weed and flotsam that could tangle in the cables, carry out any maintenance work necessary on the pontoon legs and watch out—together with the patrol above—for intruders. Even with periodic returns to the surface, this would be long enough for experienced divers.

Since his arrival on the top deck, the warrior had prowled cautiously around the whole installation. There were indeed two guards on the outer walkway, but it was easy enough to remain hidden in the patches of deep shadow between different areas of the plant when one or the other of them neared his position. He had nevertheless found nothing more to explain the existence of the phony rig.

The two frogmen exchanged greetings with the men on the walkway and made it down the ladder that led to the lower deck.

Any moment now, Bolan thought. Once they're wise to the fact that neither of the first pair is going to show, all hell will break loose.

At 0213 he heard an urgent shout from somewhere below. There was an answering call from the walkway, and a spotlight at the edge of the platform dazzled into brilliance. Heavy footsteps rang on the iron catwalk as the second guard hurried to join the first. The spotlight beam tilted downward, then began to sweep across the surface of the water.

More shouts, tinged with alarm this time. One of the guards ran to the control bunker, opened a door and went inside. Lights sprang on behind the windows. A Klaxon ululated into an alarm call.

Clearly they had found one of the bodies.

Lights glowed and then flared into life all around the perimeter of the rig. Men spilled out from the living quarters, some still in dun-colored pajamas, others pulling on jeans and sweatshirts. There was a babble of voices, then one authoritative one calling out orders.

Once they started looking, Bolan knew, it would be only a matter of minutes before they discovered the scuba gear he had lashed to the girders just below the surface of the sea. He had to get lost, fast.

He had to determine the means and method. The helipad? He looked out over the rails. No way. Two of the riveting crew were still up there, the electric lamps lit, staring down across the platform.

He checked out the other possibilities in his mind: the roof of the bunker, the living quarters, the mess hall?

Negative. Half a dozen men had already swarmed down the ladder to the level below, but there were still ten or twelve milling around between the bunker and the powerhouses. One of them would be sure to see him if he tried that.

Someplace in among the drilling rig complex? Up one of the cranes?

Uh-uh. He shook his head. The central flood was too near and too bright.

The raucous seesaw blare of the Klaxon stopped. Bolan could hear one of the diesel generators thumping away to keep the current flowing and the lights bright. He was standing, poised for action, in the shadow cast by one of the false crude reservoirs. He moved farther back as three men with nets approached, on their way to the central ladder.

Was he going to have to make a run for it, to dive forty feet into the sea, a strike out for the cruiser on the surface a mile away? With the submachine guns that some of the men now carried trained on his back?

An involuntary shiver spasmed Bolan's muscular frame. The breeze blowing through the tear in the damp neoprene was cold. Moving, shrugging his shoulders to keep the circulation toned up, he touched inadvertently the wooden side of the camouflaged tank.

The wood moved, sliding laterally a couple inches away from him.

Frowning, he explored with both hands, and an entire panel moved. It shifted silently to one side, leaving a dark space. He tested it again, and found that the panel was like a door that led to the inside. He stepped in and pulled it shut behind him.

The sounds of the awakened rig—questions, answers, shouted orders, footsteps, the generator, a bumping of metal against the girdered pontoon leg that vibrated the whole structure—were all muffled, distanced inside the false tank. There was something else, too, a new stimulus that actuated another of the Executioner's senses: a thin, sour, slightly metallic odor.

Machine oil.

And with it, very faint but still discernible, the sweetish stink of used gasoline.

The fake tank was roughly put together. In a dozen places, through small holes in the planking, between the edges of panels that did not quite fit, light penetrated in beams and rays. Once his eyes were accustomed to the artificial dusk that these created, Bolan saw with astonishment that the tank was used as a kind of garage or hangar.

Inside it were parked two jeeps and a wide, squat, tracked vehicle. With increasing bewilderment, the warrior edge around them. The jeeps looked like normal American M-151s. The tracked vehicle—he walked around it twice to make sure—was indeed American Army issue: an amphibious M-548 cargo and personnel carrier packing a light-weight folding missile launcher just forward of the tailgate.

On the floor of the M-548's hull were one dozen TOW antitank missiles, complete with U.S. Army stencilings and part numbers.

What the hell, Bolan thought, was going on? He recalled that the four powerboats he had seen slung from davits were American KrisKraft. Like the vehicles in his hiding place, they were painted a dull olive color.

The mystery deepened with every step he took.

But before he allowed his mind to dwell on the latest discovery, he determined to find out more. If that was possible.

Making a quick recon, he found there were loose planks in the corner of the false reservoir opposite the entrance door. Twenty minutes later, working soundlessly and with great care, he had pried them aside enough to slip through into the shadowed corridor between the "storage tank" and the one beside it. Maybe here, too, there would be a sliding door... with something surprising behind it.

His expectations proved correct.

At first, after he had edged in and closed the door, he thought the place was empty. Then he saw in the dim light that filtered through the cracks that there were several large wooden crates stacked at the far end.

Behind them was a smaller trailer. He recognized it as a lightweight M-740 missile launcher, the type that could be towed behind a jeep or a 4X4 truck.

The largest crate was sixteen feet long and maybe twelve wide. The lid, which was almost level with his shoulder, was loose. He raised it and peered inside.

Sleek and finned, they shone dully in the gloom: Lance missiles, maybe a dozen of them, ready to fire but so far minus warheads.

Staring at the deadly cylinders, Bolan knit his brows. Somehow it didn't quite stack up. But he had to ignore the question of why they would be stashed on a Bulgarian offshore rig, miles out in the Black Sea, and concentrate on what they were to be used for.

The TOW—tube-launched, optically tracked, wire-guided—missiles in the first hangar could be launched from the M-548 carrier or fired from a chopper. They were three feet ten inches long, weighed forty pounds and had a maximum range of four thousand yards.

The MGM-52C Lance, on the other hand, was over twenty feet long and weighed a ton and a quarter when the warhead was fitted. Its maximum range was almost ninety miles and it was capable of shooting one hundred fifty thousand feet into the stratosphere to make it.

The TOW, with its shaped-charge HE warhead, could knock out a tank or breach a defense wall; the Lance, whether it transported HE, tactical nuclear or TGSM—terminally guided submissile—cluster warheads, was a weapon for long-distance bombardment.

Bolan couldn't think of any way the two could logically be used together on a relatively small-time, one-off operation. For it was clear that this material must have been collected for a military purpose—and equally clear, whatever that purpose was, that it would be in the nature of a raid rather than a battle.

What it all had to do with an oil rig, he had no idea.

By now, nevertheless, the rig itself was jumping. He heard the motor of the launch moored to one of the pontoon legs roar to life. Judging by the commands and sound effects penetrating the woodwork, a full-scale search of the platforms was under way. They must have found the bodies of both divers as well as Bolan's scuba gear by now.

He went to one of the smaller crates. It was full of clothes, neatly pressed and packaged in cellophane. Olive uniforms, camous, combat fatigues, U.S. style. GI steel cellophane. Olive uniforms, camous, combat fatigues, U.S. style. GI steel helmets filled another crate, webbing equipment and M-16 rifles a third, combat boots a fourth.

Bolan was already suspecting something lower than low. But it was the last crate that was the clincher.

As he had half expected, it contained warheads for the Lance missiles. Streamlined, tapering to a fine point, the shells with their graze fuses were not packed the way warheads for most delivery systems were packed. They were packed more like bottles of priceless vintage wine, each one cushioned in a shaped polystyrene nest, with the nose cone wrapped in cotton wool that was kept in place with a kind of single-finger chamois leather glove. Foam mattresses separated each row of three from the ones above and below, and the walls of the crate were padded with rubber.

Bolan was unable to read the red-lettered warning notices inside and outside the lid, but the black skull-and-crossbones motif that accompanied them was explicit enough. His flesh crawled as he scanned the six-language handling instructions stapled to the crate.

He knew now...and if he didn't know, the letters and figures stenciled on the warhead casings would have told him.

*A secret fund for the production of specially designed 500-lb bombs*, Ben Yassir had said before he died. The normal weight of a Lance warhead was 467 pounds. For bombs, read missiles—a simple translation error.

So the Bulgarians, who had end-user certificates, were processing the MPD themselves—they weren't passing it on to the Iranians, whose secret fund was targeted for the purchase of chemical weapons.

The Executioner was looking at a part, at least, of the deadly chemical consignment he had come so far to track down!

And the ironic thing was, Brognola's mission, which he had tried to turn down, and his own personally motivated operation had turned out to be one and the same!

## 9

Bolan decided to move out. The sounds of the search came from the far side of the rig, but they'd be checking out the fake storage tanks soon enough, and he also wanted to conceal the fact that he knew about the hardware inside.

He eased back the sliding door, slipped outside and then closed off the gap. Situation analysis could come later— right now the number one priority was survival. Escape from the platform and survival. He'd start thinking how best to act on his discoveries when he was safely out of range.

The cabin cruiser was one mile away. Without scuba gear, how could he make it?

Surface swimming? Not with a launch, four KrisKraft and a chopper at the enemy's disposal.

Taking one of the boats himself was the only answer. And it would be no joyride.... There was no chance of sabotaging the bird and the other boats before he left. Plus the camouflaged naval guns.

He shrugged. Those were the cards, and he was going to play the hand.

It was impossible to lower a KrisKraft without being seen, since there were between twenty and thirty Bulgarians disposed over most of the rig's surface. It would have to be the slower launch, but at least it was already in the water with the engine warm.

He couldn't hear it anymore. Maybe they had brought in both the frogmen by now. That should make it easier for

him, there was no way he could board the boat and overcome its crew if it was still circling around in search of the
missing guards.

One other thing—the only one—in Bolan's favor: having
found the flippers and scuba gear lashed to the underwater
girder, they would know the intruder had come aboard the
platform. The majority of the personnel would be above the
water level searching for him, and they would not expect any
overt action to come from the sea.

Which was one good reason for the warrior to be there.

Between the two false reservoirs, he paused and listened.
The nearest searchers were on the far side of the derrick.
There were no guards on the walkway on the near side of the
upper deck.

Bolan took a deep breath, glanced rapidly right and left
and ran lightly out, across a gangway and past the living
quarters to the outer catwalk.

There was a slim chance that he might make the water
without raising the alarm.

Just one thing, though... He had figured the drop for
forty feet, but that was from the lower deck; this one was a
good twenty feet higher.

The Executioner shrugged again. That was just too bad.

He climbed up onto the guardrail, took a final look
around and dove into the dark water.

He broke the surface cleanly, plunging deep with scarcely
a splash, but the shock drove the breath from his body and
the impact tore open the ripped wet suit, stripping it away
from his lower limbs.

He kicked free of the clinging neoprene, wrenching off the
last undamaged section from the small of his back. Then,
remaining under water as long as his breath held out, he
swam with powerful strokes in beneath the lower platform.

Surfacing when he saw the girdered network of one pontoon leg shimmering a few yards ahead, Bolan shook the
water from his eyes and looked around. He was beside one
of the legs with no ladder, safe from observation so long as

he made no move. The launch was tethered to a ladder on the far side of the rig. Two Bulgarians standing in the stern were handing the body of a frogman, wrapped in net, to another pair perched on the lower rungs of the ladder. Higher up, three men maneuvered a second corpse toward the opening in the deck above. The action was lit by two powerful floodlights, one above each ladder, and the upper-deck spotlight still shone down onto the swell outside the rig.

A confusion of voices echoed between the ripples washing through the pontoon legs and their reflections dancing on the underside of the deck. At the top of the second ladder, a man in uniform appeared, shouting orders and waving his arms.

Bolan reckoned it was as good a time as any to make his play.

With five men and two dead bodies blocked on one of the ladders, pursuit would be hindered—and they wouldn't be able to drop the corpses back into the boat. If things panned out the way he wanted, he'd already be steering the launch toward the open sea. He took a deep breath and submerged. He had the width, not the length, of the platform to traverse, but two hundred fifty feet without replenishing the oxygen was a long way to go. He would be gasping when finally he came up for air, but he hoped the element of surprise would counterbalance the disadvantage.

Only partly. They were shouting when he surfaced; someone must have registered him as a dark shape underwater while he was arrowing toward the launch.

He took in the whole scene: the five men on the ladder, frozen into immobility with their gruesome burdens; the officer type with his submachine gun hip high, ready to fire; the guys in the launch leaning forward to peer into the water.

*Now!* Bolan thought. I can use that!

He thrust himself up with raised arms, grabbed the nearest man and pulled him overboard.

The Bulgarian splashed into the swell, and Bolan shoved him under with a single powerful heave. The top half of the damaged wet suit was still secured at the waist with the scuba belt, and in the belt were the two diver's knives. He snatched one free, pushing the struggling boatman deep down below the surface with his feet. After that it was one more lungful, a duck-dive, and a sudden savage thrust with the knife.

The blade slid into flesh, the water crimsoned in front of Bolan's eyes and then he was under the boat and coming up on the far side.

He heard shouting and the explosive rattle of the SMG as he hauled himself over the gunwale to fall on the duckboards, grabbing the remaining boatman around the knees.

The guy swung around, cursing, staggering against the warrior's prone figure as the SMG spit fire a second time. The lethal stream caught him high up on the right shoulder, spun him around and pitched him over the side into the sea.

Bolan was already up in the bow, slashing at the painter with his knife. The rope parted and the boat backed off. He dropped into the well and stabbed the starter button.

The engine started with a roar. Lying on the duckboards, he selected reverse gear, shoved the throttle fully open and reached up to twist the wheel. The launch corkscrewed out from beneath the rig in a swirl of foam.

A third burst from the stuttergun momentarily drowned out the motor. The windshield erupted. Splinters flew from the tear at the stern. There was gunfire from the installation's upper deck, too, Bolan saw as he slammed the stick into forward gear and the launch careered away in a broad zigzag.

When he was out of range, Bolan sat up on the leather bench to steer, using his compass and what he remembered of the rig's configuration, lighted up beneath the night sky, to make it as near as possible to the position where he had left his own boat.

The lights of the rig receded, but for a while he would still be close enough to notice the KrisKraft when they were lowered from the davits.

But they were not being lowered.

Two minutes later he discovered why.

A sudden burst of flame printed the outline of the rig against the darkness. A thunderous report rolled across the sea, and at the same time there was an express-train screech, a second earsplitting explosion and a fountain of white water jetting from the waves two hundred yards ahead.

Why bother to lower powerboats when you had six-inch naval guns ready to fire?

A second shell burst a little nearer, and then a third. Bolan throttled back the engine until the bow wave creaming away from the launch subsided. Before the towers of steam and water had collapsed into the sea he had turned through ninety degrees and headed away at right angles to his former course.

But the next salvo—he thought there were two, if not three, guns firing now—bracketed the motorboat more closely still.

Bolan bit his lip. It was as he feared. Clearly the gunners were not laying visually, homing on the phosphorescence of the foam that was visible through the dark. They were using radar, and the launch showed up as a blip on their screen.

Three shells erupted together, so near to the launch that the Executioner was showered with icy spray. While his ears were still ringing from the multiple detonation, he stood up and dove again into the water, striking away from the boat in a fast Australian crawl.

The maneuver was only just in time. A giant fireball billowed into the sky as the gunners scored a direct hit. Deafened anew by the colossal blast, he plunged beneath the surface to escape the splintered planking and fragments of metal raining down into the boiling sea.

When he resurfaced, a portion of the wreck was still floating, blazing fiercely. Roaring flames leaned sideways, painting a lurid red light on the underside of a column of black smoke teased away by the wind. Then, quite slowly, the hulk turned over and sank with a hiss of steam.

Bolan was alone in the darkness.

The launch had been clinker-built, with overlapping blanks. A curved length of teak, part of the savaged hull, washed against the warrior as he tread water. He clung on to it gratefully, kicking out with his feet to propel himself in the general direction of the cabin cruiser. If he failed to locate it in the dark, he could stay afloat until dawn, then make it back there when he saw the boat rising above the swell.

No dice.

The guns opened fire again, bellowing out tongues of fire. Shells exploded in the sea four or five hundred feet ahead of Bolan. He cursed, but there was nothing he could do. For the Bulgarians, the *Aruba Sport* would make a blip on the radar screen just as big as the launch. Maybe even more definite. They would find the boat long before he could.

This time they were really on the ball—they hit paydirt with the second salvo. Again, a direct hit. Once more the thunderclap of explosions rolled across the surface of the water. For the second time he saw the livid flash, the sudden fountain of blazing debris, trailing spirals of smoke as the target disintegrated.

Five minutes later he heard the turbo-whine of an aero engine and then the clatter of rotors as the chopper lifted off the rig's helipad.

It flew fifty feet above the waves, sweeping the surface of the sea with a searchlight. Bolan let go of the driftwood and floated facedown with his arms and legs spread-eagled. With half the wet suit ripped away and his naked legs and buttocks pale against the dark water, he hoped he would look sufficiently corpselike to satisfy the spotters.

The dazzling beam swept over him and went on to the place where the cruiser had sunk. The chopper circled a couple of times, dropped down almost to sea level and then winged back above the charred flotsam that marked the launch's grave. Holding his breath with his head underwater, Bolan felt the muscles of his back contract, tensed for the leaden whip that would thrash the life out of him in a single blinding burst of pain.

But no shots were fired. The bird circled once and then returned to the rig. He must, he guessed as he gratefully gulped in air, look just about as dead as he felt!

The wind was rising. The swell was breaking up into short, steep waves that slapped his face. It took him ten minutes to locate the plank, or one like it.

Buoyed up by the single piece of wood, he was adrift in the dark, in worsening weather conditions, forty-six miles from the nearest land.

**10**

Rum, scalding hot and piquant with spices and lemon, burned down through Mack Bolan's throat and burned through the top half of his body. He choked, gagging on the fiery liquor, and then looked up as life began returning to his numbed limbs.

He was lying in a four-bunk cabin, wrapped in a blanket, in a small boat making it fast through a choppy sea. The bow smacked down, each time the craft lifted, in a hiss of spray. Through a circular porthole he could see low clouds veiling a watery sun.

"What the hell . . . ?" the warrior croaked.

The man holding the mug of grog smiled. He was compactly built, clean shaven, with bright, keen eyes beneath close-cropped curly hair. "Feel better, sport?" he asked. "Bit of lead back in the pencil? You just sank half a bottle of Chanel No 5!"

Bolan gaped. It was the Australian smuggler, O'Riley. If it hadn't been for the voice, he would never have related this spruce character with the unshaven dropout he had last seen on the water's edge in Istanbul. "How did you . . . ?" he began hoarsely.

"Pick up the damnedest flotsam in my racket," O'Riley remarked conversationally. "Forty kilos of weed drifting in a waterproof package once—and I don't mean from the Sargasso. Corpse strangled with barbed wire another time. Off the east coast of Cyprus."

Bolan stared at him.

"Got me a live one this time, didn't I?" The Australian grinned.

The warrior's face, hollowed by fatigue, mirrored disbelief. "You're telling me that in one hundred and fifty thousand square miles of inland sea, you just happened . . . ?"

"Tell you the truth," O'Riley said, "we were kind of looking. For survivors, I mean."

"Survivors?"

"Gunfire at night. Flashes on the horizon. Shells bursting and a chopper aloft. Interesting, I thought. Why not take a look-see."

"You figured there might be some kind of pickings?"

"Do you mind!" O'Riley said with reproach in his voice. "We found wreckage. First rule of the sea—even the baddies respect it. If a ship sinks, you look for survivors."

"And you found me?"

"Only just, cobber. Clinging to a spar, half-dead. Been there for several hours, I reckon. My surprise when we fished you out."

"Mine, too." Bolan cleared his throat. He freed a hand from the blanket and held it out. "I'm obliged."

"All in the night's work," O'Riley said. He shook.

"Okay," Bolan said, "so how come you happen to be in the area, anyway? If that's not a secret."

"No secrets among friends. But don't tell the customs police. The answer is smokes."

"Smokes?"

"Cigarettes, the Yankee brand. The Russkies go for them in a big way. So would you if you could only buy that horseshit at the end of a cardboard tube that they smoke. There's a PX 'somewhere in Europe' where it seems they have more than they need, so I run a few cartons in to Ivan, in the marshes west of Odessa."

"You mean you recycle merchandise that fell off the back of a truck?"

"You got it." The Australian looked out the porthole. The sun was trying to break through the clouds, and there was a patch of blue sky off to one side. His manner suddenly became brisk and businesslike. "You did me a favor there in Istanbul. This is my round. We can fix you up with a sweater and jeans, a little of the ready, a gun if you need one. But *I* need to know where we can put you ashore. We have another operation in hand that's kind of... delicate... and—"

"You want I should get the hell out of here before."

O'Riley nodded. "Well, yeah. Where would it suit you? You won't want to go back to Sinop."

"Not really."

"And I wouldn't think—from my own experience—that you'd have any special reasons for wanting to make it back to Istanbul."

"You can say that again. Anyplace else, any country that has a public phone system."

"Okay. Well, for personal reasons, Romania's out, as far as I'm concerned. That leaves us with a choice of one. How does Bulgaria grab you?"

"Bulgaria," the Executioner replied, "would suit me just fine."

THE CAB DRIVER LOOKED at Bolan a little strangely. "Perestrek 32," he repeated. "You sure that's the address you want?"

"Sure I'm sure." Bolan's eyebrows were raised. "Why do you ask? It's not far from here, is it?"

"Not far, no. It's near the Place Lénine, a cul-de-sac off the Boulevard Georgi-Dimitrov." The cabbie shrugged his shoulders and eased the Moskva taxi into the traffic flow outside Sofia's central station. "Whatever you say."

Bolan settled back against the threadbare Bedford Cord seat. It was two days since the smuggler O'Riley had made a dawn landing on the Bulgarian coast somewhere south of Varna, and twenty-four hours since Hal Brognola's courier had contacted the Executioner with the clothes, weapons and papers he had demanded in his urgent coded phone call to the Fed. In the meantime he had made the one-hundred-fifty-mile journey across the country's central highlands without any interference. According to the papers he now carried, he was Mike Blanski, a member of the Soviet-American Cultural Friendship Society on a fact-finding trip to check out Eastern bloc methods of collective farming. He even had a brand-new visa from the Russian Embassy in Washington, D.C., allowing him access to any Warsaw Pact country.

Mr. Blanski, it seemed, was a journalist in his own country, which was why he carried a Nikon camera to supplement the written investigations he would publish on his return. Nobody so far had thought to investigate the expensive black hide camera case in which he carried the lenses and meters and other high-tech accessories of the photographer's art. The false bottom of the case hid a new Beretta 93-R with its shoulder rig, the Turkish-made Walther PPK given to him by O'Riley and a number of nonexplosive martial items that were only slightly less lethal.

Bolan looked curiously out the window as the cab sped toward the center of the city. It was the first time he had been in Sofia, which, until the Soviet takeover at the end of World War II, had been one of the least industrialized capitals of Europe. There was plenty of modernization now. A ring of factories, chemical works and refineries surrounded the old town, and there were many new office buildings and apartment blocks, solidly built, with small windows in the Eastern European style, but impressive enough in their way.

The strongest impression the warrior had—as he did in all the Eastern cities—was the lightness of the traffic flow. There was an ancient domed building surrounded by trees in the center of the wide square named after Lenin, but pedestrians could cross over at any point without hurrying or having to leap aside, and the broad paved parking areas on either side of the Boulevard Georgi-Dimitrov could have taken as many cars again and still looked empty.

On a bluff a quarter of a mile along the boulevard, the sixteenth-century Banja-Basi mosque raised a cupola, three small domes and a minaret skyward above Moorish arches fronting the street. The cabbie turned abruptly left, swearing at the driver on a tramway car rocketing along the tracks in the middle of the road. He shot into a narrow lane opposite the bluff and braked violently to a halt fifty yards along, between two rows of gray, dormered buildings that were five stories high. "That's the place," he growled, pointing ahead, "the one after the street lamp, with the sentry outside."

Bolan paid and started walking as the Moskva backed noisily up and turned into the boulevard. Why, he wondered, hadn't the driver taken him right to the door?

He knew nothing about No. 32 on the street called Perestrek. It was only by chance that he had the lead at all. Without going into detail, he had inferred, talking to O'Riley, that there was something odd about the Black Sea oil rig. And he had asked, casually, if his rescuer happened to have any contacts in Bulgaria who might provide a handle.

At the time, the Australian had made no reply. Then, right at the last moment, when the rubber dinghy that had landed Bolan was already disappearing into the dawn mist, he had called out: "If it's contacts you want, sport, make it to Sofia and knock on the door at Perestrek 32. If they don't know, nobody will."

Knocking on the door, Bolan reckoned as he approached the building, was not to be taken literally. The place had a central courtyard approached through an archway in the front facade. There was a uniformed sentry there, as the cabbie had said. Inside the arch there were four more; two on each side of a flight of steps that led up to the main entrance. They all carried Russian Stechkin machine pistols, and each man looked as if he knew how to use the gun. At one side of the yard a black ZIL limo was parked by three camouflaged Lada off-roaders.

Bolan walked on past. Seventy yards farther on, the lane turned a corner and ended facing a high brick wall.

An old man with a pail and a broom was sluicing the sidewalk outside a dingy tavern. Bolan stopped in front of him. The bar looked empty. "Tell me, friend," Bolan said, relying on his limited language ability, "that place around the corner, at No. 32. What goes on there, exactly?"

The old man stared. He looked nervously over his shoulder. "You must be new in town—or a foreigner," he said, licking his lips. "I thought everyone knew—that's the headquarters of the Secret Service's wet affairs unit."

**11**

Bolan's own contact, the only one he had in Sofia, had been set up by the Bulgarian dissidents on the coast who'd been checking out arms shipments for him.

The guy was leader of a guerrilla band, the kind of group whose existence the Communist rulers of the country preferred to forget. His name was Vasil Stojkov. He represented a tradition deriving from the haiduk people who had for centuries rebelled against the authorities.

The meet was in a taverna outside the city, in a medieval village overlooking the Iskar River, and Bolan could see at once that Stojkov had a hell of a lot going for him. He was a big man, as tall as the Executioner and a good deal heavier. His fierce blue eyes, staring out of a seamed peasant face above a bushy iron-gray beard, took in the warrior's outward appearance in a single scorching glance. And accepted him as a kindred spirit, while reserving judgment on his moral qualities until experience marked up a score. Bolan liked him immediately, and felt an element of trust that was tempered with caution.

"Wet affairs," Stojkov said when the Executioner had put him in the picture, "is something of a simplification. The Secret Service as a whole will certainly deal in such matters. Witness the broadcaster murdered in London with the Rycin-smeared umbrella tip. It will carry out operations for the KGB with which the Russians do not wish to be involved—helping the Italian Red Brigades kidnap Brigadier Dozier in 1981, for instance. It will allow free passage to terrorist groups and, if necessary, supply arms. The mad Turk's attempt on the life of the Pope is an example. But the unit operating from Perestrek 32 is rather more specialized, and its aims are specific.''

"You're saying it's a Bulgarian equivalent of No. 2 Dzerzhinsky Square, in Moscow?'' Bolan asked.

"In a way. But not precisely. The unit is known as C.4—like the RDX-based plastic explosive—and its task in general is disinformation, with the specific aim of destabilizing Western society.''

"Even the KGB doesn't have that as its principal aim anymore,'' Bolan objected.

"No. But our hard-line Marxists here do. They don't like this phasing out of the old Cold War. They think Moscow has cold feet!'' The Bulgarian's deep voice erupted into a rumbling laugh at his wordplay. "If their destabilizing maneuvers embarrass Moscow, so much the better, eh?''

They were drinking beer out of one-liter tankards. Stojkov banged his on the wooden table and roared an order for refills to the white-aproned barkeep. "It is quite possible, of course,'' he said, leaning confidentially toward the Executioner, "that such maneuvers may involve what you call wet affairs. Or result in them. But that is not the main purpose of them. The unit is not a school for hit men. It is much more sophisticated than that.''

"Okay,'' Bolan said. "So why would section C.4 of the Bulgarian Secret Service stockpile missiles charged with MPD or Sarin nerve gas on a phony oil rig in the Black Sea? If that section is in fact responsible. I don't know for sure that it is.''

"It sounds like one of their schemes,'' the Bulgarian said.

"And if it is responsible,'' Bolan pursued, "why would the guys on the rig also have a supply of GI uniforms, helmets and U.S. Army hardware? Tell me that.''

"I can think of one reason.''

Bolan nodded grimly. "The obvious answer,'' he said, "is to embarrass the United States in some way, to pull off some military coup, using American material, and have the U.S. blamed for it. You agree?''

''As you say, it seems obvious.''

''Which is why I have to find out pretty damned quick what these guys are up to. Specially if it involves chemical warfare.''

''I understand,'' the guerrilla leader said heavily. ''But there is only one way to answer these questions, to find out if the C.4 people *are* responsible and perhaps to get a line on their plan, if they are.''

''And that is?''

''Enter Perestrek 32 at night and go through their files.''

''Oh, sure,'' Bolan said. ''You mind if I look around here a little, Colonel, check out the paperwork and maybe stay late after the office closes? All I need is a few photocopies.''

Stojkov smiled. ''You can laugh, my friend, but that is not impossible. We have plans, quite detailed plans, of the interior of the building.

''No small feat!'' Bolan said appreciatively. ''You're not putting me on?''

''By no means. We have friends, allies, in many places. What we lack is individuals with the courage, the initiative, to make use of the information they supply.''

''When can I see the plans?''

''In exactly...'' Stojkov looked at his watch. ''In forty-five minutes, when the government servants start their one-hour luncheon break.''

''You mean the city?'' Bolan drained his second tankard. ''Let's go.''

''We have to meet two friends of mine,'' Stojkov said. ''It is better if we ride there on bicycles. There is a machine outside that you can borrow.''

''Suits me. There is one other thing. To make use of the plans, I have to be inside the building, right? You got any ideas on that?''

"It is guarded night and day, of course, with many warning systems. But there is a way in—dangerous, difficult, but possible. It involves crossing roofs and lowering oneself down an air shaft."

"That's my scene," Bolan said. "Do I need backup?"

"You already have it. I will make myself responsible."

"I appreciate that." Bolan put money on the table and rose to his feet. "What really bugs me," he said, "I mean I can understand the rest, but why the hell would they need an *oil rig*?"

"Perhaps we shall find out," Stojkov replied.

His two friends proved to be burly countrymen perspiring in tightly buttoned suits of cheap material. Clearly, with their red faces and hardblock felt hats, they were farm workers up for a day among the bright lights. "Our secret police," Stojkov told Bolan, "are dumb enough to believe that anyone who looks like a hick from the sticks is going to behave like one!" He himself was wearing a sleeveless leather vest over a collarless shirt and mud-stained corduroys.

They met, as if by chance, in a public garden outside the National Archeological Museum, which was housed in an ancient mosque. Children played on the grass nearby as Bolan and his guide leaned their bikes against a slatted bench where the two men were already sitting. On the far side of a wide graveled pathway, flights of pigeons circled a stall selling bread rolls stuffed with mountain ham and hot *Parkis* sausages. It was, Bolan thought, a sufficiently innocent place to plan a raid on the headquarters of a murderous espionage organization.

Stojkov's confederates were introduced as Aleksandar Botev and Boris Levski. Botev, it seemed, was an armorer, and his companion a quarryman who was the group's explosives expert.

They had been there less than five minutes when the bread roll vendor looked their way and nodded from behind his counter. Stojkov rose to his feet and stretched. "That means our man is leaving his office," he told Bolan. "If we go now, that should be about right."

Bolan followed him without asking questions. He had no doubt Stojkov knew what he was doing.

Levski and Botev walked off in the opposite direction, but organized their pace in such a way that they approached the garden's exit gate a few yards ahead of the two wheeling their bicycles.

On the far side of the street that passed the garden, clerks and secretaries hurried down the broad flight of steps that would have been visible to the vendor at his stall. The steps led to the stone-pillared portico of a block of government offices. Stojkov came to a halt, resting the bike's frame against his thigh. He took an orange from his pocket and began peeling it. The other two men went out the gate and stood talking on the sidewalk.

A small man wearing a black jacket and striped pants crossed the street from the government building. His eyes were hidden behind circular, steel-rimmed shades, and there was a wisp of mustache on his upper lip. He appeared to be reading a letter as he walked.

Stojkov touched Bolan's arm and began strolling toward the gate once more, steering the bike with one hand. The small man passed through the gate, still reading. Then, with a shrug that could have been disappointment, he crumpled the letter into a ball and tossed it into a litter basket attached to the railings inside the gateway. He passed Bolan and the guerrilla leader without a glance.

At the litter basket, Stojkov dropped in the orange peel. When his arm returned to his side, the crumpled paper was hidden in his huge fist. Outside the gate, he ate the orange, unfurled the paper and used it to wipe his hands. Afterward he tore it into small pieces, which he dropped down a grating in the gutter. It would have seemed, to anyone watching, an innocuous enough series of actions. But it had given him time to read and memorize the single line of handwriting on the paper.

"Quite smooth!" Bolan acknowledged.

"We have to be very careful," the Bulgarian said. "Anything we have on paper is kept moving. That message was to indicate today's address."

Bolan nodded. "That's good security. What's the strength of the secret police?"

"Very strong. They are not all that intelligent but they have unlimited powers. They are cruel, merciless, and they are answerable to nobody. Fall into their hands, and your friends can kiss you goodbye."

"And the guys at Perestrek 32, the men of C.4?"

"They work only outside the country. The planning is here, but the building is guarded by the military, who are answerable, in this case, to the secret police."

"And just how well they guard it," the Executioner said, "we shall find out tonight."

THE SAFEHOUSE was sandwiched between a joiner's yard and a bicycle repair shop at the end of a street of run-down buildings in the medieval quarter of the city. They had reached it, leaving their bikes chained to a rail outside a school, via a warren of lanes and alleys, one of Stojkov's companions riding shotgun on the far side of each narrow street, the other playing backup one hundred yards behind.

They were stopped by uniformed police once. A routine check.

"Papers," the tallest of the three-man patrol demanded, holding out his left hand. His right was wrapped around the stock of a machine pistol, the first two fingers laid alongside the trigger guard. The butt of a Tokarev automatic protruded from the unflapped holster at his waist. Stojkov, Bolan and the guy across the street produced their papers. Levski, who had been bringing up the rear, walked on past without being challenged.

The cop handed the papers to the man on his left without looking at them. The machine pistol, slung on a webbing strap from his right shoulder, covered Bolan and his friends very steadily.

The man with the ID documents read each one slowly, pausing to check faces with photos, turning back a page from time to time. The third policeman kept staring at the three men, watching their expressions for signs of nervousness, for a bead of sweat on a brow or an upper lip. Then he switched with the second guy, scrutinizing the papers while his mate handled the stare. It was the classic Eastern bloc ploy, designed to intimidate and expose.

"What are you doing in the city?" the cop who had first looked at the papers asked Stojkov.

"The trade fair in the Socialist Agricultural Hall," the bearded man said. "There's a new Soviet-designed combine harvester—"

"And you?" the policeman interrupted, turning to Botev.

"It's cabbages, cabbages, cabbages on my collective," Botev answered. "I've been sent to inquire about chemical fertilizers that promise a better yield."

The man with the machine pistol had taken Bolan's papers. Now he put in his own bid. "A stranger?" he said. "A foreigner? And just what is your interest, Comrade, in this city at this time?"

"I am here to investigate modern methods of collective farming. As you can see." Bolan nodded toward the Soviet visa and its attached document, which the cop had been reading.

"But surely you would be much better off talking to the commissar in charge of increased production, or even the party secretary with responsibility for agriculture? These country bumpkins will be able to tell you nothing." The cop was contemptuous.

"One can," Bolan said smoothly, "learn a lot from the men who actually do the work."

"You can say that again," the man who first read the papers said. "Just try asking the pen pushers up at headquarters what police work is really like!"

The man with the machine pistol grunted, then waved Bolan and his companions on.

"The Farm Directorate Committee Member will be speaking at the fair tonight," the third policeman called after Stojkov. "Mind you don't let the manure on your boots foul up the red carpet!"

All three of the cops burst into loud guffaws. "You see the kind of thing we have to put up with?" Botev said bitterly as they rounded a corner and the patrol was lost to sight.

Levski was waiting for them in the hallway of the safehouse. He was with a frail, elderly man with wispy white hair and a haggard face. "This is Hristo Stambolijski," Levski said to Bolan, "and don't be fooled by the exterior—there's wiry strength still in those skinny limbs!"

The old man grinned. "A pleasure," he said in a high, fluting tenor voice. "I understand we shall be working together tonight."

"That so?" Bolan said. He looked inquiringly at Stojkov.

"I'm just the pointman, the backup, the minder," the guerrilla leader explained. "Stambolijski here is the inside man, on account of his trade. He's the real professional, you see."

"His trade being?"

"He's a burglar," Levski said proudly. "The best second-story guy Sofia ever had, not that there's much worth stealing in this socialist democratic paradise."

"He's an archivist," Botev corrected. "He...acquires documents of various kinds that people prefer to keep private—"

"And will pay a lot of money, hopefully, to get back," Stambolijski cut in with a twinkle in his eye.

"And among these documents," Bolan said, "are details of the security arrangements at Perestrek 32?"

"Correct. Although this is one item I wouldn't suggest the interested parties buy back!" The burglar smiled again.

"Now we take a look, no?" Stojkov said.

Levski and Botev produced pistols from a closet beneath the house's rickety stairway. They went, one to the front window, the other to a door opening on a yard, to keep watch. Stojkov, Bolan and the old man went upstairs.

The place was shabbily furnished with pieces, many of them worn out or broken, that could have come from a run-down junk shop. Stambolijski moved aside a trundle bed that was the only item in a second-floor bedroom at the back of the house. He peeled back a threadbare rug and pried up on of the dusty floorboards with a screwdriver. In the dark hollow beneath was a zippered canvas valise about eighteen inches long. Stambolijski took out a wad of tightly rolled papers secured with elastic bands. He slipped off the rubber retainers and began spreading the papers out on the floor.

Bolan and Stojkov knelt down beside him. Bolan saw photostats of official documents, roughly sketched plans of military installations, grainy blowups of men with undressed women, a sheet of paper crammed with handwritten columns of statistics.

The floor plan of the Secret Service headquarters was fuzzy and indistinct in places. It had clearly been rephotographed several times from an original architect's blueprint. Additional notations had been scribbled in green ink, and certain areas on the plan were outlined in red marker.

"The red sectors," Stambolijski explained, "indicate certain areas inside the building that are protected by a specialized volumetric alarm system. The house as a whole is equipped with the more usual type of warning—magic eye beams, pressure pads under windows and inside doors, electric circuits guarding all the entries and exits."

"Except," Stojkov said, "one very small transom window halfway up the wall of the air shaft I told you about."

"Got it," Bolan confirmed.

"The window lets air into a washroom cubicle. It's only around nine inches deep, but it's a couple feet wide. It's hinged at the top, and even a husky guy like you should be able to squeeze through.''

"Okay," Bolan said, "and to reach this window...?"

"Like I told you—down from the roof on a rope."

"No downspouts? No ledges? No way at all from the bottom of the shaft?"

"No way."

Bolan nodded. "Right, I'll buy that. Now, this red sector—" he indicated the plan "—that you marked. The top secret material is all kept inside there, I guess?"

"Correct," Stambolijski confirmed.

"A *volumetric* system, you said?"

"That's right. Once the windows and doors have all been shut, the last man out presses a switch and a computer reads the atmospheric pressure inside the closed area. The smallest change in that figure—something that could be caused by the opening of a door, a current of air set up by a moving body—trips a contact and the alarm goes off."

"How is the system deactivated?"

"The switch is a push-button affair. Push it a second time, and the computer is disarmed. You can do this manually, if you happen to be near enough, or with a telecommand gadget if you happen to have one on the right wavelength. It's like the alarm system on some automobiles."

"The way you describe it," Bolan said slowly, "it seems the alarm is only going to be effective against an intruder *trying to enter through a window within your red area.* Otherwise, if you're in the building already, you could just walk up, press the button and—"

"Not quite," Stojkov corrected. "The computer's a black box fixed to the wall outside the main entrance to the area. It's at the far end of a forty-foot corridor blocked by a steel grille gateway. And there's a separate alarm system wired to that. Force the gate, and the red-sector alarm is activated automatically."

"The guy setting the alarm, once he's pressed the button, has twenty-five seconds to make it down the passage and close the grille before the computer's armed," Levski said.

"So, how do the people from C.4 get back in?" the warrior asked. "With a telecommand box?"

"That's right. And, no, we don't have one. Only the top three officers running the unit do. So far we haven't been able to get anywhere near them."

"Okay," Bolan said. "Now let's check the whole building out, floor by floor. We'll deal with the computer when we come to it."

He listened carefully as the two dissidents went over the plan in minute detail, questioning and requestioning when something was not quite clear or the drawing imprecise, storing each possible entry, exit and escape channel in his memory.

The guerrillas who assembled the Intel had done their work well. The number of guards at any given time, the frequency of indoor patrols and the route they took, the arms they carried, details of the shift rotation—it was all there, neatly docketed and keyed in to the floor plans.

"You guys sure know your business," the Executioner said warmly when at last the rundown was complete. "So, what say we move on one space, start working on a plan of attack that'll get us in there—and leave me enough time to sift through every goddamned file they have?"

It was two hours later, rain was falling and street lamps shone through the dusk already along the deserted lane when finally he reckoned every angle had been covered. "I'll split now," he told Stojkov, "eat at my state-run, foreigners-only hotel and turn in early. No point raising suspicions by staying up late. I already took enough photos at the trade fair to add up to a day's work for a visiting news hawk. Did you say you were interested in combine harvesters? I can offer you pictures full face, rear elevation or profile of every machine in the show!"

Stojkov grinned. "How will you get out again?" he asked. "You know the desk clerks and janitors at those hotels are all members of the secret police. They report every movement."

"So long as they don't keep watch on the downspout outside my window..." Bolan replied.

## 12

Toward midnight the rain fell more heavily. By the time Mack Bolan climbed out his bedroom window and swarmed down the downspout at 1:00 a.m., the city streets were awash and the downpour had reached almost tropical proportions.

That was both good and bad news: good because foot patrols from the army, the police and the militia, along with any stray nightlifers, would have run for shelter; bad because he was soaked to the skin before he made one-tenth of the five hundred yards between the hotel and his rendezvous with the dissidents. And he would have to work throughout the night in clammy, wet clothes.

The rdv was in a bus shelter between the old tramway tracks in the center of the Boulevard Georgi-Dimitrov. To Bolan's annoyance, there were already several people there when he arrived. He squashed into a corner, making himself as inconspicuous as possible, but he was aware that the skintight pants of the combat blacksuit he wore beneath his lightweight windbreaker were already drawing curious glances. There was no sign of Stojkov or the burglar.

The rain drummed heavily on the shelter roof, bounced calf-high off the flooded pavement and gurgled in the gutters at each side of the road. A closed truck splashed past, spraying wide fans of muddy water from its front wheels. Several people leaped aside, cursing as the liquid mud fell like a whip across the glass panels of the shelter and spattered them from the knees down. A young man and his girl opened a cardboard suitcase, took out a tartan rug, held it over their heads and ran off into the storm.

Bolan looked at his watch. It was almost a quarter to two. The meet had been scheduled for one-thirty.

Some minutes later, as the headlights of a homegoing cab swept across the facades of the buildings across the street, he recognized a bulky, bearded figure huddled into a recessed doorway. Stojkov was waiting over there.

Pantomiming the reactions of an impatient man finally pissed off waiting for the rain to stop, Bolan consulted the watch again, sighed heavily, peered out of the shelter and up at the sky, then shrugged and made a dash for it.

He sprinted across the roadway, bounded up the steps, and joined the guerrilla leader in the doorway. "My fault. I didn't see you before," he panted. "You been waiting long?"

"Since one-thirty. Those folks in the shelter loused up the schedule, but it doesn't do for me to be recognized after dark and I didn't like to signal you from here."

"No sweat," Bolan said. "Where's your second-story man?"

"Around the corner in the dry. The rain's bad for his rheumatism."

The warrior grinned. "He's plenty game, that one! How old is the guy?"

"Sixty-seven. Yeah, he's one of a kind, all right. They don't come that way anymore."

The Secret Service, Bolan had been told, had requisitioned the buildings on either side of No. 32, so the approach to the roofs had to be made two houses away. The place Stojkov had chosen was a rooming house. All the boarders had been vetted, screened and okayed by the secret police before they were permitted to stay there. "But there are always ways," the guerrilla said, "if you have the right kind of handle."

Nobody was asking the roomers to help out, but it had been arranged—whether by threats, bribes or blackmail

Stojkov did not say—that nobody would pay any mind to the comings and goings that night. "It pays sometimes," he said, "especially in a socialist paradise, to be looking the other way."

Bolan nodded. He knew the tune.

Stambolijski, looking heavier, fleshier than he had the previous afternoon, was waiting in the lobby. The three of them crept upstairs. Behind different doors, they heard the sound of snoring, the muted sounds of a radio relaying Greek bouzouki music, the tapping of a typewriter, a murmur of voices. But they saw nobody.

On the top floor a stepladder leaned against the wall. Stojkov opened it out and placed it beneath a trapdoor in the ceiling. He climbed up and raised the trap. Mentally Bolan awarded five on five for good preparation—the trap lifted soundlessly on oiled hinges. Rain lanced down into the stairwell. "We're on our way," Stojkov whispered.

The roofs of the row houses along Perestrek were steeply pitched, slippery with wet soot and exposed to the relentless pelting of the rain. For the three intruders, creeping along six floors above the ground, ducked down behind the ridgelines to avoid being seen from the street, the traverse was perilous. A misplaced foot could result in a chute down the slope of wet slate and a drop to certain death on the flooded cobbles ninety feet below; a stumble and a tile displaced could bring the guard running from the courtyard of No. 32.

A narrow lane lined with garbage cans ran behind Nos. 28 and 30, but the Secret Service building with its inner courtyard ran back into the neighboring block, and there was a bewildering confusion of gables and dormers to be negotiated before they arrived above the air shaft. The trip took them almost a half hour.

At one side of the shaft a chimney stack supporting a dozen pots rose ten feet above the roof. Stojkov leaned his back against the wide stone slab and produced a soft nylon backpack from beneath his sodden raincoat. "You can stash

# POW!

## THE MOST GENEROUS
## FREE OFFER EVER!
### From the Gold Eagle Reader Service

# ACCEPT FOUR BRAND-NEW

# YOURS

We'd like to send you four free Gold Eagle books, worth $11.80 retail, to introduce you to the benefits of the Gold Eagle Reader Service. We hope your action-packed free books will convince you to subscribe, but that's up to you. Accepting them places you under no obligation to buy anything, but we hope you'll want to continue!

So unless we hear from you, we'll send you five additional Gold Eagle books every second month on free home approval (Two Mack Bolans, and one each of Able Team, Phoenix Force and Vietnam: Ground Zero). If you choose to keep them, you'll pay just $2.49 per book—a saving of over 15% off the suggested cover price for five books. There is NO charge for shipping and handling! There are NO hidden extras! And you may always return a shipment at our cost, simply by dropping it in the mail, or cancel at any time. The free books and gift remain yours to keep, in any case.

Why is the Gold Eagle Reader Service so great? Because here's what you'll get...

- Hot-off-the-press Gold Eagle books BEFORE they're available in stores
- All titles delivered in sequence—you never have to miss a title in the series
- Hefty savings off the retail price
- Always with the right to cancel and owe nothing
- Free copy of *AUTOMAG* newsletter in every shipment
- FREE convenient home delivery

## PLUS... A SURPRISE MYSTERY GIFT FREE!!!

As a free gift, just for accepting four free books, we'll send you a surprise mystery gift—ABSOLUTELY FREE!!

# GOLD EAGLE® NOVELS
# FREE!

## *Gold Eagle® Reader Service*

AFFIX
FOUR FREE BOOKS
STICKER HERE

**YES,** send me my free books and gift as explained on the opposite page. I have affixed my "free books" sticker above and my "free gift" sticker below. I understand that accepting these books and gift places me under no obligation ever to buy any books; I may cancel at any time, for any reason, and the free books and gift will be mine to keep!     165 CIM RABT

NAME
_____
                    (PLEASE PRINT)
ADDRESS _____ APT. _____

CITY _____

STATE _____ ZIP _____

Terms and prices subject to change without notice. Offer limited to one per household and not valid for present subscribers. NY and IOWA residents subject to sales tax.

AFFIX FREE SURPRISE
MYSTERY GIFT STICKER
HERE

# WE EVEN PROVIDE FREE POSTAGE!

It costs you nothing to send for your free books—we've paid the postage on the attached reply card. And we'll pick up the postage on your shipment of free books and gifts, and also on any subsequent shipments of books, should you choose to become a subscriber. Unlike many book clubs, we charge nothing for postage and handling!

your outer stuff in here," he murmured. Bolan stripped off his windbreaker and rolled it up. The blacksuit was already glistening with moisture, but the thermic material maintained his body temperature at the optimum operating level.

When Stambolijski stripped off his coat, the warrior saw why the old man had looked heavier than he did before—a rope ladder was coiled around his waist and midriff.

He unwound it carefully, testing each rung of the thin, tough nylon cord in the diffuse light thrown up by the street lamps below. Beneath it a leather carpenter's belt held an array of steel tools. Bolan was harnessed into the shoulder rig that held the Beretta and its silencer. A small but powerful electric flashlight and the Nikon camera were clipped to his waist belt.

Working in semidarkness on the slippery tiles was nerve-racking for all three of them, but in less than ten minutes they had located the transom window, revealed in a single quick flash of the warrior's torch. They positioned the unrolled ladder beside it and belayed the support cords at its upper end around two iron hoops cemented into the stack for the use of chimney sweeps.

Stambolijski touched Bolan's arm. The old man's thin hair was plastered to his skull, the thick-lensed spectacles were pockmarked with rain, his pants wrapped around his legs like waterlogged rags. But Bolan could have sworn he surprised a gleeful smile creasing the haggard face. He nodded, and Stambolijski moved toward the shaft.

Stojkov had been on the far side of the ridgeline to check out the building's courtyard. He returned as the burglar was letting himself down into the shaft on the first few rungs of the ladder. "Seems fine," he whispered. "The guard detail are playing cards in a glassed-in kiosk beside the main entrance. The night sentries—there are only two after midnight—are sheltering beneath the portico. The man on duty by the arch is in the dry, too—smoking a cigarette in a doorway."

"Swell. We'll see you when we can." Bolan swung himself over the stone rim of the shaft and felt with one foot for the upper rungs of the rope ladder.

Stojkov raised a hand in farewell and ducked down out of sight. His job as a minder was to check as far as possible that the personnel guarding the building made no alteration to their normal routine, that the relief detail due to take over at 4:00 a.m. arrived in the usual truck, that the guys being relieved did leave in the truck...and of course to give covering fire if Bolan and the burglar were discovered and had to flee.

Swaying on the flimsy ladder in the darkness of the shaft, with the rain needling fiercely through the hair on his bare head, Bolan felt in some ways more vulnerable than he had on many adventures that were theoretically far more hazardous. There were no windows opening onto the shaft on the six, fifth or fourth floors. The transom was on the third. Below that there were two windows, heavily barred, on each floor, and an armored door at the area level. From any of these, if the alarm was raised, the two of them would be sitting ducks, clamped to the nylon ladder. Bolan was agonizingly aware that thirty or forty feet of nothingness lay between the final rung and the concrete floor. Each small scrape of material against the wall of the shaft, every little knock or thump of elbow, knee or knuckle, seemed abnormally loud to his ears. Even the asthmatic rasp of Stambolijski's breath made the hairs on the nape of his neck tingle.

Fingers momentarily gripped the warrior's ankle. The old man had arrived at the level of the target window.

Now came the difficult part. The transom was hinged at the top. It opened outwards. With one hand grasping the nylon cord, and one foot hooked through a rung, the burglar had to manipulate his tools, slip the catch, pull the window toward him, and then transfer himself to the sill and squeeze through into the room beyond.

And the warrior could do nothing to help him. Marooned six feet higher up against a blank wall, with no ledge, no crevice, no protrusion to grab, he was powerless to steady the ladder, incapable of supporting the old man during his one-handed contortions.

The nylon shivered and shuddered. Bolan heard a small splintering sound, a metallic snick, the squeak of a hinge. And then the ladder twisted and knocked him against the wall as Stambolijski threw himself sideways and scrambled into the opening. But instead of grasping the window frame with both hands and hauling himself in headfirst as Bolan expected, he had swung up a leg, still holding the rope, and turned himself so that he could slide in backward, facing the ground.

Smart, Bolan thought. That way the guy could feel for the floor, exploring with his feet, instead of tumbling with outstretched hands into the unknown.

He was continuing his own descent when a sudden loud thump echoed in the shaft. Bolan froze. The old man's elbow had knocked aside the metal stay holding the transom open, and it had dropped down and hit the top of his head.

Bolan held his breath, listening to the rain splash into the area far below. From over the rooftops he heard a whine of gears and the snarl of an exhaust from the boulevard. But none of the barred windows opened, and no light blazed into the dark.

Thankful, he lowered himself to the sill, reached out and pulled himself through the opening.

Stambolijski's hands emerged from the dark, supported his weight and lowered him gently to the floor. The window was in fact set between five and six feet high in the wall, and anyone tumbling straight through would have made enough noise to alarm even the sleepiest night-watchman.

As they had been told, they were in a men's washroom. Easing open the door, they traversed what seemed to be a small mess hall, avoiding the plastic-topped tables and chairs with small stabs of light from Bolan's flashlight, whose lens was now covered with a mask that only allowed a tiny beam to escape.

The door of the mess hall sighed shut behind them against its hydraulic stop. They were in a long windowless passage. Halfway along, a broad flight of stairs curled down to the lower floors. And at the far end a barred steel gate blocked the way.

"That will be it," the burglar muttered. "The computer should be beyond that. And then the suite protected by the volumetric alarm."

Treading warily, they approached the grille. Bolan lanced the flashlight beam through the bars. Beyond them the corridor continued for a further forty feet and then opened into an empty hallway. The black metal box housing the computer that controlled the alarm system was cemented into the wall beside a heavy oak door. A red pilot glowed above a small switchboard. Below it, attached directly to the wall, was the circular boss that housed the ivory-colored control button.

Bolan unleathered his Beretta. "I have to tell you," Stambolijski breathed, "that the button has to be hit dead-center, smack on the nose—hit it partly on the button, partly on the surround, and you trigger the alarm."

"Now he tells me!" muttered the warrior.

He had been well briefed on the exploit, but it was going to test his skill to the utmost.

The button—the target—was perhaps the size of a man's fingerprint, not a large one. The shot must be one hundred percent accurate, dead center; if the bullet that drove the button home and destroyed it also fouled the side of the casing, it would be a fatal error. And there would be no second chance.

Bolan smiled sourly. He was a professional, an expert, but he remembered reading some wiseguy's statement about people being experts only at dying: we only do it once, and we get it right the first time.

Well, this was the other side of the coin: he had to get it right first time—but the reward was living!

Hitting a half-inch button with a 9 mm handgun at forty feet is no big deal for a marksman. But in such circumstances, in the dubious illumination of a flashlight beam, with so much depending on it . . . Bolan was sweating despite the chill night air and the clammy clasp of his blacksuit.

He had spent an hour in his hotel room modifying the one round he could afford to fire: he reduced the charge, and altered the bullet's profile. It would of course flatten, but the smaller the initial point of impact, the more chance there was that the alarm system would be deactivated in the hundredth of a second before the switch as a whole was destroyed.

Bolan flicked on the torch, checking in the masked beam that the right slug was in the breech. He drew a deep breath. He unscrewed the mask and handed the flashlight to Stambolijski. "Here we go," he said.

The old man directed the powerful shaft of light through the steel bars of the gate. Glaring reflections winked off the shiny black computer casing, and the polished ivory button glittered. "Hold it off to one side," Bolan ordered.

The beam shifted, killing the dazzle.

Bolan approached the grille. He was about to lean his wrist on one of the crossbars when Stambolijski spoke softly. "You cannot fire the gun while you are touching the gate. The vibration could transmit through the metal and trip *that* alarm."

"Even with a suppressor?"

"Even with a suppressor."

Bolan sighed. He had to assume the local talent would know what they were talking about. "That's all I need!" he murmured.

Another deep breath. He held it. He raised the Beretta, left hand supporting the right wrist, eye squinting at the sights, trigger finger curled. He took up the first pressure.

The barrel wavered. Raindrops from his wet hair ran down his forehead and trickled into his eye. He could feel

his heart thumping. Air hissed out between his teeth. He
lowered the autoloader, brushing the blacksuit sleeve over
his face. Somewhere outside, a distant siren warbled.

Bolan filled his lungs again.

He concentrated every atom of his finger's determination on the white button centered in its brown Bakelite casing. If he smashed the entire switch before the circuit was
cut, it would be the signal for the old man's death, his own
death and probably Stojkov's, as well.

The responsibility was frightening.

It was the thought of others depending on him, of what
he owed to these people risking their lives for him, that
steeled his resolve. He relaxed deliberately, then froze into
a statue. The white button grew large in his sight. His trigger finger squeezed gently once, twice.

*Chunnnng!*

An eternity of silence, ringing in his ears, followed the
soft subsonic thud of the silenced Beretta. Then there was a
loud metallic click, and the steel gate swung slowly open.

The flashlight beam hadn't wavered. The red pilot light
above the computer switchboard was no longer illuminated. Stambolijski put up a hand and squeezed the warrior's shoulder. "Bravo!" he said.

"Only a brave man could have stood there the way you
did," Bolan replied. "And don't think for a moment that I
wasn't shit-scared."

Together they pushed the gate open wide, walked through
to the hallway and tried the heavy door beside the savaged
alarm switch. It opened silently and easily.

The burglar was examining the switch. "Beautiful!" he
enthused. The button had been pistoned through to the interior of the mechanism; the brown casing wasn't even
cracked.

"Some days it works out right," the Executioner said. He
passed a hand over his face to brush the sweat from his eyes.

The suite of rooms on the far side of the door opened off
a lobby furnished with a desk, a chair, an intercom and a

closed-circuit video screen. The screen showed a profile view of Stambolijski and himself. It had presumably recorded their traverse of the hallway outside. He hoped the screen was not twinned with another in the guardroom below.

No. Why would it be? It was for the guy behind the desk, so that he could check who—among the people already in the building—wanted in. In theory the guard would have been tipped off to the presence of intruders before they made it as far as the hallway. Just the same...Bolan held up his hand, halting the burglar before he penetrated any farther.

He heard no rush of footsteps, no elevator whine, no shouted orders. Nothing but the swirl of water in the gutters outside and the steady drumroll of the rain.

Should he sabotage the cameras—he discovered the lenses, half hidden in plaster curlicues decorating the ceilings—in case they were recording the images on tape?

Negative again. There might be separate alarm systems wired to the video circuit. If the faces of those who had broken in were on record...well, that was a risk they had to take.

Bolan waited a full two minutes before he was satisfied that their entry remained secret. Then he jerked his head, and they passed through into the other rooms.

There were four of them: a comfortably furnished inner sanctum with an anteroom that contained a secretary's desk and a PBX telephone switchboard, and two offices lined with steel filing cabinets.

The cabinets, a row of box files, three glass-fronted cupboards stuffed with documents and a small safe built into the wall were all locked with varying degrees of security. Bolan gestured with his right hand. "Over to you," he muttered.

Stambolijski walked around each room once and then began to select shining instruments from the collection in the leather belt around his waist. In less than a minute he had the first of the steel cabinets open.

Bolan rolled out the drawers and began flipping through the folders inside.

Time was all too short. Each floor of the building would have been patrolled shortly before they broke in. The guard detail was due to be relieved at 4:00 a.m., and there was another patrol due one hour later. One of the tasks the watchman had to attend to would certainly be to check that the volumetric alarm was still correctly set.

In addition to which, Bolan had to climb the downspout and make it back to his hotel room before daylight.

Put it another way: they had to be out of there and back on that rope ladder by a quarter to five. Because it would be evident, once the sabotaged computer was discovered, that the files had been searched—and all hell would break loose at once. Bolan and the burglar must not only be out of the building but away over the roofs and clear of the Perestrek neighborhood before a cordon was thrown around it.

Many of the different classification systems could be discarded at once. The box files, for instance, contained nothing but cards on individuals—informants, criminals, black marketeers, suspected persons and known dissidents, as well as those ticketed "reliable" and Intelligence colleagues from neighboring Eastern bloc countries. Some of the entries, especially those relating to agents of hostile Intelligence services, were cross-indexed to full dossiers in the glass-fronted cupboards. These included photographs, MOs where known, aliases, idiosyncrasies, sexual habits, probable contacts and lists of operations in which the agent was known to have been involved. One box was devoted entirely to mercenaries. Another detailed the private lives of men and women with a high-security clearance who might be possible subjects for blackmail.

Riffling through hastily, Bolan was amused to see many names that he knew. He had no time to search for his own. None of the entries he found was cross-referenced to current operations or disinformation schemes under consideration. One of the steel cabinets did contain files referring to past operations, but since Bolan's command of the Bulgarian language was limited, and the code names—in English—meant nothing to him, he left them alone.

An hour passed. Stambolijski had opened everything but the safe. He was crouched, listening for tumblers to fall when the warrior swung the flashlight his way. "I don't know that I can do it." He frowned. "It's a seven-figure—"

"Forget it," Bolan cut in. "The safe will be for money to finance wet affairs, false ID papers, that kind of thing. A place sewn up this tight, they don't keep files in there. It's just a question of finding the right reference. In any case it's five to four—we have to kill the light now and wait until the relief detail has taken over down below."

A few minutes later they heard the truck arrive. Regulation-issue army boots clattered in the courtyard below. Voices exchanged coarse pleasantries about the rain. Then the truck drove away and silence returned. "Okay," Bolan said. "We have to keep trying."

He continued to open drawers, ransack files and dump the used material on the floor. "We can't hide the fact that the place has been gone over," he told the burglar, "so why waste precious time shoving it all back?"

The two offices were knee-deep in paperwork, and Bolan had found nothing remotely resembling a reference to an operation involving an offshore oil rig. And then suddenly—it was almost four-thirty—he had the hunch. Immediately, too, he knew it must be right. He went through into the inner sanctum and pulled out the drawers of the boss's desk. Right enough, the guy—whoever he was—kept a personal notebook, a kind of ringback scribbling block on which he jotted down memos relating to the operations in hand.

Bolan carried the book back to the office in triumph.

The secret was no great intellectual discovery. In contrast to the meticulous orderliness of all the other classifications, the files on current plans were kept in the same drawer as those on operations already completed. They were stacked alphabetically. All you had to know was the code word for the scheme. And for Bolan that was no great sweat, either.

Operation Baseball.

Base because of the rig. Ball because it was already rolling. Baseball because, hell, it was American, wasn't it?

Laboriously the warrior began to go through the document. It was honeycombed with dates and geographic references and map coordinates, with comments from the control officer scrawled here and there in red ink in the typescript margins.

The more Bolan read, the more concerned he became. "This is dynamite!" he breathed. "I've got to set up the camera and photograph every single page!"

Stambolijski's reedy tenor interrupted his train of thought. "It is already four-fifty. By the time you arrange your camera and the lighting..." He left the sentence unfinished.

Bolan sighed. "You're right. I'd hoped, if we left everything strewn about the floor, they'd never know exactly what we came for. But we'll have to take the risk that they'll tumble, after all." He stuffed the folder, along with several others, into the waistband of the blacksuit and clapped the burglar on the shoulder. "All right, old friend, we're on our way!"

Back on the rope ladder, they made it as far as the fifth floor before the shooting started.

## 13

Bolan never knew what it was that tipped them off. An impatient NCO who sent off the patrol a little early because he wanted to get back to his card game? A closed-circuit video camera that he himself had missed? A sentry who had spotted Stojkov on the roof? Or it could have been something that Stambolijski and the warrior had overlooked.

Whatever, one of the windows opening onto the lower part of the air shaft was flung up, and the dazzling light that Bolan had feared on the way in was projected skyward through the bars.

Somebody shouted. A handgun spit flame, and then another. A second window opened.

Bolan, bringing up the rear, turned and fired two 3-shot bursts down the well. He heard a yell of pain and a tinkling of glass. But the light remained, crucifying the intruders against the night.

None of the first shots from below had scored. But now gunmen started firing from the second window. Bolan felt a jolt that nearly tore him from the ladder as a slug carried away the heel of one combat boot. Stambolijski, about to hoist himself over the rim of the shaft onto the roof, uttered a choked exclamation and sagged. If Bolan hadn't flashed up one hand to support the old man's limp body, he would have plummeted to the concrete floor at the foot of the well.

Stojkov's head and shoulders appeared above the rim. He emptied a heavy-caliber revolver in the direction of the windows, the shots echoing thunderously in the narrow shaft. "Take the old guy," Bolan panted. "I think he's hit. I can't shoot while I'm holding him."

The guerrilla leader leaned over and seized Stambolijski's shoulders. He hauled him up and off the ladder as Bolan turned again to empty the remaining rounds in the Beretta's short 15-shot magazine.

The guards had ducked back during the fusillade from Stojkov's revolver, but now they were blazing away again, at least three of them. The Nikon slung from the harness at the warrior's waist disintegrated. The shoulder rig jumped as a bullet passed between Bolan's left arm and his ribs. Stone chips gouged from the wall of the shaft raked the knuckles of his left hand where he grasped the nylon cord, drawing blood. Then he, too, was out of the shaft, crouching on the wet roof in the rain beside Stojkov and the prone figure of Stambolijski.

"Is he hurt bad?" Bolan asked.

"Right shoulder," the old man croaked, answering the question himself. "Wrong side for the heart, and I don't think it touched a lung."

"It's bleeding pretty bad, just the same," Stojkov said. "We've got to get him out of here."

"Okay," Bolan said, "let's go." Thrusting the stolen files more securely under his belt, he helped the Bulgarian lift Stambolijski. Together, with the wounded burglar slung between them, they started stumbling toward the open skylight three houses away.

In the street below, on the far side of the ridgelines, there was a lot of noise now. Whistles shrilled, several people shouted commands, heavy boots clattered on the wet cobbles. Bolan and his companions were still only halfway across the roof of the house next to the C.4 headquarters when a detail charged into the alley that ran behind that and No. 28. Half a dozen soldiers took up position along the narrow lane, and an officer and two men carrying submachine guns burst into the rear door of the first house backing on the alley.

Hunched down behind a chimney, Bolan pulled Stojkov's sleeve. "We'll never make it," he whispered. "Not in a million years. In five minutes they'll have this whole neighborhood sewn up tighter than a—well, tight. And we'll still be up here on the roofs. And they'll have found the open trapdoor."

Stojkov was shivering. "And so?"

"So we'll do the only thing we can do. We'll go back."

*"Back?"* The guerrilla leader was dumbfounded.

"Sure. Where's the last place a search party will look for guys who escaped from them? Back in the place they escaped from. You dig?"

"You're telling me that . . . ?"

"We pulled up the ladder and left it on the roof by the shaft. It's still belayed to the rings in that stack. I'm telling you that we let that ladder down again, go in the way we did before, make it down to street level and deck any guys they left behind. There won't be many—they're all blocking the other end of the street!"

"It might work," Stojkov admitted after a moment's silence.

"It's going to work."

"And what happens then? We overcome any guards left in the building—how do we get out from there?"

"You leave that to me," Mack Bolan assured.

Painfully, trying not to hear the increased activity below, they worked their way back to the shaft. Bolan threw the ladder over the edge. Stambolijski's shoulder was hurting too much for him to lock hands around Stojkov's neck; the guerilla had to drape him head-downward over one shoulder in a fireman's hoist and hold on to the ladder with one hand.

Military trucks—two or three—roared up Perestrek and halted with squealing brakes as they began the difficult decent. Bolan went first. The transom was still propped open.

He reached out to grab the sill, transferred his weight, and scrambled in. Then he balanced himself with his hips on the ledge and stretched out his arms to help Stojkov with the difficult task of loading the old man off the ladder, across the yawning gap, and into the building. Sweat was pouring off all three of them when the job was done and they were safely in the men's room. "He's lost a lot of blood," Stojkov said quietly. "We've got to get him to a doctor pretty quick."

Bolan had already noticed the acrid, metallic odor and the dark patches staining all their clothes. His own hands were sticky, black with it in the beam of the masked flashlight. "We'll do our damnedest," he said.

On the far side of the refectory, they took the stairs curving down. There were elevators behind a second exit from the mess hall, but the shaft was closed off with old-fashioned steel latticework gates. Calling up a car would have been the easiest, quickest way to convey Stambolijski to street level, but also, Bolan was convinced, the surest way of tipping off anyone still below that there were strangers in town. Because the mechanism of such an old installation would whine, the gates would clang and the cage would creak.

But reaching the floor below and approaching the second flight of stairs, he had second thoughts. Right now they had no idea how many guards—if any—had been left at the entrance. By using an elevator, he would tempt them to show their hand.

Motioning Stojkov to support the old man and stay where he was, the warrior soft-footed back upstairs and ran to the steel gates. He pressed the call button at the side of the shaft.

At once there was a heavy clunk from somewhere below, followed, as he expected, by the whine of machinery and a metallic rattling as the cage labored upward.

It was followed also by a distant shout and a flurry of footsteps at the bottom of the stairwell.

Bolan sprinted back to rejoin Stojkov, taking the stairs—spattered with drops of blood from the old man's shoulder—three at a time. "Pick him up again and follow me," he ordered. "But keep your distance until I wave you on, okay?"

The Bulgarian nodded. He patted the revolver stuck into his waistband. "You want me to...?"

"No way." Bolan shook his head, showing Stojkov the silenced Beretta. "If we're going to make it out of here, the guys down there must be wasted before they have a chance to shoot. The sound of gunfire would bring the whole damned army running back into the courtyard."

Lifting his hand in a gesture commanding silence, he glided down toward the final bend in the stairway.

There were two of them. Each man carried a Polish-designed M-63 machine pistol with a box magazine packing twenty-five 9 mm rounds. In each case the dark secret police uniform was surmounted by the fairly vacant features of men blessed with toughness and guts but used to command and not efficient in actions on their own. They were facing the elevator shaft, weapons at the ready. In seconds—a heavy click shuddered down the shaft as the car halted outside the refectory—they would realize that nobody was opening the gates, nobody was going to use the elevator.

And then they would start looking elsewhere.

Bolan had eased a new clip into the Beretta while he was still on the roof. He could have picked off the two of them from behind, with a single shot each. And neither of them would have known what happened. But that wasn't the Executioner's way.

He had been crouching. Now he rose and stepped out into the center of the stairway.

Hearing the footfall, the nearer of the men swung around with a curse. He canted up the stubby barrel of the M-63. But before even a nervous reflex could tighten his finger on the trigger, Bolan's autoloader had choked out a lethal 3-shot burst.

The first slug drilled the guy just below the throat, and as he pitched forward, the second channeled a deep trench in the top of his skull. He fell spraying blood and brains.

The second soldier had no luck. He was quicker to react, but in the instant that he whirled toward the menacing figure on the stairway, his companion blocked his field of fire. It was as he sprang sideways that the third round of the Executioner's trio burst took him in the left shoulder, spun him around and flung him to the checkerboard tiles of the entrance hall. He twitched, writhing to sit upright, his mouth open wide to yell.

Bolan made it easy for him, flicking the 93-R onto single-shot and slamming a 9 mm hollowpoint through his heart before he could utter more than a strangled croak.

Stojkov came running down the stairs with the semiconscious burglar over his shoulder. Bolan led the way, and they raced through the doors, past the deserted, glassed-in guardhouse and down the steps into the rain.

But here trouble lay in wait.

The two night sentries posted on each side of the steps had not been ordered away with the rest of the soldiers cordoning off the street. They were sheltering in doorways a few yards away from the main entrance. And something had alerted them, perhaps just the unexpected noise of the doors bursting open. One of them was already out in the courtyard, covering the steps as Bolan appeared.

Bolan was on the alert, too, shooting as he ran. And he wasn't half blinded by the driving rain. He dropped the guard where he stood, but not before the man had blazed out an explosive burst from the Skorpion machine pistol he carried. The deathstream flew wide, but the rasping concussion of the multiple detonations echoed thunderously off the walls of the courtyard.

In the same tenth of a second, the other man dropped to one knee outside his doorway and blasted off half a magazine in the direction of the steps, and Stojkov, hefting the heavy revolver in his free hand, fired a single skullbuster that flung the sentry several yards back to lie with outstretched arms on the wet cobbles.

The twin fusillades, one following so closely on the other, drew a reaction from the street on the far side of the arch.

Shouts. Whistles blowing. The blare of a Klaxon. Running feet.

Bolan's single glance took in the details of the courtyard. Doors—probably locked—flanking the arch, shuttered windows on either side, three military personnel carriers and a scout car.

Bolan's mind homed in on the vehicle with lightning speed. The scout car was like a jumbo jeep, with a sloping hood that supported the spare, jerricans and entrenching tools clipped to the back, a Stechkin machine gun strapped to the nearside fender. The vehicle had clearly been developed from the Wehrmacht's World War II, VW-based *Kübelwagen*. Bolan hoped that, like that rear-engined maid-of-all-work, this machine required no key but started with a simple press on a button. Most European military transport—in France, for example, in West Germany, in Holland—was designed without supposedly "thief-proof" ignition locks. No key was needed to fire up the motor. The reasoning was that who in their right mind would want to steal an army truck?

Bolan was backing a hunch that the Eastern countries would follow suit. The penalties for theft, especially theft of official property, were much more severe in Communist countries, anyway.

He leaped for the open-side body and ducked in beneath the canvas roof. And the hunch paid off. On the Spartan steel panel behind the wheel he saw three dials: fuel, oil pressure and speedo—and a black button.

Turning to wave Stojkov on, he saw with dismay that the Bulgarian was staggering. In milliseconds he was by the man's side, relieving him of Stambolijski's burden an instant before he slumped onto one knee.

"What is it? Are you hit?" Bolan rapped.

"Bastard got one in first," Stojkov said weakly. His face was chalk-white in the light of the lamps around the courtyard. "It's only a flesh wound—clean through the calf, I think—but it's difficult to walk carrying a load."

"In the back of the car," Bolan said. "I'll take care of the old guy." He releathered the Beretta, quickly bundled Stambolijski and the old man onto the rear seat and jumped in behind the wheel. He thumbed the starter button.

The warm engine started with a roar, and the warrior slammed the stick into first and careered through the archway, out into the street.

Stojkov was crouched behind the three front seats, leaning outward so that he could wrap one hand around the stock of the Stechkin. He couldn't lift the machine gun out of its retaining straps, but he was able to squeeze the trigger, firing short bursts straight ahead as Bolan wrenched the scout car into Perestrek and headed for the boulevard.

The third sentry had jumped out of a recess in the archway before they approached, firing his Skorpion blind as the hurtling vehicle bore down on him. Glass exploded behind the steel grilles protecting the headlights. The windshield shattered. The driving mirror disintegrated. Then the offside fender caught the soldier across the hips, breaking his spine and flinging him aside like a discarded rag-doll.

Bolan floored the pedal, laying down rubber as the rear wheels spun on the slick pavement. Punching broken glass from the windshield frame, he saw that there were a dozen armed men running toward the arch from the far end of the street, where movable guardrails had been dragged across the roadway. Steel-helmeted soldiers with submachine guns stood at each end of the barrier, and an officer with a drawn automatic had posted himself halfway across.

But the roadblock was designed to halt fugitives fleeing on foot, not to stop a one-ton armored vehicle traveling at nearly fifty miles per hour.

Some of the men, too, seeing one of their own scout cars in the street, were kind of slow catching on that the guys aboard were the ones they were supposed to arrest. By the time they got it together, Bolan was in third, holding the pedal against the floorboards as the scout car raced for the barrier.

The rails were the kind used as crush barriers to control crowds at football matches. They were made of lightweight tubular steel that was not intended to withstand an assault by heavy machinery.

For a quarter of a minute there was chaos in Perestrek. Some men fired at the speeding car, others leaped aside as Bolan rocketed the vehicle toward them. Some fell, wounded by the stream of bullets sprayed ahead by Stojkov's machine gun, and two more were struck by the runaway scout car and tossed lifeless onto the sidewalk. By the time the military vehicle was fifty yards short of the roadblock, both SMGs were hammering out a stream of lead and the officer was sighting his handgun low, aiming deliberately at the tires.

Metal screeched and spanged and boomed as slugs struck different parts of the bodywork, but miraculously none of the occupants was hit. Crouched low behind the armored scuttle, the warrior zigzagged furiously, running the vehicle up onto the sidewalk as if he was trying to squeeze past the block. Then, at the last moment, he tweaked the wheel to send the scout car roaring straight for the center of the barrier.

The maneuver fazed the soldiers completely. The gunners on one sidewalk had flattened themselves against the wall, fearing they were going to be annihilated as the vehicle squeezed through. The men on the other side held their fire, afraid of mowing down their companions. The officer dived to the ground as the scout car changed direction.

The cast-iron bumper, rigid as the blade of a bulldozer, struck two of the rails simultaneously, spinning them aside as easily as splintered matchwood, scything down three of the enemy running up from behind. The officer was left kneeling on the wet cobbles, emptying his automatic uselessly at the jerricans and entrenching tools on the back of the retreating car. Then they were broadsiding left into the boulevard, slewing across the wet streetcar tracks as Bolan steered past the mosque and headed for the outskirts of the city, where the sky was already paling above the eastern rooftops.

"Don't let's do that too often," Stojkov said after a moment from behind Bolan's seat.

Bolan grinned. "There are times," he said, "when you have to push your luck some. Now, which way do we go?"

The guerrilla directed him onto a ring road and then through a maze of narrow streets in one of the older suburbs. "There's a doctor you can trust somewhere around here?" the warrior asked, hearing Stambolijski stifle a groan on the rear seat.

"Sure," Stojkov said. "But it's some way. Guy lives in a village up there in the hills." He pointed toward the heights of the Vitosa massif, frowning above the rainswept city in the dawn light.

"Okay," Bolan agreed. "But we have to junk this battlewagon pretty damned quick and find alternative transport. I can hear at least three sets of sirens behind us already."

Soon after that, on the far side of a vacant lot, he parked the scout car outside an auto junkyard. Half a block away the driver of a taxi, emerging from his cottage to take his Lada sedan into the center for the early shift, was astonished to see a bizarre trio approach through the downpour.

The burly, bearded man was limping badly, dragging one leg. The frail old guy was slung over the shoulder of the tall, husky character with the cold blue eyes. All three of them were soaked through, smeared with soot and covered with bloodstains.

The tall man carried a gun with a perforated extension screwed to the barrel. It was pointing at the cab driver. "What say the four of us take a little trip into the mountains?" the tall man said curtly.

## 14

Bolan's first reaction, reading the blueprint for the Bulgarians' Operation Baseball, was one of stupefaction.

How a responsible state, even a Stalinist hard-line state, could deliberately activate a plan so irresponsible, so malevolent, so utterly evil, was beyond him.

Reading through it unhurriedly for the first time, some of the details escaped him: there were Bulgarian technical terms with which he was unfamiliar; certain passages had been almost obliterated by rain soaking through the folder; a postscript was written in Serbian, which he didn't understand.

But the main outlines of the scheme were clear enough.

This was no ordinary disinformation project. Disinformation was certainly involved, but it came after the inhuman part of the plan had achieved its object. The role was to furnish a false explanation for the horror that had gone before.

And the horror, of course, was the firing of those specially designed missiles with warheads crammed with Sarin nerve gas.

The fake oil rig, Bolan discovered, had been built as a base from which undercover military operations could be rehearsed in secret. Baseball was to be the first of these.

It involved a seaborne assault on the Turkish coast, in which a handpicked squad of experts would be landed, together with the vehicles and launchers Bolan had seen. The missiles would be fired, from Turkish soil, at targets in

Iran—the city of Tabrīz and a military installation on the shores of Lake Rezāīyeh being cited as "desirable" examples.

And, as the Executioner had deduced, the United States would carry the can.

The raiders would be wearing American uniforms, the camouflaged KrisKraft were American-built, the vehicles, the launchers and the other weapons were U.S. government issue, and the American-pattern missiles carried U.S. Army markings.

The operation was to be delayed until a time when Middle East friction had raised the temperature of Washington-Tehran relations—always hostile—to near boiling point.

Bolan's flesh crawled. There was enough Sarin packed into the missiles he had seen on the rig to annihilate the entire population of Tabrīz, wipe out the military base and decimate the inhabitants for fifty miles around. More if the wind continued to blow from the north.

The thought of what might follow such a catastrophe appalled him.

There were nevertheless points that puzzled him. Why fire the missiles on Turkish soil when the U.S. was to be blamed instead of dropping them from a plane with American military markings? He didn't know what was in the seaborne assault routine or the rehearsals preceding it.

He decided to seek a second opinion.

He was holed up, along with Stojkov, the burglar and the two guys who had kept watch at Stambolijski's safehouse, in an isolated hill farm. Bolan had released the cab driver three miles out of town, and abandoned the Lada at a mountain intersection five miles farther on. A horse-drawn wagon crewed by friends of the guerrilla leader had taken them to the village and the doctor. And later, when he had extracted the bullet from the old man's shoulder and patched up both their wounds, the medic himself had driven them to the farm.

Stojkov was lying on a divan in an upstairs room with his bandaged leg stretched out in front of him. "Did you find what you wanted to?" he asked.

"I found what I'd rather not have found," Bolan replied grimly. And he gave Stojkov a brief rundown on Operation Baseball so far as he had been able to decipher the documents in the stolen file.

"My God," the Bulgarian exclaimed when he had finished, "a deal like that could set the Middle East on fire! If it succeeded."

"It doesn't even have to succeed," Bolan said. "That's the wicked part of it. If the raiders fail, and it can be shown that they *meant* to succeed, the damage will be just as bad as the real thing."

"But surely your country would be able to show—"

"With the attackers in American uniform, using genuine U.S. Army equipment? Oh, sure, they could probably prove it was a setup, eventually. But there's always mud that sticks. And it wouldn't bring back the dead. In any case," Bolan said, "the aim of the operation is simply to create instability in the West, whether or not folks believe my country is responsible. Even the fact that someone's mean enough to dream up such a plot would be disruptive. And just imagine the reaction of the Imams and the hothead extremists who listen to them if such a story broke! There'd be a renewed epidemic of revenge killings all over the world—unless World War III had already started." Bolan shook his head and lapsed into silence. Outrage at the perversity of the Bulgarian plan had provoked him out of his normal taciturnity.

"I fight against the Party, the Central Committee," Stojkov said a little later, "but even then I don't believe, I *can't* believe, that this diabolical plan is official...that it has government approval."

"Hell, no," Bolan said emphatically.

"Then, what...?"

"It's a wildcat operation, for sure. My guess would be that it started with the KGB or that part of the KGB that's still anti-Gorbatchev and anti-*perestroika*. They'd be as happy to see the soft-line Moscow bosses in deep as they would be to louse up the West."

"And the people in Perestrek?"

"Being used as tools by Big Brother's hard-liners."

"Yes," Stojkov protested, "but it costs a fortune to set up something like an offshore oil rig, for God's sake! Don't tell me the Party votes that kind of money to the boys in C.4!"

"I reckon," Bolan said, "that the *rig's* 'official,' if you like. I mean that it's been okayed as a secret base for some kind of military or naval operations. But not for this specific operation."

"So, why don't we just tip off the government—blow the whole thing wide open and let them work it out with their own rebels?"

"Because nobody would believe us, Vasil. Face it, who is going to take your word, the word of an outlaw, and a foreign spy's—a mercenary, they'd most likely call me—on a deal like this? Against the country's own security service? The spooks would lie until they were blue in the face. The evidence on the rig could be ridden or disposed of easily enough. This evidence—" he tapped the stolen folder "—could be faked. We'd be in jail before we were halfway through the scenario."

"And if we didn't do the blowing ourselves? If the evidence was presented anonymously, or through a third party?"

The Executioner shook his head. "No way."

"So, what do we do?"

"Kill the whole stinking thing stone dead." Bolan opened the file and riffled through the damp pages. "But there are things in here I don't understand—Bulgarian military terms, some of the handwritten comments, a whole passage in Serbian. At least I think it's Serbian." He handed Stojkov a sheet from the file. "I'm not one hundred percent sure I have the whole picture."

"We'll check it through together," Stojkov said.

The military terms related to ballistics, guidance systems, infrared targeting and such. They were of little interest, since the terrain over which they were to be used was not specified. "This page in Serbian—you're right, it is Serbian," Stojkov said, "seems to be a military analyst's report on a contingency plan to raid some kind of outpost or defense position."

"To raid?"

"To raid, to attack, to overcome, to capture—the term could be interpreted several ways. Clearly it's part of your Baseball operation that was submitted to an outside expert for evaluation, and this is his appreciation, with comments and suggested improvements."

"I don't get it," Bolan said. "I don't see how it fits. What outpost? Where?"

The guerrilla leader spread his hands. "That's the problem. Obviously the plan was submitted in the form of a theoretical exercise, since the objective is referred to simply as 'the site' and topographical features, along with place names, are indicated by numerals and letters only."

"And there's no key in the file?"

Stojkov shook his head.

Bolan swore. "So the whole passage is meaningless, unless—"

"There is one other thing."

"Yes?"

"You're not going to like this one bit," Stojkov said. "But there *is* a reference in the folder to the original plan on which the exercise was based. It seems there is in fact an annex to this file."

Bolan stared at him. "Are you telling me that I overlooked . . . ?"

"It was the same master number," Stojkov said, "but, on account I guess of the outside expert, it's filed in the correspondence section."

Bolan groaned. "And there wouldn't be one chance in hell of making a second entry to Perestrek 32. Not now!" He picked up the Serbian sheet again. "But there's something else here that I don't dig. Look, here at one side of the text, in red ink—'Arafat' and a few more words. What the hell has Yasser Arafat to do with all this? I should have thought the last thing the PLO wanted was to get on the wrong side of the Iranians!"

Stojkov was examining the document. "The rain has smudged the handwriting," he said at length. "The word is not 'Arafat' but 'Ararat.' The whole phrase reads, 'Uncle Sam's replacement Ararat.' It seems to be a subsidiary heading, for insertion halfway down the page."

Bolan was quiet, trying to pin down the connection. And then he had it. Of course! Mount Ararat! But why did the geographical reference start alarm bells ringing in back of his mind? Because that was where the jetliner carrying Brognola's man Shapiro and his fellow victims had crashed.

Surely it must be more than a coincidence that it should show up again now, dead center in the Operation Baseball investigation?

"Look," Bolan said, "I have to make phone calls, mainly to the United States. But they'll be on to me here, since I left my hotel room in the middle of the night and never showed again. What do you think I should do?"

"Leave it to my friends," Stojkov said. "They'll take you into Romania."

"Romania?"

"Safer there and no questions asked. There's jealousy involved, see. Romania has the oil, and it's the most Western-oriented, the most technologically advanced Balkan state. In comparison we're just emerging from the feudal system. Even if Sofia put out an international alert for you,

I doubt if Bucharest would pay it any mind. In any case every overseas call made here is monitored.''

"Okay," Bolan argued. "How do we get there?"

"There are two ways. There's a river that joins the Danube, which forms the frontier between the two countries in the north. It's foolproof if you go hidden among the freight on a barge, but it's slow—you'd have to count on at least two days and nights. Or we could take you through the mountains into Yugoslavia. The nearest point on the border's less than fifty miles. There's a...contact...we have near Dimitrovgrad who runs a flying school to train civil pilots. He could land you in a field near Bucharest in one of those YAK-52 trainers in a couple of hours."

"I'll take the mountain hike and the flying machine," Bolan said. "But, look, I relied on you guys more than enough already. I can't—"

"Any debt you think you owe us is already amply repaid," Stojkov interrupted.

"Come again?"

The guerrilla leader chuckled. He picked a dozen five-by-four-inch pasteboard rectangles covered in typescript from a shelf beside the divan. "While you were amusing yourself playing baseball," he said, "Stambolijski was doing a little research on his own. These boxfile cards contain Intel on him, on me, on Levski and Botev and all the members of our group. Without them as a cross-reference, the secret police won't be able to check us out with anything they have on us in their own files. As of last night, thanks to you, we ceased to exist."

"As a unit, you mean? As a threat to the People's Democracy? But that's great. How do you think—"

Bolan broke off as Aleksandar Botev flung open the door and burst into the room. His normally ruddy face was pale. "Chief," he said breathlessly, "there are two APCs loaded with infantry and a couple of jeeps with mortars advancing up the track from the village!"

## 15

"That's one hell of a task force to weed out three guys and two wounded," Bolan observed. "The question is, how did they know?"

"There's a couple dozen hardmen hiding out—maybe I should say resting up—in one of the barns," Stojkov admitted. "As to the rest—" he shook his head sadly "—there's always someone, Bolan. However safe you figure you are, there's always someone. An old woman noticed the horse and buggy set out a lot earlier than usual. A stoolie who turns over gossip to the cops in return for a blind eye on his own chickenshit scag. Someone who thinks his woman has been putting it out to one of our guys. You name it."

"How far away?" Bolan asked Botev.

"Half a mile. Maybe a little more."

"What do you have?"

"AK-47s, the old model, maybe nine or ten, some smoke grenades, couple of Skorpions, handguns, and one RPG-7 with half a dozen rounds."

"Give me a rundown on those hardmen. How many? Where? Holding what?"

Stojkov and Botev gave him the goods, and Bolan nodded curtly.

"Show me," he said from the window, and when the outbuildings were pointed out to him, he slid a final glance through the window at the land dropping away toward the village and the dun-colored procession winding its way up in the direction of the farm.

"Leave this to me," he told Botev, "and do what I tell you as soon as I give the signal."

Soon afterward they heard an authoritative voice relayed through a bullhorn. The soldiers were deployed in a ring around the farm. One jeep with its mortar crew at the ready was behind the outbuildings; the other was in front. The two armored personnel carriers were drawn up fifty yards away with their 7.65 mm machine guns trained on the farmhouse windows.

"Let us have the American Bolan," the amplified voice bellowed. "We have no quarrel with the rest of you. Hand over this foreign spy, and you have our word that no action will be taken against any of you."

Stojkov snorted. "We have heard, as the British say, that one before," he riposted. "The moment they laid hands on you, the rest of us would be in jail quicker than you could unlock a cell door!"

"Just play it my way, and let them *think* that's the way it's going to be," Bolan said. "And don't forget the signals."

He walked to the front door and jerked it open. For a moment he stood there, a tall, rugged, apparently unarmed figure in the bright light. The rain had stopped, and the sky was clear. "I am Bolan," he called. And then he began walking steadily toward the guns.

"Approach the nearest half-track with your hands raised," the bullhorn voice ordered.

Bolan obeyed. He walked very slowly, seemingly a man in whom wariness and mistrust warred with bravado. He hoped the picture jibed with what the soldiers had been told about him.

In front of him, the dirt road snaked down between stoney vine terraces and patches of green where crops grew or sheep grazed. The village was hidden below the lip of an escarpment. Behind the farm buildings, close-packed firs rose to a jagged skyline.

The warrior's plan, formed during his swift recon with Botev, was based on the age-old cliché that attack is the best method of defense. Surrounded in a shut-end situation, it was better to leap out and strike rather than wait for the vise inevitably to close.

The plan depended on surprise and the unexpected, but Botev had a long way to run, crouched down out of sight behind the terraces, before it could be put into operation— and Bolan had only a short way to go before he was grabbed by the soldiers. He must give the guerrilla the signal before he made it that far.

Twenty yards short of the personnel carrier, a furze bush grew beside the track. Behind it a pile of small rocks had been stacked to repair a breach in a stone wall.

That bush was the limit of Bolan's advance.

The officer had lowered the bullhorn. "Move it!" he snapped. "We don't have all day."

Bolan carried a whistle on a string looped around his neck. The whistle was between his lips.

He blew a piercing blast and dived for the rockpile.

The peaceful mountainside erupted into action. Botev hadn't made it to the preferred position; he was below but still a little to one side of the APCs. But it was good enough in the circumstances. The single round from the breech-loaded grenade launcher attached to his Kalashnikov spiraled lazily up into the air and bounced to the rocky ground ten yards in front of the carriers. The 40 mm smoke grenade immediately poured out a dense, choking screen of black that rolled up the hillside in front of the deployed soldiers, cutting them off from the farm buildings.

A second smoke grenade, Bolan knew, would have been launched at the mortar crew behind the outbuildings. At the same time, the guerrillas posted at windows and doors around the farmhouse opened a withering fire from Skorpions and AK-47s that had been aimed in the direction of the attackers before the smokescreen erupted. The tinkle of sheep bells was drowned in a rattle of gunfire.

The officer was shouting orders, and the carriers' machine guns blasted into action. Soldiers shot blindly through the smoke in the general direction of the farm. Bolan heard the thump of mortars fired from the jeep behind the APCs, and then the tearing crack of explosions somewhere behind him.

He filled his lungs and blew two more shrill blasts.

That was the signal for the active guerrillas to come out fighting. Safe from the mortars, which would be launched at the buildings, they were to mow down anything and anyone they saw through the smoke. The two wounded men had already been carried to an ancient grotto beneath one of the vine terraces.

Bolan was on hands and knees behind the rockpile. His Beretta had been tucked out of sight into the waistband of his jeans, above the hip pocket. Now it was in his right hand, ready to fire. In his left he held a stun grenade that Boris Levski had found among the guerrillas' weapons collection. It had been suspended on a length of string down one leg of his borrowed pants.

Beyond the shelter of the furze bush, the warrior crawled along the track toward the enemy vehicles. Through the billows of smoke, he could hear a babble of voices between bursts of gunfire. The officer was somewhere over to his left. Ahead of him the mortar coughed.

Shells burst farther up the hill. The clatter of slates and stonework showering back onto the hard ground showed that at least one of the mortar crews had found the range, but then Bolan heard the detonation of the defenders' RPG-7, fired from a terrace off to one side of the farm. After three of its rocket grenades exploded, the mortar fire behind the building was silenced. Bolan continued crawling toward the second jeep.

Wind gusting across the mountainside suddenly thinned the smoke, rolling it momentarily off the dirt road, revealing two steel-helmeted soldiers with machine pistols ten yards ahead of the Executioner. They spun his way, lowering the stubby barrels as he lined up the Beretta and choked out two 3-shot bursts.

Concealed in his waistband, the 93-R had been deprived of its silencer. The three weapons spit fire simultaneously, a sudden harsh blast that cut across the background noise of the battle. One of the soldiers hinged forward over the red ruin of his chest and died quietly before he hit the ground. The other whirled away with a bluish heave of intestine visible through a gashed belly before the wind dropped and the smoke closed in again and swallowed him up.

Bolan had twisted violently aside as slugs furrowed the surface of the track and sent stone chips flying. But he had seen enough while the smoke screen thinned to locate the jeep and the second mortar crew. He rose to his feet, primed the stun grenade, and lobbed it in that direction through the obscurity.

Flat on his face once more, he covered his ears to minimize the concussive effect of the grenade. Even at thirty yards the thunderclap of the burst was painful.

He sat up when he was sure there were no more sounds of movement from the jeep. The carriers' machine guns were still hammering away on the far side of the smoke, but now it was time to bring on the third wave and finalize his hastily improvised plan.

He blew the whistle again—three blasts this time.

At once there was a flurry of activity between the outbuildings and the farm. Bolan kept low—Botev was enfilading the confused, smoke-blinded soldiers with his Kalashnikov—but he could see as the screen lifted momentarily in another gust of wind that Levski was directing a small group of men dragging a four-wheel farm wagon out into the open.

Four men hauled the shafts, digging in their heels to brake the wagon when it reached the top of the slope.

The wagon was loaded ten feet high with bales of hay.

Levski ran to the front. He was carrying a twist of newspaper and a box of matches. Between the shafts he struck a match and lighted the paper. When it was well alight, he passed the flames along the bottom of the stack of hay bales. The tinder-dry fodder blazed up at once.

Within seconds, the whole front of the stack was an inferno. In no time the fire had spread along each side, and the wooden wagon itself was burning.

Levski snapped an order. The four men put up the shafts and ran to the back of the wagon. Levski took out a clasp knife and cut the ropes securing the towering stack of hay bales. He raised his hand. The four men pushed, and the wagon with its fiery cargo began to roll down the mountainside.

The faster it moved, the higher the flames roared, until the whole load was transformed into a blazing torch that had been accurately aimed down the slope, increasing speed as it hurtled with murderous precision toward the hollow where the two armored personnel carriers were parked.

Levski and the four guerillas, sheltered by the flames, raced behind the wagon, firing their Skorpions and AK-47s as they ran. Shooting from the hip, they scored hits among the soldiers milling through the smoke screen, but it was the blazing wagon that wreaked havoc.

Bouncing into the depression, it struck a rock outcrop, broke a wheel and tipped over onto its side, spilling the flaming hay bales over the APCs.

Two of the guerrillas fell, cut down by the carriers' machine guns, before the crews leaped screaming for safety with their hair and uniforms ablaze. Bundles of burning straw set fire to the undergrowth, exploded boxes of ammunition and transformed the depression into a searing, hellish cauldron as the bales disintegrated. Infantrymen ran, choking, from the inferno or rolled on the ground, beating with bare hands at the flames devouring their clothes.

The end came when the fuel tank of the second APC, which had been smothered by half the blazing wagon's load, exploded with a dull roar to send a crimson fireball, veined with black, boiling skyward through the smoke. The guerrillas closed in with a ragged cheer, gunning down any human torches still writhing among the charred debris.

Only the officer commanding the assault group remained. Bolan, standing with his empty autoloader on the rock outcrop, saw him rise from behind the pile of stones, raging eyes staring out of his blackened features. A Skorpion machine pistol, steady in a two-handed grip, was leveled at Botev, who was clambering up over the wall retaining one of the vine terraces.

Bolan yelled a warning. He leaped from the rock, throwing his useless handgun at the officer and hurling himself across the intervening space to collide violently with the man as the Skorpion spit fire. The two of them fell to the ground, scrambling for a hold in a cloud of dust and dislodged pebbles.

Bolan stayed close, pinning the gun between them with the weight of his body, wrapping one steely arm around the Bulgarian's shoulders in a bear hug so that the muzzle was trapped, pointing upward. Flame singed his cheek as the guy's trigger finger emptied the magazine. Then he had jerked the wire circlet with its two wooden toggles out of his hip pocket with his free hand. He thrust himself away from the struggling man and dropped the wire noose over his head, pulling the toggles savagely apart.

The officer gagged, clawing at the garrote that was already sinking into the flesh of his neck. His eyes bulged. His tongue protruded between drawn-back lips.

Bolan maintained the ferocious pressure until the man sagged and his eyes rolled up. He lowered the body to the ground and shoved himself upright, a muscle in his cheek twitching. It was a quick way to die, but not one the warrior cared to hand out. If it hadn't been a simple choice between the soldier's life or Botev's...

He shrugged and hurried across to the terrace wall. The guerrilla was nursing a grazed arm, but otherwise he was unhurt. "That's one I owe you!" he said warmly.

Bolan clapped him on the shoulder. "Let's go see how the guys who are really hurt made out," he said.

Stojkov and the wounded burglar were safe in their grotto. Four guerrillas had been killed, and three more injured, one of them seriously. "The hill people will take care of them—and of us," Stojkov told the Executioner. "By nightfall, the only trace of a battle will be a ruined farmhouse." He gestured toward the bullet-scarred walls and blackened joists where mortar shells had ripped apart the fabric of the buildings.

"I'd still like to know," Bolan said, "exactly how they pinpointed us so quickly and so exactly."

"I told you," Stojkov said sadly. "There's always someone. The important thing now is to get you over the border into Yugoslavia before they send another squad to find out what happened. The RPG-7 destroyed the jeep in back of the farm, but the other's okay, and the second APC is usable—charred but in working order. Which would you like?"

"The jeep's faster," Bolan said.

"But the carrier's tracked. It can make it over terrain where the jeep would be blocked. And the guys who will take you to the airfield know mountain shortcuts where the trail peters out."

"Sold!" Bolan smiled. "I'll settle for the APC."

Levski emerged from beneath the sagging rafters of the farm's shelled facade. He was carrying a small black valise.

"Arriving by plane in Romania," he said to the warrior, "it looks kind of... well, more kind of regular, if you bring in a little baggage with you."

He handed it to Bolan.

Bolan glanced at the zippered, black hide valise in astonishment. It was the camera case he had left in his hotel room in Sofia.

He opened it and rummaged inside. The Nikon camera had been pulverized in the air shaft during their escape from the Secret Service headquarters in Perestrek. But the lenses and meters were still there, and so were the warlike accessories hidden beneath the false bottom. Someone had even thought to add a basic shaving kit, a spare shirt and clean underwear. His photographic accreditation and ID documents for both the Blanski and Belasko characters were safe in a zippered pocket at one side of the case.

"Hey, this is a good move!" Bolan exclaimed. "How in hell did you guys get around...?" He broke off, shaking his head in mystification.

Stambolijski, his arm in a sling and his face still pale from loss of blood and fatigue, favored the warrior with a crooked smile. "As Comrade Stojkov admits," he said, "there's always someone."

**16**

Four lines of trees separated the boulevard, the two sets of walkways and the two service roads along the wide avenue that arrowed toward the Palais de la République on Place Gheorghiu-Dej in the center of Bucharest.

As in Sofia, the traffic was light by Western standards. But the twin lines of white stone buildings, receding in perspective like the facades of an architectural drawing, lent the place a brighter, more modern air than the facades in the Bulgarian capital. The subway stations, with their looping, overhead connecting galleries, were marvels of engineering married to contemporary art. Three blocks from the terminus at the end of the line, Bolan stared at a crumbling terracotta portico topped by a reddish cupola supported on squat stone pillars. The house behind it looked like a back-lot mockup from some rejected project for Disneyland. For a moment he thought he must be in the wrong city, or the wrong neighborhood, or at least the wrong street. But no—he checked the address he had jotted down—this was the place the Embassy had sent him to. He passed two sets of windows hidden behind peeling shutters and yanked at a rusting bell handle.

Crazy, Bolan thought, waiting for the distant jangle to be answered. As a cultural exchange official, Mike Blanski had been warmly welcomed by any Romanians he had met. Press officers, diplomatic advisers, junior ministerial staff had all been anxious to interest him in the Rombac aerospace complex, the Central Chemical Institute, the Tractorul agricultural machine factory. He could have been shown around a dozen exhibitions, displays and trade fairs with official sponsorship. The only folks who didn't want to know were the official representatives of his own country!

They wouldn't have him anywhere near the Embassy; even at the Consulate he was fobbed off with a third secretary, who got rid of him as soon as possible with instructions to go to this derelict building that was clearly some kind of safehouse for the local head of station.

The man who opened the door was young, with fair hair and a wispy mustache. He was wearing a Brooks Brothers suit with a button-down collar and a narrow necktie. He was no more welcoming than the third secretary.

"Frankly," he said when they were sitting on threadbare chairs in a shabby parlor at the rear of the house, "you people are a pain in the neck to us."

"I'm not 'people,'" Bolan said. "I'm me. And all I want is some action from you guys."

"Spooks!" The young man sniffed. "Treading all over the shop with their great flat feet. One misstep, and you can louse up a whole year's work organized by our fellows."

"Is that so?" Bolan replied. "Well, number one, I'm not what you call a spook. And number two—"

"Undercover operative, then. What's the difference? Whatever it says on the label, the product's basically the same."

"Look, sonny," Bolan said, "I may be a pain in the neck to you, but unless I get some cooperation pretty damned quick, I'm gonna be a pain in the ass. And guess whose ass is gonna be in a sling."

"Oh, very well." The words were accompanied by an impatient toss of the blond hair.

"I want two cables sent to Head of Sensitive Operations, in Washington, D.C. Slugged 'For Your Eyes Only.' They'll be in five-figure cipher groups, and I'll expect immediate transmission and answers within the briefest delay."

There was an audible sigh first. "Can do. If you'd like to call back tomorrow morning, around ten o'clock..."

"I want both answers in less than an hour," Bolan said. "Whatever pressure you put on is up to you. But let me tell you one thing—any complaint I make to Sensitive Operations goes straight to the Oval Office, without any 'diplomatic channels' crap whatsoever."

The young man took the coded signals Bolan had prepared and left without another word.

He was back in exactly fifty-nine minutes. Bolan had the impression that he'd been waiting around to delay his return as long as he dared.

Brognola's reply to the first of the warrior's queries read: *One Mercedes one Jaguar coupé Stop Fifteen-room house with five-hundred-yard frontage Long Island Sound two powerboats Ends.*

The second was even shorter. Deciphered, the message read: *Dimbovita canal footbridge university end tomorrow noon.*

THE CANAL, wide, placid and tenanted by swans, ran straight as a die between the faculty buildings and the usual line of flat-roofed, seven-story, white stone blocks that characterized the new city. The iron bridge spanned the water in a low, flat arch with ornamental lamp standards at each end. It was a sunny day. Bolan leaned on the rail and gazed down at the birds as students strolled up and down behind him discussing electronics, civil engineering, Michael Jackson.

Soon after midday, a professorial type with a bushy mustache and rimless glasses installed himself a few feet away from the warrior. "A pleasant day," he said conversationally. "Sunlight, the reflections on the water...they help one to muse on the eternal verities, do they not?"

Bolan agreed that they did.

"On such a day perhaps," the elderly man pursued, "the dove flew back across the water to Noah, with the sprig of olive in its beak."

"The time he was on vacation on Mount Ararat?"

"Precisely."

"Okay," Bolan said. "I guess the answer was too long to encapsulate in a cable. I'm listening."

"Mr. Brognola was anxious that you should receive the fullest possible answer to your question. And that any additional queries you had should be attended to at once. The matter could be . . . delicate."

"Damned right it could," Bolan said. "At least from my end. So tell me, what is there of specific U.S. interest in that area?"

"An American missile silo, for starters," the man said who looked like a professor.

Bolan schooled his features to suppress the surprise that flashed across his face. "What's its status," he asked.

"It's not armed. But the bunker, the operating gadgetry and all the software are in place. It could be activated very quickly."

"Explain."

"Turkey's been a member of NATO since 1951. Mount Ararat lies in the eastern corner of the country, flanked by Iran, Iraq, Syria and Russian Azerbaijan. The missile site was constructed at the time of the Cuban crisis—and it was in fact one hell of a sight more of a menace to the Soviets than Castro's rockets were to Uncle Sam. Turkey's like a finger poking into the Russian belly—IRBMs based on the Ararat site could hit Odessa, Kiev, Kharkov, Volgograd . . . maybe even Moscow, with a following wind."

"You said 'could.'"

"I said the site was disarmed. The hardware was removed years ago under the SALT trade-offs. But when Greece pulled out of NATO in '74, the decision was made to keep the place in running order. Just in case. It's guarded by a skeleton military crew, and regularly visited by maintenance technicians who check that, theoretically at least, all systems are go.''

"Yeah," Bolan said. "Well . . . thanks for the message.''

"My pleasure. Do you have any questions?''

"One. How many men in your skeleton crew—and when's the next maintenance visit scheduled?''

"Twelve men. They will be relieved at the time of the next maintenance visit, in two weeks' time.''

"Okay. I guess that wraps it up for now.''

The courier's hands—he wore black kid gloves—were resting on the flat-topped rail. When he removed them, Bolan saw a small book of matches bearing the name of a club in Istanbul in their place. "An emergency number for Mr. Brognola, operative for the next two weeks," the courier said. "In case you should need it. Behind the matches.''

Bolan nodded, pocketing the little pasteboard folder.

"Good day to you, sir. Always nice to exchange greetings with a fellow traveler," the professorial man said with a perfectly straight face. He raised his hat politely and sauntered off toward the university.

"My pleasure," said Mack Bolan.

Two swans took off from the canal, their great wings whooshing, fracturing the reflection of the white stone houses with their trailing feet. Bolan memorized the handwritten number and dropped the matchbook into the water. A third swan swam rapidly across and seized the pasteboard in its bill, dashing it repeatedly beneath the surface in the hope that it would become sodden enough to eat. The inked figures, Bolan knew, would have smudged at once and then become obliterated.

He crossed the bridge, walking slowly toward the city center. But his mind was racing. Now the full horror of the evil plan spawned by the men of Department C.4 was revealed to him. Now the meaning of the mysterious phrase in the Serbian military analyst's report was clear.

*Uncle Sam's replacement Ararat.*

It was no longer surprising that the Sarin nerve gas was not to be dropped in the form of bombs from an airplane with U.S. markings.

The planners had a better idea.

The assault group training on the offshore rig was not going to launch the missiles from any old place that happened to be on Turkish soil; it was going to launch them from a genuine American site.

The combat they planned was not against any Turkish forces that happened to get in their way; the pseudo-Americans were aiming to waste genuine GIs . . . and then take their place.

The Serbian analyst, without knowing the true identity of the two sides, had been evaluating the blueprint for that operation.

Bolan could see it happening.

The relief detail on its way, along with the maintenance experts, to the old missile site . . . the ambush, probably in the wild, uninhabited foothills below the 17,000-foot peak of Ararat . . . the skeleton crew ready to welcome the guys they imagined to be their replacements . . . the massacre once the phonies were inside the perimeter.

And then the launching of the missiles.

At Tabrīz? At Amadiyah, in Iraq? At Amāz, on the Syrian border? It didn't matter. The damage to the United States—and to the fragile stability of the Middle East—would be the same.

Apart from the appalling cost in human lives and human suffering.

Once it was known where the missiles came from—and the Bulgarians would make sure that it was known, because the existence of the site was no secret—all hell would break loose.

Oh, sure, there was a chance that the Administration could straighten it out somehow, could present a convincing case for the defense.

But there *was* a missile site on Ararat. There *were* American troops there. The natural explanation would be that what everyone had feared for years had finally happened . . . a madman had pressed the button.

The U.S. would be discredited throughout the Arab world. Relations between Washington and all the Muslim capitals would sink to zero. Even within Nato the ''special relationship'' would be soured if America's European partners believed the U.S. had reactivated the site without consulting them and in defiance of all existing treaties.

Because whether or not it was believed that Americans had in fact actually fired the missiles, *it would remain true that a stock of chemical warfare weapons had been available on that site*. That was the diabolical second phase of the plan.

And in the meantime a lot of innocent people would be dead.

Dropping into a chair at a sidewalk café table and calling for a beer, the Executioner sighed. He would kill the whole stinking thing stone dead, he had told Stojkov. Suddenly it seemed a lot to ask of one man within a space of two weeks.

## 17

The truth of course was that there was no way that Operation Baseball could be killed stone dead by one man.

For the tenth time, sipping beer at his café table, Bolan went over the options.

He had agreed with Stojkov that it would be useless tipping off the Bulgarian government. Warning the Pentagon or the White House would be equally counterproductive: a preemptive strike at the oil rig could prove as damaging as the success of Baseball itself, especially as there was no firm proof that the C.4 plot existed. Apart from which, military action could result in the release of a deadly cloud of Sarin.

Remaining, then, was undercover action executed by Bolan himself: destroy the raiding party before the relief detail was ambushed on its way to the Ararat site.

Bolan weighed the pros and cons for success. Negative. Four powerboat loads of seasoned combat veterans, plus two jeeps, an M-548 and a launcher with a dozen TOW antitank missiles, ruled out singlehanded heroics.

Even with help, even if the raiders could be exterminated, the battle would leave plenty of evidence that supposedly American troops had been engaged in some kind of warlike activity. They couldn't make all that identifiably U.S. Army issue hardware vanish into thin air. And they certainly couldn't destroy the Lance missiles with their Sarin warheads.

Perhaps the men guarding the site should be warned that their relief detail would be a phony?

Or maybe a way could be found to contact the genuine detail and warm them.

Negative again. Even if they fought and won, the same objections would apply. And if they were warned too much in advance, they would call in Washington, for sure. The earlier arguments about that route being counterproductive applied here, too.

Bolan knitted his brows. The two-stage operation, with short-range hardware to take care of the men guarding the silo and their replacements, and long-range missiles to do the damage afterward, meant there was only one way to deny the Bulgarians at least some measure of success.

The raiding party must never be allowed to leave the fake oil rig.

Trouble was, Bolan reasoned, that even if the party itself was decimated, along with its weapons and the crew on the rig, there was nothing to stop the evil geniuses of C.4 from planning a repeat performance at some time in the future.

It followed, therefore, that the whole rig must be destroyed.

Bolan drained his beer tankard and held up a finger to summon a white-aproned waiter. On the boulevard, Jugos, Ladas, Polski Fiats, Pobedas, Romanian-built Dacias and an occasional ZIL limo passed and repassed in the sunshine. A light breeze ruffled the leaves of the acacia trees lining the sidewalk. Bolan concentrated on the problem.

Was it possible, assuming that he could once more anchor a small boat within one mile of the rig without being blown out of the water, that he could make the underwater swim with enough explosive to sabotage the platform legs and bring the whole structure tumbling down into the sea?

No way.

Not even if he was prepared to make it a one-way, suicidal kamikaze assault. Not against those odds.

Next he considered executing his objective with a shallow-draught boat packed to the gunwales with explosive.

No, he deduced, not with the radar defenses they had.

In any case none of those alternatives would allow for the certain, safe and final disposal of the deadly Sarin warheads.

Turned around any way, the problem circled back always to the same basic point: the maximum score would never be chalked up unless outside help was involved.

Bolan ordered another beer.

THE LAST THING Vasil Stojkov had said was: "Do not hesitate, my friend, to call upon us if you should need help. Any kind at all, not excluding a short sea voyage!" And he had laughed his great rumbling laugh and punched the Executioner on the shoulder.

"You sacrificed quite enough already," Bolan had protested. "You lost men, others are wounded and the old man's hurt bad. You yourself got a slug through the calf, and your safehouse in the hills is finished. I can't ask you to risk your lives, your liberty, again—not just because it would help out in my private war. I owe you as it is."

"With all due respect..." Stojkov, as lame as he was, had drawn himself up to his full height. "This is no longer your private war. Not this time. I understand your concern for the good name of your country. Also your desire on humanitarian grounds to prevent a massacre and the consequent risk of war. But you must remember one thing—we may not agree with the present system of government, but we are Bulgarians, after all. And this...this beastliness is being done in our name. We have as much interest, and as much right, in preventing it as you."

"Okay," Bolan said. "Point taken. I won't forget."

"And when it comes to the repayment of debts," Levski had added, "we have already told you that anything you owe us in connection with the plans for the raid on the C.4 archives in Perestrek is more than repaid by the fact that we ourselves are no longer on file there."

"Which is one reason," Botev had said, "why we would be freer to move from place to place and assist you, if the question should arise."

Bolan had laughed. "Okay, okay. You twisted my arm. I promise I'll call on your guys if the job gets too big for me."

Sitting in the sunshine in Bucharest a couple of days later, well aware now that the job was indeed beyond the scope of one man, he reckoned that maybe it was time to keep that promise.

Later that evening, he left his hotel and went to a pay phone—one of a row outside the terminal at the city's central bus station.

He fed in money and punched out the international prefix, the code for Bulgaria and the number of a private house in Sofia. The man who answered was the insignificant government office clerk who had dropped the safehouse address into the litter basket for Stojkov to collect in the public park.

Bolan relayed a guarded message in the verbal code that he had established with the guerrilla leader before he left the country. If he had played it right, he should be contacted within the next twenty-four hours.

## 18

Bolan spent several hours that night poring over a large-scale map of the eastern part of Romania.

The Danube River, he saw, having linked Linz, Vienna, Bratislava, Budapest and Belgrade, swerved suddenly south of Bucharest and then turned abruptly north again to form the border between Romania and the Soviet Union, before it spilled into the Black Sea. It was here, 1,770 miles from its source, that the great river separated into several branches and flowed through a huge estuarine area of swampland and lagoons.

And that was where, the warrior reckoned, he could find the space and the solitude essential to the rehearsals he would need if the assault on that oil rig that he planned was going to succeed.

From the capital to the swamps was a distance of one hundred fifty kilometers—ninety-five miles, give or take a few—most of it across a plain that lay between the wooded crests of the Transylvanian Alps and the sea. He would need at least a couple hours there to check out the best places for the operations he had in mind. Allow four hours each way for the drive, which should take care of bad roads, hold-ups, police checks, whatever. He concluded that it was possible to make it there and back, do what he had to do and still be in Bucharest in time to receive Stojkov's reply to his message. He was up early and waiting outside the State auto rental office when the reception clerks reported for duty at eight.

The car was a locally made Dacia sedan, a slope-tailed hatchback with lines similar to the larger French Renaults. The two-liter engine was a little sluggish by Western standards, but it pulled the car along willingly enough, and by nine-thirty he was twenty miles out of the city and speeding northeast across the flatlands.

The highway, which passed under the twelve-foot pipeline carrying oil from the Ploesti field to the port of Constanta, on the Black Sea, ran for thirty miles along a shallow valley between a river and the railroad, then crossed the Danube at Giurgeni. After that there was a range of low hills and then the thirty-five-mile-wide strip of marshland separating Lake Razelm from the Russian frontier.

Bolan stood on a wooded hillock and stared across the gray landscape. He saw lakes, ponds, wide waterways and narrow, twisted creeks, all separated by areas of swamp grass and islets of stunted trees. Occasionally the square sails of a grain barge glided above the dun vegetation, and away to the north, the upperworks of an ocean-going freighter steaming upriver to the Danube ports of Galati and Braila.

Bolan drove out across the marsh. Soon the crushed-stone roads petered out in a network of tracks and trails, many of them axle-deep in mud. There were few signposts, and the maps he had gave no more than a general indication of landmarks. It took him a lot more than two hours to find a place that was suitable for the maneuvers he planned: a saltmarsh surrounding a sheet of open water hidden by head-high reeds. It was an isolated location, a couple of miles inland from the Sfintu Gheorghe lighthouse. Huge clouds of migratory water-birds rose screaming into the air each time Bolan neared the fringe of reeds. He hoped he would be able to find the place again as easily as they did.

It was a quarter to four before he made it back to the highway and headed south. Eight minutes later he realized he was being tailed.

Briefly he wondered if he was right, but with traffic so light, it would be easy enough to make a mistake. But it wasn't too difficult to check. Bolan hung the speed-up-slow-down routine on them; he tried the stop-start-stop pattern. The suspected tail remained the same distance behind him. Finally he took four consecutive turns, bringing him back to the place he started from. The image in the driving mirror was still there.

Okay, so now he was one hundred percent sure.

What was certain also was that the people operating the tail would know now that he was on to them. His mind was working away at the question of what he should do.

He could try to lose them. He could turn and fight, or—if the interested party turned out to be no more than secret police checking out a Western foreigner—he could wait for them to make their move and then play it by ear. Let them stop him. Answer their questions. Honest Mike Blanski, cultural rep—all political colors welcome.

Bolan didn't think they were secret police.

He looked more carefully at the vehicle reflected in the mirror. It was a Duster off-roader, the Romanian equivalent of a Land Rover or Toyota Landcruiser. It looked as though there were at least six men on board. A tall whip aerial sprouted from the center of the roof, but none of the men wore uniforms, and the bodywork of the Duster was a bright primrose yellow; neither—despite the radio—was characteristic of a cop wagon in Bolan's book.

He decided to treat the natives as hostile.

But before he could do anything decisive, there was a more immediate problem: the needle on the Dacia's fuel gauge was quivering over the zero mark.

There was a solution to that one almost at once. The road skirted a stand of young birch trees and then widened to run through a small village. The houses fronting the main street, typical of the Danube delta, were thatched, with blue-washed walls and intricately carved eaves and porches. At the far end of the street was a tin-roofed shack with a rusting tow truck parked out front, and a single gasoline pump. Bolan pulled off the road and cut the motor, signalling to a youth in a New York Giants sweatshirt that he wanted the tank filled.

The youth had begun metronoming the lever of the hand-operated pump when the Duster swung around the curve circling the birch trees and the driver came unexpectedly on the mark he had believed still a quarter of a mile ahead.

Instinctively he braked . . . and then, realizing that Bolan had stopped only to refuel, lifted his foot and accelerated away toward another curve some way beyond the village.

It would be no sweat for the driver to pull off the road and pick up the trail once more when Bolan passed, providing final proof that the warrior was indeed being shadowed—that is, if proof were still needed after what he'd noted as the car had passed him.

Bolan had seen the glint of sunlight on gunmetal as the off-roader swept on. He'd also seen six swarthy faces ostentatiously not looking at the refueling Dacia, and he'd seen something that was still more of a giveaway.

The shadows were hostile all right—but they were not natives.

The Duster had Bulgarian plates.

Bolan was frowning as he drove out of the village. He was puzzled as to how they had gotten onto him. Nor did he know which of the various Bulgarian factions he had run up against had sent them or what their orders were. To waste him or just to keep tabs on him?

And it was of acute interest how they had been able to pick him up, in that part of Romania, with such perfect timing.

There was only one answer to that: the description and number of his rental must have been radioed to them. The implication was that he had been under surveillance in Bucharest, which in turn implied a pretty big-time operation if the hardmen had been called in from another country.

Bolan had ideas of his own on who might be behind that operation. Some of the other questions could be answered by the characters in the Bulgarian off-roader. He decided it was time for the hunted to turn hunter, therefore, and time to squeeze the truth out of someone as soon as he could. The Duster had, after all, picked him up again and was keeping station a quarter of a mile behind, as before.

Soon the country road joined a macadam highway that was narrow, but smooth and straight. Bolan crammed on as much speed as the Dacia could make, gradually outdistancing the heavier utility vehicle. There was a good half-mile between them when the road twisted down into a shallow valley, crossed a bridge spanning a stream and then looped up the far side of the depression to resume its crow-flight line across the Danube plain.

There were trees in the valley—beech, birch, pine and gray oaks covered in creeper that looked almost tropical. Bolan screeched the sedan to a halt immediately after the curve in the roadway, backing up into a shadowed arcade formed by two curtains of creeper. If he allowed any more time to pass, the men in the Duster would wonder why the Dacia was not visible climbing the grade on the far side of the valley; he would have to act the moment the off-roader appeared around the bend.

He waited, the shift locked into first gear, his left foot flat on the clutch pedal, the motor idling. He heard the whine of the Duster's engine, the boom of its large-bore muffler, a familiar squeal of brakes as the driver slowed for the corner.

Still holding the clutch out, he gunned the motor, his head tilted, listening. What he was going to do was dangerous and difficult. But he reckoned it was the best way to build up enough surprise to give him an edge over six armed men.

The off-roader appeared, slewed sideways in a cloud of dust. Bolan floored the accelerator, lifted his foot from the clutch as the engine roared and sent the sedan leaping out from behind the creeper curtain to block the route.

He had gambled—remembering that sudden dab at the brakes when he was sighted at the gas station—that the pursuing driver was impulsive rather than collected, somebody who could be panicked perhaps.

The gamble paid off. The tall, unwieldy, fat-tired Duster was already going too fast when it made the corner. Suddenly seeing the bulk of the sedan shoot across in front of him, the driver did panic. He swerved violently, found that the tires had lost their grip, overcorrected, and then—wrenching at the wheel with the steering on full opposite lock—spun off the road.

The Duster hurtled through ten yards of underbrush, smashed sideways against the trunk of a pine, rolled over, hit a fallen tree and finally came to rest canted over on its side at the top of the riverbank.

Bolan was already out of the stalled Dacia, crouched down in the undergrowth. He had brought the black hide camera case with him on his trip, and now the Turkish Walther PPK, given to him by the Australian smuggler, O'Riley, and hidden in the false bottom of the case, was in his hand. He could see inert figures inside the capsized Duster—dead or only stunned, he had no idea. But one beefy character had crawled out through the exploded windshield and ducked down behind the crumpled hood. Bolan saw eyes glaring malevolently out of a bloodied face...and then birds flapped angrily out of the treetops as the silence of the wood was shattered by the searing eruption of automatic fire.

The thug was hosing a stream of death into the underbrush from a Skorpion machine pistol. Plunging to the ground, Bolan was showered with stalks, twigs and savaged leaves as bullets ripped through the greenery above his head.

Moving swiftly, the gunman dodged behind a tree.

Immobile, Bolan waited.

Second passed. The stream burbled over flat stones. Steam hissed from the off-roader's burst radiator. Bolan saw an arm, a shoulder, the muzzle of the Skorpion and finally enough of the killer's face to sight the machine pistol he was poking out from behind the tree. Belching flame flickered at the muzzle, and a second hellfire burst zipped through the bushes.

Bolan's single shot—it was a tough one—grazed tree bark and plowed into the gunman's shoulder. But the impact was strong enough to spin him out from behind the tree, cursing and clutching at his arm. It was then that the warrior fired again, another single burst, coring the Bulgarian's throat. He fell, gargling blood.

The Executioner rose to his feet. He walked over to the wrecked vehicle. One of the men inside had a broken neck, the guy sitting beside the driver had fragmented the windshield with his face and two more had been knocked out— they weren't going to wake up for a while.

Bolan had accounted for the fifth man.

So where was the driver?

He swung around...a fraction of a second too late. A booted foot, iron-hard, smashed against his wrist and sent the PPK spinning away into the undergrowth. The driver had been thrown clear as the vehicle keeled over, and had tumbled down the bank into the river. Half-stunned, it had taken him a couple minutes to recover. And now, drenched from head to foot, he faced the warrior with a long-bladed knife in his hand.

Disarmed, Bolan kicked out with one foot. His toe caught the wrist of the knife hand, but the guy twisted away, riding the blow. He was a dark-featured forty-year-old with a ragged black mustache. Blood from a gash on his forehead trickled down one side of his face.

Momentarily off balance, Bolan had staggered, putting a hand to the ground to stop himself from falling. As the warrior steadied himself, knees bent, fingertips touching the stones that floored the underbrush, the knife-holder swung forward again, his blade glinting in the sunlight that filtered through the branches overhead.

It slashed sideways, point slightly uptilted, aimed at the warrior's head.

There was only one thing he could do. He allowed himself to collapse on his back, dropping beneath the wicked sweep of the knife. At the same time he drew up his knees, and then, while his assailant was unbalanced, violently straightened his legs.

The heels of his combat boot caught the man below the chest, reeling him back several paces. By the time he was ready to rush in again, the Executioner had scrambled upright and backed off. He held a stone the size of an orange in his right hand.

The knife was now grasped by the tip, its shaft slanted backward, ready to throw. Five or six yards away, Bolan was a target too big to miss; if he wanted to live, he had to act first. And fast.

Past experience came to the rescue. At one time in his military career, Bolan had been selected as pitcher for his divisional Army baseball team. The forgotten skill returned to him now. There was no mound, no time for a proper windup, but he pitched—hard and fast and accurately.

The rock hit the knife-thrower's wrist, knocking his arm back. The weapon fell to the ground. Before the guy could reach it, Bolan leaped in and grabbed him by the lapels in steely hands. "All right," he grated, "give while you still can. Why were you and those other killers tailing me? Who sent you?"

"I don't know what you mean." Then the man fell quiet and shrugged, but when Bolan shook him violently, he let out a stream of obscenities and spit at the warrior's face.

Bolan released his grip, drew back his arm and slashed the guy backhand across the face. The blow carried all his weight. The knife man catapulted backward, crashed to the riverbank and slid down into the water in a shower of earth and stones. Bolan leaped after him, his big hands spread.

Before they could close around his quarry's throat, there was an angry shout from the bridge, and he swung around.

Three militiamen stood there holding submachine guns. Behind them a fourth sat at the wheel of a jeeplike car parked by the Dacia sedan that still blocked the roadway. "What's going on here?" the tallest of the men demanded.

Bolan decided to play the outraged tourist with all the stops pulled out. "I demand to know the same thing!" he shouted. "Sonofabitch here tries to force me off the road—then, when he's overcooked it and crashed that wreck of his among the trees and I give chase, bastard pulls a knife on me!"

Another of the militiamen joined in. "You can't leave your car blocking the road like that, whatever your complaints are."

"Well, what the hell am I supposed to do...?" Bolan began. But the man he was chasing broke suddenly away, ducked beneath his outstretched arms and ran wildly away upstream, stumbling, splashing and scattering stones right and left.

The warrior let him go. He wasn't going to find out anything with the militia watching, and the killer's flight lent credence to his own story. With luck they might assume the man had been alone in the Duster. The bodies would not be visible from the bridge.

"You better show us your papers," the tall militiaman said.

Bolan scrambled up the bank and handed over the Mike Blanski ID, together with the Cultural Friendship documents. He supplied the soldiers with an edited version of the events that led to his fight with the knife man on the riverbank.

"Why should this man have been following you in the first place?" the tall guy asked when he had finished.

"Search me," said Bolan. "I don't know for sure that he was. But it sure looked that way. Then he was drawing alongside and doing his damnedest to push me into the trees. Unfortunately for him, I was able to turn the tables and... well, you saw what happened." He shrugged, then in an appeal to the Balkan sense of national rivalry, added, "Bloody Bulgarian!"

"Well, in that case..." the third man began, turning away. Several cars and a truck held up on the far side of the Dacia were hooting impatiently. The driver of the jeep shouted: "Look, we haven't got all day! We're supposed to report at the Hirsova camp by five. We don't have time to mess around with private quarrels. Tell him to get that heap off the road!"

"But what about the wreck there among the trees?" the second militiaman said dubiously. "Shouldn't we—"

"There's a gas station in the next village," Bolan interposed swiftly, "with a tow truck out front. If you were to drop by on your way and wise them up, they'd probably drive out here and take care of the wreck."

The tall one nodded. He handed Bolan back his papers, and then jerked his head at the Dacia and snapped, "Make it fast, eh? You wasted enough of our time already."

Bolan breathed a sigh of relief. He didn't like to think of the consequences if he'd had to explain the bodies. He backed the sedan in among the screens of creeper as the militiamen clambered into the jeep and drove away. He allowed the blocked traffic to pass and then went back into the wood to recover his Walther. He picked up one of the Skorpions and concealed it in the camera case. He released the magazines of the others, emptied the clips and dropped the shells into the pockets of the bush jacket he was wearing. Then he fired up the engine of the Dacia and resumed the return journey to Bucharest.

On the banks of the stream, the birds settled back in the treetops and started to sing again.

BOLAN WAS twenty miles outside the capital, not far from the town of Trziceni, when he caught on that he was being tailed again. This time it was a powerful Tatra fastback—a wide, low Czech limo with American-style coachwork that was twice as heavy as the Dacia. He cursed. One of the stunned killers must have recovered consciousness earlier than he expected and alerted his base by radio.

Next time, Bolan told himself savagely, if there is a next time, you make damned sure.

The driver of the Tatra was making no pretense; the big car was hanging in no more than a yard from the Dacia's rear bumper. So close that Bolan could see in his mirror that below the black shades, the driver's face was pockmarked; that the guy beside him had a fringe of beard and a scar on his upper lip; that there was a third man, a thug with a cloth cap pulled down over his eyes, leaning forward from the back seat.

It was the man sitting next to the driver who held the SMG.

The Executioner thought fast. There would be no question of outdistancing this car. The traffic was a little heavier here, but the road was straight. There was no chance that he could put a slower vehicle between them, since the Tatra would always be able to spurt past and catch up again before he had the opportunity to get lost up some unexpected dirt road or side street.

He wondered again what their orders were. To take him alive and bring him back, to eliminate him with a burst of fire from the SMG as the faster car overtook? Of course, they could always fake an accident or force the Dacia off the road, take him prisoner to dispose of more discreetly.

He didn't have to wait long to find out.

The road was running beside a double pipeline that channeled natural gas from the Ploesti oilfield to the Danube port at Braila. In the distance derricks and drill rigs and pumping machinery were outlined against the jagged mauve crests of mountains in the interior. On the other side of the highway an embankment carried railroad tracks. And ahead ripening corn that covered the flat landscape was already punctuated by gas stations, hamburger stands for truckers, potteries, a cement factory and the gaunt pylons of the country's new hydroelectric grid.

The Bulgarians made their play just after Bolan had accelerated past a line of semis hauling containers packed with fruit from the orchards on the lower slopes of the Transylvanian Alps. The road stretched ahead for more than a mile, with no traffic in either direction, then twisted out of sight around a line of trees that bordered a canal.

He reckoned they might try something as soon as he was around the curve and out of sight of the leading semi. So he slowed as much as he dared, hoping to keep the sedan in the truck driver's field of view as long as possible, steering with one hand while he picked the Walther from his camera case and laid it on his lap.

But the hoods didn't aim to wait that long. The Tatra roared up behind Bolan while he was halfway along the straightaway. A moment later he was jerked violently forward against the seatbelt as the heavier car's bumper slammed into the rear of the Dacia. The sedan staggered, slewed half across the road, and finally straightened up as Bolan spun the wheel.

The big limo crashed against him again, harder this time, and once more with a shriek of tortured metal as something ripped away from the Dacia's trunk and clattered onto the pavement.

Bolan had no options. There was no way to out-accelerate the Tatra. He couldn't brake fiercely and hope to bring the two vehicles to a standstill, because the powerful limo would just keep pushing until the smaller sedan broadsided across the road and finally rolled over. He was stuck with the situation, shunted along as helplessly as a freight car in a railroad siding. Again and again the Tatra battered the Dacia's rear until, level with the trees, it drew alongside at last.

The hood with the pockmarked face shifted down, and the sound of the engine rose to a scream. He tweaked the wheel fiercely to the right. The limo's nearside front fender crunched against Bolan's car. The Dacia skated across the road, ran onto grass and bounced off one of the trees. The driver's window imploded, showering the warrior's knees with granules of toughened glass.

Bolan coaxed the sedan back onto the macadam. He didn't dare pick up the Walther and fire at his attackers; he needed both hands and all the strength he possessed to wrestle with the wheel.

The Tatra's trunk was beside the broken window. Bolan saw its brake lights blaze. The big car fell slightly behind, and then, viciously accelerating, raced up again and side-swiped the Dacia's rear wheel-arch with stunning force.

This time the Executioner couldn't retain control. Trees, sky, canal bank and buildings streamed past the windshield as the lighter car's tires lost traction. It spun twice amid a shriek of rubber, plunged between the trees, canted up over the raised towpath and dropped with a shattering crash into the water.

It sank almost at once, huge air bubbles gurgling to the surface while water gushed in through the smashed window and welled up from the engine compartment.

Bolan had taken a deep breath when the car was in mid-air and grabbed the waterproofed camera case. The Walther he had to let go with the tide. When the water touched the roof, and the Dacia was resting on the canal bottom, he swam out through the open window.

Fifty yards away a bridge that led a service road to an unfinished factory site arched over the waterway. Still submerged, he swam that way. The water was muddy, opaque and icy cold.

When he judged he was beneath the bridge, Bolan surfaced with his lungs bursting. In fact he was on the far side of the bridge.

Shaking the water from his hair and eyes, he headed for the bank, towing the camera case behind him. Soon his feet touched bottom, and he was able to wade ashore and hoist himself up onto the towpath on the side of the canal far-thest from the main road.

He crouched down, looking back beneath the arch of the bridge. The three men from the Tatra were standing on the bank by the scarred earth where the sedan had made its death plunge.

Bolan glanced over his shoulder. The service road led to a fenced-in compound lined with single-story workmen's shelters and an overseer's hut. Dump trucks, bulldozers, earth-moving machines and concrete mixers were parked here and there in the yard. Beyond stacks of bricks and piles of sand and cinder blocks, the skeleton of the factory building stood by a gravel pit filled with yellow water. The structure was eight floors high, but only the red steel framework had been erected. There was no roof, no sheathing, and it was floored only on the three lowest levels, where tubular scaffolding spined the outer girders.

Bolan heard a shout from the other side of the canal. The killers had seen him and were now running toward the bridge.

He turned and raced across the rough ground in the direction of the yard, unzipping the black hide case and opening the false bottom as he ran. By the time he made the gateway, the Skorpion was in his hand.

Fifty yards of open ground lay between him and a stack of lumber, which had clearly been offloaded from a nearby dump truck. There were no workmen in sight, either the construction site was temporarily deserted or the gangers stopped work at five o'clock. Bolan sprinted for the lumber.

The pursuers appeared in the open gateway, then immediately fanned out to cover the widest sector of fire.

The husky guy in the cloth cap dropped to one knee and started shooting while the others were still running. Bolan was maybe thirty yards ahead. The stream of slugs was dangerously close, scuffing the beaten earth beside his feet, gouging splinters from the lumber. He dived behind the stack.

Folded forward over the Skorpion's ten-and-a-half-inch length, the wire stock left the machine pistol highly maneuverable. The stubby, cylindrical wooden butt fit snugly into Bolan's fist, and the short curved magazine, projecting downward in front of the trigger guard, allowed him a second, stabilizing grip to counteract the gun's tendency to climb. He set the selector lever to auto, flattened himself on the ground, and edged his head and shoulders around one corner of the stack to squeeze off a short burst at the man with the pockmarked face, who was moving out to enfilade him from beneath the dump truck. The guy dropped out of sight behind the truck's treble line of ribbed rear wheels.

Bolan scrambled to the far side of the stack and sent the bearded man diving for safety in his turn with another burst. Then he was on his feet and running again for the next piece of cover—the nearest pile of cinder block. The bearded man's SMG, he had seen, was a Russian PPSh-41—the 35-round box magazine type issued to sailors of the Soviet Black Sea Fleet based on Odessa. The other two thugs were armed with ex-Soviet army Stechkin pistols.

Now Cloth Cap was running, too. He leaped up on top of the lumber and hosed a long 9 mm deathstream at the zig-zagging warrior a moment before he dodged behind the pile. Gray chips fountained up from the blocks, and Bolan felt the camera case leap on its shoulder strap as the black hide was cored in several places.

He fired again, twice, reloading the Skorpion's 7.65 mm magazine during the temporary lull. Out in the open, with only occasional cover, he could do no more than make the hunters keep their heads down; spread out as they were, he had no chance to score until he made it to the complexities of the incomplete building. The driver of the Tatra was in among the earth-moving equipment, still thirty yards away but closing in. The man with the SMG blasted off half a magazine from the top of a sand heap.

But Bolan was already on the move again, hurling himself down beside the caterpillar tracks of a bulldozer and then rolling through puddles of water to a tin shack by the factory entrance. Another ten yards, and he was through the scaffolding and under the unfinished concrete arch where the main doors would be.

There were no doors now. Planks laid from girder to girder made a dogleg walkway crossing the open space above the factory basement. Bolan dashed over until he could round the central core from which the structure's floors were cantilevered out.

The driver of the Tatra was shouting curt orders. The three killers were already within the framework of the building. Shots echoed thunderously among the ironwork, and a hellfire spray splatted against the concrete core and rattled between metal stays above the warrior's head. Soaked as he was from the canal, filthy from the puddles on the site, he was leaving traces wherever he walked on the planking. He heard the hollow ring of boots on metal. One of the Bulgarians was climbing the scaffolding; the other two had only to close in and follow the damp footmarks, flushing him out of cover so that he could be shot down from above.

The last burst had come from the SMG, locating the bearded guy someplace near the entrance. The driver was yelling in back; he must have circled the block outside. So it was Cloth Cap swarming up the scaffolding. That suited Bolan—he figured that one for the dumbest of the trio. He decided to go aloft himself.

Treading as lightly as he could, he ran for the tubular framework. He had made only a few yards when a double firestorm erupted right and left, forcing him to drop to the planks and empty the Skorpion's magazine a second time. He looked over his shoulder. Maybe it would be smarter to go back the way he came?

It was then that he saw the electric cable.

Wide coils of it, with heavy-duty insulation, lay outside the central core. And although two elevator shafts visible from his former position were empty, from where he was he could see a service cage designed for goods in a wider shaft.

It was possible that the cable was connected to the elevator and the main supply.

Still lying flat, he inched back toward the elevator. One end of the cable arched down into the basement, where the hydraulic machinery was. He couldn't see the other end; from the coils outside the shaft it snaked around the core of the building and disappeared. He decided to take a chance.

He turned stealthily around on the planking boardwalk and crawled into the elevator cage. Once inside, he rose to his knees, reached up with one hand and pressed the button on the control panel.

There was a sudden clunk from below. The elevator floor shook. The concertina gates clanged shut, and the cage moved upward.

Bolan breathed a sigh of relief. The current was switched on!

Over the shrill whine of the mechanism, he heard a shout from the boardwalk. Gunshots reverberated. Bullets flattened themselves against the concrete shaft, ricochetted off the steelwork radiating from it and thudded into the freight elevator's thick wooden floor.

The cage went on climbing. One floor sank past the open grille, two, three. After that there was nothing but open girders. He stared through the steel tracery at the flat countryside. Beyond the blue, serrated silhouette of the mountains, the sun was setting.

Bolan stopped the elevator at the fifth floor. The gates slid apart. A narrow catwalk led to the outer framework of the building. He walked warily out along it.

His thinking was based on mechanical differences between his 7.65 mm VZ-61 Skorpion machine pistol and Cloth Cap's 9 mm Stechkin. The Czech weapon's ultralightweight bolt and consequently high rate of fire was countered by an inertia system within the pistol grip that effectively delayed the return of the bolt and reduced the rate to manageable proportions. There was no such compensation in the 750-rounds-per-minute Stechkin, which was chambered for a wildcat Russian cartridge, known as the 9x18 Soviet, that was shorter and less powerful than the 9 mm parabellum.

At anything beyond close-combat distances, therefore—and Bolan was already two stories higher than the top of the scaffolding—the Skorpion was the more accurate weapon.

The catwalk ended in a steel grid perimeter gallery that circled the building. Bolan was almost there when Cloth Cap opened fire. He ran the last few feet and threw himself down on the metal grille as the leaden hail drummed on the girders and screeched off into the sky.

He peered over the edge of the iron footway, staring down through two levels of nothingness at the cement surface of the third floor. And at the bulky, cloth-capped figure darting from the scaffolding toward the central core.

The hood turned as Bolan eased the Skorpion into position. Both men opened fire at the same time. The first two or three slugs from the blowback Stechkin struck the grid inches from Bolan's elbow, the remainder of the long burst being dispersed harmlessly upward by the rapid-fire pistol's climb.

Blasting downward simultaneously, the Executioner's killstream was lethal. Half a dozen steel-jacketed bullets ripped across the Bulgarian's chest, and he dropped heavily, spraying crimson over the chips of cement and staining the dust. In the silence that followed the exchange, Bolan heard the cartridge cases ejected from his gun tinkling down among the ironwork.

He hurried back to the elevator, feeling vulnerable as a spiderman balanced on the girders. He had jammed the gates open with the camera case, so that the cage could not be recalled. He had to decide how far to take it down—or accept a stalemate that could last until nightfall.

Negative on that one, since he needed to be back in the city in time for the message from Stojkov. He chose the second floor. If one or the other of the remaining killers was making it up the scaffolding now, he should still be above them at that level.

The elevator sank down at the center of the skeletal building, and the action suddenly speeded up.

The Tatra driver yelled to his companion as he heard the gates of the elevator clash open on the second floor. The voice came from the outer framework of the factory, a little below the level of the cage. Bolan dropped the case again and sprinted across.

It was too easy. The guy's head and shoulders were just rising into sight as he left the elevator. The Stechkin was in his right hand, but in no position to aim. Bolan fired as he ran, leaving the machine pistol on auto, stitching a left-right-left pattern across the target before the killer had a chance to shoot.

The driver threw up his arms, the pistol dropped from sight and a moment later the Bulgarian careened backward and fell after it. The tubular scaffolding shook as his body hit a spar lower down and stayed draped across it. Two down, and one to go.

Bolan soft-footed back to the shaft. He removed the camera case, took off his squelching combat boots, then held the gates open while he pressed the button for street level. The gates closed with a metallic rattle. The elevator started down. Silently Bolan ran, his stockinged feet leaving damp footmarks on the gritty cement.

Before he reached the planks laid across the scaffold tubes, he heard a shuddering jar as the elevator halted. The man with the beard must have made it to the emergency button and blocked the cage between floors. Now he would be dashing toward the shaft, ready to blow away the captive in the cage with the remaining rounds in his magazine.

It didn't work out quite that way.

Bolan dropped from the scaffolding, sped noiselessly up behind the killer and leaped...one-tenth of a second before the guy could peer up at the lower part of the halted elevator and realize it was empty.

The warrior's left arm circled the bearded man's head, the wrist and forearm jammed up beneath his chin to cut off the air supply. At the same time a broad-bladed commando knife, recovered from the false bottom of the camera case, plunged into his back.

The razor-sharp point grazed a rib and then slid home in soft tissue. The killer's body became rigid, stiff and he made a snorting noise like a man underwater. Bolan felt the throat constrict against his arm. The SMG discharged the rest of its load to scar the ceiling, then clattered to the floor. The killer's whole body went limp as blood spilled from the corners of the mouth and jetted from the nose.

Bolan lowered the dead man with his red-frothed beard to the planks. He unblocked the elevator and rode it up to collect the camera case and his boots. After riding back to street level again, he walked out of the unfinished factory. On the far side of the canal, he climbed into the Tatra limo and drove it back to Bucharest. The owners wouldn't be needing it any more.

He left the car two blocks from the special foreign visitors' hotel and walked the rest of the way. The reception clerk was busy at the phone. While he was waiting to ask for his key, Bolan turned to scan a notice board advertising conducted tours, exhibitions, trade fairs and theater programs.

His own face stared back at him from a printed bill pinned to the center of the board. It said in large black letters:

Mack Bolan. Wanted by the police in connection with two murders in Istanbul, crimes against the state in

Sofia, multiple assassinations on a Black Sea oil rig and illegal entry into Romania.

"This man," the notice advised, "is dangerous."
He calmly turned on his heels and beat it out of there.

**19**

Bolan went back to the central bus station and called the secret number that had been written on the book of matches given to him by Brognola's courier. The Fed himself was not available—a meeting of the National Security Council in the Oval Office, the woman who took the call informed him—but she promised that his demands would be met as speedily as possible.

How speedy was that? Well, seeing that it was technically east of the Iron Curtain, it would be better to allow three days.

"I need the stuff in two," Bolan said. "Before nightfall, day after tomorrow, at the map coordinates I gave you. Without fail."

She said she would do her best. Bolan knew that was good enough.

He couldn't be at the hotel to take the call from Stojkov, but there was a fallback number that the Bulgarian guerrilla leader would call exactly one hour later if Bolan missed out on the first one. The number identified a pay phone in the foyer of the Athene theater. Bolan paid for a ticket admitting him to a performance by a Russian company of a play by Gogol, mingled with the crowd streaming in beneath the huge pillared portico and slowly drifted along beneath the dome of the rotunda until he located the phone—one of a row housed in booths at one side of the cloakroom.

A very young blonde was already using the instrument. He waited in an agony of impatience while the girl, giggling, grimacing and lighting cigarette after cigarette, gossiped interminably with a friend, evidently determined to keep on talking until the performance started. He dared not draw attention to himself by urging her to hurry up, especially as two of the neighboring booths were unoccupied. When at last the bells rang and she left, Bolan's call was twelve minutes overdue.

He stepped into the booth, leaving the door open to allow stale cigarette smoke to escape. The phone rang.

He snatched up the receiver before any of the theater personnel noticed, and made the necessary arrangements with Stojkov.

The call took several minutes. "You're too late—the curtain's already up," an usherette said severely as he emerged. "It's forbidden to enter once the play has started. You'll have to wait until the second act now. I'm sorry, but I have my—"

"No problem," the Executioner assured her. "The lady I'm waiting for is obviously delayed. I'll call her home and then take a breath of fresh air until the intermission."

He went back into the booth and dialed the number of the American Embassy. "Is Mr. Zabriski in this evening?" he asked the switchboard.

"I don't believe so," the operator said. "Hold on . . . I'll check."

Bolan nodded to himself. One hunch paid off. His assumption had been correct; the CIA man was in town.

The girl was back on the line. "Hello? No, I'm sorry. Mr. Zabriski is not here at the moment."

"Do you know when he's coming back?"

"I can't say, sir. There's no message on the board."

"No sweat. Which hotel's he staying at?"

"I don't think he's . . . I'm sorry, we are not allowed to reveal the whereabouts of diplomats. I can't give you his address."

"It's very important. It's vital I see Mr. Zabriski to-night."

"I'm very sorry, sir. That's the rule."

"People say they're meant to be broken. Couldn't you at least bend it? Just this once?"

"Uh-uh," the girl said. "May I know who I'm talking to, please?"

"The name's Brognola," Bolan said. "I'm from the Justice Department, Sensitive Operations Group. I shouldn't even be telling you this, but Zabriski needs the Intel I have."

"I *told* you, sir!" The woman was growing angry. "There's nothing I can do. I'll put you through to the duty officer or the vice-consul, if he's still in his office. If you'll just hold—"

"I don't want the vice-consul—I want Zabriski!" Bolan said sharply.

"Then I can only suggest that you call by in the morn-ing," she replied icily. "The office is open at eight."

That was the last thing the Executioner intended to do. "Forget it," he said. He hung up and walked out of the theater.

The slight slip at the beginning of the conversation gave him the clue he needed. From what the woman almost said, it seemed clear enough that the CIA man was *not* staying at a hotel. So, where would he be? He wasn't based in Ro-mania, so he wouldn't have a pad of his own in Bucharest. One of the station's safehouses, then?

That seemed a reasonably safe bet, and since Bolan knew of only one safehouse, he had no trouble deciding where to start checking. He drifted with the city center crowds until midnight, and then began the long walk out to the subway terminal. He was leaving it until late because he wished to make sure Zabriski would be back from wherever he had been, and in any case the subway could be dangerous if those "Wanted" posters had been widely distributed.

He waited until two o'clock before he made his play. The crumbling terra-cotta house with the cupola lay in a shadowed section of the street between two overhead arcs. A prowl car had traversed the street at one-fifteen and again at one-forty-five. Bolan reckoned he had fifteen minutes free of official observation, assuming the police would be around again at a quarter after.

He had already checked out all the angles, waiting in the darkness of a recessed doorway of an empty building across the street. The safehouse would be protected by the normal burglar alarm systems: electrical circuits, Chubb-style window locks, magic eye beams, floor pressure pads inside each door and window. But he was counting on the fact that there would be nothing more sophisticated, nothing whose installation would draw official attention to the place.

If he was right, the way in for him was via the cupola.

He ran across the road and ducked in under the portico. From the camera case he took out heavy-duty suction pads, which he strapped tightly to his elbows and knees. Then, leaving the case in the darkness behind the top step, he moved to the rear of one of the squat stone pillars and began to climb.

With the pads to aid his steely grip and the fingerholds offered by the numerous decorations, curlicues, rosettes and other stone carvings above the pillars, it was no great sweat making it to the cupola.

The cupola was segmented, like an orange, with each section filled by curved panels. At one time the panels had probably been copper, or even glass, but People's Democracy horror of ostentation had decreed that they should be replaced by asphalted roofing material. On the side of the dome away from the street there was, nevertheless, as the warrior had hoped, still one panel designed to slide down over the one below it to allow entry.

The panel, clearly, hadn't been moved in years. Bolan had thought of that. He produced an aerosol tin of thin machine oil and sprayed generously all around the panel and along the grooves in which it should slide. While he was waiting for the oil to penetrate, he heard the prowl car make its half-hourly patrol along the street below.

That meant it was two-fifteen.

It was only on the third attempt, when most of the oil in the aerosol was exhausted, that he was able to feel the panel shift. It dropped a quarter inch then jammed. It was fastened on the inner side with a catch.

Bolan took the commando knife from his belt and slid the blade between panel and frame. He maneuvered the knife to pry back the catch. He heard a loud snick, and the panel moved easily under his hand.

Freezing momentarily because the noise had seemed very loud, he waited, holding his breath. There was no reaction from below.

He lowered the panel to its full extent and stared into a dark oblong just wide enough and deep enough to admit a man's body. Warm air, spiced with stale cigar smoke, the odor of cooking and a hint of after-shave rose through the hole.

No lights showed inside the house. Bolan risked a rapid examination with his penlight. A small circular gallery ran around beneath the cupola. Below that was the building's second floor. As he had guessed, remembering the layout from his meeting with the consular official, this floor was basically a mirror image of the first: a central hallway that included the staircase; two rooms opening off each side; a storeroom and the offices, with the second-floor bathroom above the first-floor kitchen, at the rear.

The cupola framework was cast-iron. He tested it for strength and then lowered himself through the opening. Hanging at the full stretch of his arms, he found his toes were about four feet above the gallery floor. Holding his breath, he let go and dropped.

Although he was lithe as a spring and in outstanding shape, it seemed to him that the shock of his fall shook the house. But once again there was no audible reaction from any of the rooms.

Bolan crept down the spiral stairs from the gallery. He heard a light snoring from one of the rooms. The door was ajar. He peered through the crack, daring another swift flash of his penlight. The fair-haired man with the wispy mustache, who had badmouthed the warrior when he'd been at the house before, was lying asleep on a divan, his mouth open, one forearm across his eyes, his legs tangled in the covers.

The door of the next room was closed. Bolan eased it open. The air smelled cold, unused. He thumbed the penlight's button. An office chair, a table carrying a portable radio transmitter, a tape deck and a decoding machine. He backed out and closed the door.

A quick sweep of the thin beam around the hallway, up to the gallery floor and back. There could have been a radar eye that would signal anyone crossing from one side of the landing to the other. But there wasn't. Bolan guessed whatever apparatus there was must be concentrated at street level or around the upper-story windows. He stole around and tried the door opposite the young man's. It was closed and locked.

The fourth door was closed, too, but it opened easily and quietly. He heard heavy breathing, smelled the same cloyingly sweet after-shave. It had to be Zabriski.

Bolan slid into the room and closed the door behind him. He leaned his back against the panels and switched on the penlight.

The CIA man sat up in a single swift movement, the dapper hair mussed, the eyes red from sleep, but his right hand reaching for the stainless-steel Detonics Combat Master on the night table.

"Leave it!" the Executioner snapped. He shifted the flashlight beam fractionally to show the silenced Beretta 93-R rock-steady in his right hand.

"Bolan!" Surprise and relief were mingled in Zabriski's exclamation. "But why the theatrical entrance, man? And the gun? Why not ring the doorbell, for God's sake, at a reasonable hour?"

"Do I have to spell it out for you?"

"You most certainly do." The CIA man reached beneath his pillow, produced the rimless shades and perched them on his nose. "But let's cut out the melodrama, huh? Switch on the light, we'll call in Hoskins and behave like grown-up people, okay?"

Bolan moved a few inches to one side, flattened a shoulder against the wall and slid downwards until he tripped the light switch. A pink-shaded lamp on the night table bathed the high-ceilinged room in subdued, rosy illumination. The furniture here was newer, even comfortable. Dark blue wall-to-wall carpet covered the floor. "I don't believe Mr. Hoskins—if that's the punk snoring across the hallway—would care to hear what I have to say," Bolan added quietly.

Zabriski stared at him. He opened his mouth but said nothing.

"It had to be you," the Executioner continued in a low voice. "What bugged me finally was the fact that you were so godawful dumb about it."

"What are you *talking* about? You're out of your skull!" A thin film of sweat was visible on Zabriski's upper lip.

"Talking about that Ilyushin," Bolan said levelly. "About people knowing where it was going to crash and the loss of the black boxes. You said it yourself. In a one-horse town like Tehran, you said, it was easier to buy yourself a technician and have the dirty work done during a preflight checkup than smuggling explosives aboard. Easier, too, I guess, to locate and steal the black boxes if the precise area of the crash had already been reported to you. By a bribed Iranian test pilot, for instance, who was trying out the new Chinese pursuit plane? Easier, anyway, to hide the sabotage—or put the blame on Iran."

"Bolan, you're not making sense," Zabriski said.

"Forget all that—forget the snide tearjerkers about broken bodies. Your really big mistake, buster, was concerning me. Brognola told me, after the attempts on my life, that there had to be a mole. You fingered yourself as that mole soon enough."

"Look, I've listened to this crap long enough. I'm going to—"

"You'll continue listening." The Beretta did not waver. "The police colonel who arrested me in Istanbul called me Bolan. But I was in the country as Mike Belasko. Apart from Brognola, the only people who knew my real name were Mazuklav, the Turkish accident investigation officer, and you. Either of you could have tipped off Colonel Ecevlic. But Mazuklav knew nothing of my plans to borrow an Embassy boat from the marina at Sinop. You did. And there was a killer squad waiting for me when I got there. For God's sake," Bolan hissed, "I was dropped there by a chopper. Nobody else could have found out where I was going, and when, in time to get those hit men there before me."

Zabriski's face was white. "This is crazy talk," he said shakily. "You want to get your head examined."

"Nobody but you," Bolan continued remorselessly, "nobody in the slightest way connected with this operation could have had access to my movements, could have tipped off the Bulgarians in time for them to hit me every move I made."

"Bolan..."

"They followed me from country to country, didn't they? But how did they keep track? Only you knew that Belasko and Mike Blanski were the same guy, or that his real name was Bolan. That was the second nail you drove into your own coffin. The third was this 'Wanted' poster I see all over town."

Zabriski was plucking nervously at the sheet. "You're talking in riddles, man. I swear to you that I never—"

''That was the dumbest mistake of all. You fucked up with the name again, okay. But the photo, Zabriski, the photo! That shot's from my personal dossier at Stony Man Farm. Just Brognola and the guys at Stony Man know about that picture and name going together.''

Bolan walked across to the bed, picked the stainless-steel .45-caliber automatic from the night table and dropped it in his pocket. Zabriski cowered back, staring as if mesmerized at the silencer on the warrior's own gun.

''So it had to be someone with access to Brognola, someone with a high enough security clearance to go to Stony Man, someone with an in at our Embassies in Europe. A CIA operative fit the bill nicely.''

''This is insanity!''

''Now you're talking!'' Bolan leaned over the bed, his ice-cold blue eyes boring relentlessly through the rimless shades. ''Fuchs, Philby, Burgess and Maclean—those creeps sold out their country, but at least in their distorted way they believed in the values of the other side. They sold out for a principle. You, on the other hand—'' the contempt in the Executioner's voice stung like a whip ''—sell out for *money*. And I do mean sell. You're prepared to sacrifice the lives of thousands, perhaps millions of innocent men, women and children, blacken the name of your country and risk a Third World War to swell your bank balance! Because that was the clincher, Zabriski. When I was ninety-percent sure, I cabled home and asked for the details of your life-style.''

For a moment Bolan checked the catalog of denunciation. Then he continued. ''A fifteen-room house with a five-hundred-yard frontage on Long Island Sound, two power-boats, a Mercedes and an imported Jaguar coupé—nice going for a minor official in the Company!''

Zabriski licked his lips. ''I . . . the property was left to me by . . . by an uncle,'' he said sullenly.

''Oh, yeah? The uncle who lives at Perestrek 32, in Sofia, maybe?''

The CIA man said nothing.

"I don't know whether the loot was funnelled to you through KGB hard-liners or Department C.4 of the Bulgarian Secret Service," Bolan continued, "and I don't know how it was laundered. All I know, like you say, is that it was insanity, the act of a crazy man. And that you're not going to live to enjoy spending it." He backed away from the bed.

The spectacles fell from Zabriski's nose as he started up among the covers, his eyes filled with panic. "Bolan, for Christ's sake!" he choked out.

Bolan regarded the man dispassionately. He was not normally an angry person; the fury powering his campaign against the evil threatening the world was cold and calculated. He rarely lost that cool. He was too good a soldier to permit his tactics to be affected by emotional factors.

Only twice in his professional life had a hot-tempered thirst for vengeance unbalanced this calm deliberation. The first time was when he was recalled from Vietnam on compassionate grounds to find his parents and sister dead because of a Mafia intrigue. The tragedy had unleashed his personal—and largely successful—crusade against the tycoons of organized crime.

The second ended his career as boss of the secretly funded undercover task force based at Stony Man. April Rose, the love of Bolan's life, had sacrificed her own to save him from an assassin's bullet during an attack on the farm. Bolan had executed the mole responsible for the attack in front of the President in the Oval Office. And that, of course, was how he became an outlaw.

But outlaws do not necessarily lose their beliefs, and Bolan was a believer, a believer in decency and democracy. And also in truth and in justice.

Unfortunately, though, justice cannot always be done when the truth can't be proven.

Perhaps that was why, faced with a traitor prepared to launch the horrors of chemical warfare for personal gain, he felt within him for the third time the choking anger that stifles rational thought. Because although at last he had discovered the truth about Zabriski, there was no way he could prove it.

*I am not their judge; I am their judgment. I am their Executioner.* How often in life had events forced him to live by that personal credo? And would this not be just one more justifiable execution to add to the tally?

"Maybe this *is* in a way for Christ's sake," he said in reply to Zabriski's last cry. "Isn't there some line about suffering the little children? Maybe in this case the little children in Iran who *won't* die in agony during an unprovoked nerve gas attack?" He raised the barrel of the silenced autoloader. "I'll make it easy for you," he said.

Zabriski uttered a *no* that was half a plea, half an enraged war cry, and lunged at Bolan. The fear in his eyes had been replaced by fury, and a small blade had materialized in his hand.

But the warrior knew his kind and had been ready. The Executioner's trigger finger tightened, and he unleashed a quick and painless death. And in this case, he thought, Zabriski had signed his own death warrant.

**20**

"Do you know," Mack Bolan said to Vasil Stojkov, "that within one half mile of this lagoon you can see, between now and sundown, a polar grebe, a Siberian half-snipe, a Mongolian Saker falcon and large flocks of mandarin ducks and egrets from China."

"Is that so?"

"At the same time, if your field glasses were properly focused, you might be lucky enough to sight Mediterranean herons, ibis, pelicans, sheldrakes and sea eagles."

The guerrilla leader raised his eyebrows but said nothing.

"This part of the Danube delta," Bolan told him, "is a natural reserve for water birds. As Bulgaria is kind of a spaghetti junction for drug-runners and terrorists, so Romania is for migratory birds."

Stojkov picked up a stick and threw it into the water. "You don't say!"

"Flocks of which," Bolan pursued, "flying out daily over the Black Sea before they make the long haul, offer a radar signature virtually indistinguishable from a team of sailboarders."

"Ah!" Stojkov's interest quickened. "Now you're talking!"

The two men were standing at the inner end of the stretch of open water Bolan had located near the Sfintu Gheorghe lighthouse. It was midafternoon, the sun was shining and the tall reeds surrounding the salt marsh moved slightly in a breeze blowing in from the sea. Out on the lagoon, a dozen of Stojkov's Bulgarian partisans—smuggled into the country over the mountains—maneuvered the collapsible sails of sailboarding kits.

It was forty-six hours since Bolan had contacted Brognola's office and placed his order for supplies, thirty-seven since he left the terra-cotta house with the cupola, and it would be maybe two more before a helicopter delivered those same supplies here in this desolate swamp.

To make things easier for the Bucharest Embassy personnel and the local police, the warrior had overturned a chair, taken Zabriski's ID papers and billfold and floored the body before he left the safehouse. "Your Mr. Zabriski met with an accident," he told a surprised Hoskins, who waylaid him sleepily as he headed for the front door. "It seems he must have surprised a burglar who forced his way in through the cupola. You really should check those alarm systems."

Filling Stojkov in on the story so far, he referred only briefly to the Zabriski incident and the bad taste it had left in his mouth.

But Stojkov understood even when little was said and put a hand on his shoulder. "The man who lives large," he said, "cuts himself a large slice of trouble. The hard man gives himself a hard time."

"Too right," the Executioner replied, soothed by the unspoken sympathy and understanding. "And this year's hardest time lies right ahead! What's gonna be tough is schooling ourselves to hold back and hit out at the same time."

Stojkov nodded. "You mean—"

"I mean it would be dead easy to take out that damned oil rig in a single sweep. With your explosives expert in a wet suit, me and you as backup and enough Semtex to fill a plastic shopping sack, we could total two of the pontoon legs and have the whole shooting match under water with a couple of well-placed blasts."

"But wouldn't that leave the Sarin missiles running wild—even if they didn't get detonated in the explosions?"

"Got it. There's no more than fifty meters of water there—it's like an island coming up from the deeps. Those missiles could roll with the tides, they could get washed ashore, or they could even find their way into other terrorists' hands. And there's all that U.S. Army material. It wouldn't be as bad as Baseball, but there could be embarrassing questions if it ended up in the wrong place, in the wrong hands—and was still identifiable."

"What you're saying is that we have to take the whole base—capture it and not destroy it—and kill or immobilize the entire garrison before we even start to get rid of the evidence?"

Bolan nodded. "That's what I'm saying."

"Kind of a tall order, as the English say," Stojkov commented dryly.

"I've seen taller, pinned up on the Operations notice board. I'll draw you a plan of each deck."

Stojkov laughed. His leg still pained him, but the limp was scarcely noticeable. "Plus we got a model on the other side of the lake and one whole day for rehearsals," he said. "How can we lose?"

"We won't lose," Bolan said.

"One thing—I suppose there's no chance the rig personnel could arm and fire those Lance missiles *after* we begin the attack? I mean just fire them anywhere in revenge? Or even open the warheads up in some suicide maneuver and let the gas out?"

"No way," Bolan said. "They're fitted with graze fuses, but they have to be primed. There are so many safety precautions to *stop* them opening accidentally, you wouldn't believe it."

"And the vehicles?"

"The Lance is a two-stage rocket powered by liquid fuel, with a DC-Automet guidance system. You can't—"

"DC-what?"

"Directional Control with Automatic Meteorological Compensation. The missile is invulnerable to all known countermeasures. I'm saying you can't just arm and fire those off like revolver bullets in the middle of a close-combat assault."

"My friend," Stojkov said, the eyes gleaming above the bushy beard, "I am glad to hear it!"

"I agree it's a tough assignment, just the same," Bolan said. "But with this three-phase attack and the radio contact we'll have...well, I'll offer any odds you like that the bird will fly!"

"And talking of birds...?"

"Yeah. For the first part at least, we have to go in at dusk, when the flocks low down over the water are at their busiest. That's the most sensitive part..." Bolan paused. One of the men across the lagoon had shouted. Botev, Levski and a couple of the guerrillas standing near Bolan and the partisan chief were all pointing seaward.

The Executioner stared. Revolving radar antennae, a filigree of aerials, a dish and the top half of a glassed-in bridge had appeared above the screen of reeds. As he watched, a slim rakish bow thrust aside the tall tufted stems and an ocean-going cabin cruiser glided out from a creek and dropped anchor in the center of the lagoon.

A trim, white-uniformed figure shining with gold braid stepped to the rail and raised a bullhorn.

"Will Mr. Belasko, Mr. Mike Belasko, accept delivery of—uh—cultural artifacts consigned to this carrier by an American art dealer?"

Bolan gaped. Brognola was supplying the weaponry and hardware he had asked for by boat instead of by chopper. He focused his field glasses on the white figure, and this time his jaw really dropped.

The man with the bullhorn was the Australian smuggler, O'Riley!

"A matter of delicacy, sport," he said when Bolan had come aboard. "Your pal figured a bird over Eastern bloc airspace could've led to awkward questions . . . particularly if it was forced down by pursuit planes before the freight was delivered! Since he'd have been sending a boat, anyway, as part of the order, he reckoned it'd be smart to combine, as it were, the two.''

"O'Riley," Bolan said, "what the hell are you doing here—you yourself, I mean? Who are you?"

"Your Fed thought I could lend a hand, if you were operating a disposal team."

"So, welcome to the wrecking crew. And my other question?"

"If it's Intel you're after," the Australian said vaguely, "smuggling's a bloody good cover."

"You're into some secret service racket, aren't you? I knew you were no ordinary smuggler when you picked me up lost at sea. That was no happy coincidence, was it?"

O'Riley grinned. "You're telling the story, cobber."

"It was a slip, just a small one, but it told me something."

"Feel free to share the news."

"When you were asking where I wanted to be put ashore, you said you guessed I wouldn't want to go *back* to Sinop. I'd never said I came from there, so . . ." Bolan shrugged. "Also, you didn't ask enough questions. I mean how come I was floating there in the middle of the Black Sea in that condition."

The Australian stayed smiling. He said nothing.

"Some way, somehow, you'd been cut in on the deal. What cards do you hold, O'Riley? If you're working with me, I want to know. So teach me, guy."

"Sometimes clients sell a commodity in good faith," O'Riley said, "only to discover later that it's been ruled kind of illegal. In such cases, the manufacturer likes to keep a close eye on what's become of the product, and what use it's been put to."

"Okay, so you, too, were following up this damned MPD that was sold to Iran by the Brits. But you're not British yourself. So who contracted the job out to you—MI5? Six? The Secret Intelligence Service? Porton Down Security?''

"Something like that."

"Well, which?"

"One of the things about secret service work," said the smuggler, "is that the details remain secret."

## 21

The boat used by O'Riley was a one-hundred-thousand-dollar eight-berth Fjord 40 cruiser. Twin diesels, two-hundred horsepower each, could propel the ten-ton polyester hull through a calm sea at over forty knots. "Which could be useful," the Australian said, "if we have to fly those skiers high and there ain't too much breeze up there."

Bolan nodded. "And the tanks?"

"Just short of three hundred gallons. With a couple of forty-gallon drums stowed aft in reserve."

"Should do. If you don't aim to break any speed records on the way."

"Listen, sport, with me and you, Stojkov and his two lieutenants, twelve guys and all that hardware, we're gonna be lucky to push aside the reeds at the exit from this blasted lagoon!"

Bolan laughed. "I like to work with an optimist!"

In fact he was happy to have the Australian on the team. The guy was smart, reliable, inventive and, he knew instinctively, regardless of whoever had hired him, the kind of man he could like and trust.

They were leaving the lagoon at midnight, racing for international waters to avoid interception and the inevitable questions from Romanian coastal patrols. At dusk the following day, O'Riley would approach to within a couple miles of the rig and offload the assault force before he changed course and headed back to the open sea.

But the forty-foot cruiser would have described three-fourths of a circle around the rig before then. So the main, sailboarding body of raiders, hopefully read by the rig's radar scanners as zigzagging bird flocks, would approach from different points of the compass.

Before that, the small, flat-bottomed dinghy slung athwart the cruiser's stern would have been lowered with Bolan and the explosives expert, Boris Levski, aboard. They would drift in as near to the platform as they dared—far nearer than O'Riley could go—and then slip overboard and repeat the Executioner's previous underwater exploit, silencing both frogman sentries and emerging to take the two ladders that led up onto the rig.

Stojkov, leading nine surfers, would skim in to join them and storm the upper decks. Levski himself would stay below to organize explosive packs that would blast the whole base to hell later.

The top deck would meanwhile have been attacked from the air.

Botev, the guerrillas' armorer, with three picked men, was to be hauled off the sea by the Fjord 40 in the manner of parachute water-skiers—but with modified delta wings instead of the usual rectangular canopies. Each of these men would carry an RPG-7 grenade launcher with one spare rocket grenade. Their specific task was to silence the rig's battery of six-inch naval guns—and any other target that could menace the invaders. "But for God's sake," Bolan emphasized, "lay off anything near those dummy storage tanks, or we'll be breathing Sarin for the rest of our lives."

"One minutes and a quarter, at a conservative estimate," O'Riley computed.

"Tell me something," Bolan said. It was late afternoon, and they were horsing around, waiting for night to fall. "Why do you and your family spell your name the way you do?"

"To distinguish us from the bloody O'Reillys, of course," the Australian replied with unanswerable Irish logic.

"I'm not in so many words accusing you of being a Christian," Bolan said, "but do you have...well, let's say a given name?"

O'Riley sparked off his characteristic grin. "That's affirmative, squire. But, look, you're not going to believe this."

"Try me."

"In my business, too!" The man who used smuggling as a cover for his undercover activities shook his head. "The name is Shamus!"

Later—they were trying out the communications equipment essential to the smooth running of his plan—Bolan tried again to get O'Riley to reveal precisely whom he was working for. The warrior liked to know on whose behalf he was risking his own life. But the guy piloting the cruiser was as evasive as ever.

"The Brits have this thing about sleeping dogs," he said.

"Even if they're the dogs of war?"

"Not your bag, sport, the repartee," O'Riley said. "You're dead sure this material scores under the ocean wave?"

"Affirmative."

Sophisticated electronic apparatus supplied by Brognola was to equip each of the raiders with the equivalent of a TV lapel mike. An earplug receiver attached to the sidepiece of night-vision goggles completed the two-way system, for split-second timing was essential if the assault was to succeed.

Bolan planned to silence the sentries first, so that no alarm from below could tip off the garrison when the surfers arrived. But Botev and his hang gliders must already have opened fire from above, diverting the defenders' attention from the lower deck, where the main attack would come.

The warrior himself, of course, would not be able to transmit while he was underwater. Everything, therefore, depended on accurate position reports from the other two teams, for it was not until he surfaced that Bolan could coordinate the action.

The oil rig was a smudge on the eastern horizon when the raiders crammed into the cruiser's small saloon for a final briefing. They wore neoprene wet suits, combat cosmetic darkened their faces, the goggles were pushed up on their foreheads.

"We can't expect surprise to be total," Bolan said. "They will surely have been told that the rat who supplied the American material and wised them up on the Ararat missile site has been liquidated. They must expect some kind of countermove, sometime. Especially as they know the place has been penetrated once already. But they won't know how much we know of their operation as a whole. They'll be on the alert—but they won't know what kind of reaction to expect."

"What kind of reaction can *we* expect?" one of the partisans asked. "Outside of the people actually on the rig, I mean."

"We can't expect to take out their transmitter before they make some kind of SOS call," Bolan said. "First off, they won't know the score—they'll simply report the platform is being attacked and ask for help."

"What can they call up?"

"Gunboats, corvettes, high-powered coastguard cutters, whatever. There's nothing within the immediate sea area, we know. But we have to act fast, so we can get the hell out before anything does show."

"Having killed the rig and scuppered the Sarin shells," O'Riley said. "Fear of them should at least keep you safe from air attack!"

"Unless they really are crazy," Bolan said somberly.

He checked over each man's equipment. The delta wing flyers, who would jettison their bazooka-style RPG-7s as soon as the second rocket grenade had been fired, were armed with Desert Eagle pistols. Everyone else, including

Bolan and Levski, would be carrying a Heckler and Koch G-11 caseless assault rifle.

These modernistic West German weapons, each toting one hundred rounds of special ammunition, were perfect for the job. The smooth plastic outer case gave total protection against rough handling, shocks, dirt and—most important of all—immersion. Each round was set in a solid block of propellant, so there were no used cartridges to clear and eject. With four times the firepower of the normal SMG, the soldier had no need to carry extra clips.

"You'll see," Bolan told the guerrillas when the guns were first unwrapped from their oiled-silk packaging, "that the pistol grip here is exactly at the point of balance. The carrying handle above it is also the optical sight. And apart from the muzzle and an outlet for clearing misfired rounds, there's not a single hole or protuberance over the entire damned casing, so you can't snag it on your webbing or rip your neoprene suit."

"That's the most streamlined weapon I ever saw!" Stojkov said admiringly as he hefted the ten-pound killer in his large, hairy hand.

"The rounds are small, though," Botev commented. "What caliber—"

"Four-point-seven millimeter," Bolan cut in. "They can penetrate a steel helmet at five hundred yards. A 3-round burst takes only ninety milliseconds to clear. Any other questions?"

"Yes," the armorer said, smiling. "How soon can you get me fifty of these babies?"

O'Riley approached the rig from the east, where the sky was darkest behind the cruiser. When he was two miles away, he swung back north toward the Caucasus, circling the platform westward until he finally shaped a course southwest, as if he was heading for Istanbul. Bolan and Stojkov had been offloaded in their dinghy at the starting point of the circuit and the surfers at different points on the north and western legs. They were to float, resting on the surfboards, until the dinghy had drifted near enough for Bolan and Levski to submerge, when the Executioner would transmit the "off" signal and they could climb up and hoist the sails. At the same time, O'Riley was to turn back and lift off the flyers one by one.

The sea was less choppy this time, the longer swells carrying the tide westward, scarcely ruffled by a breeze that was forecast to freshen after dark. Birds also appeared according to plan. Dense flocks of mallard, geese and other less identifiable species swerved left and right over the surface, just visible against the afterglow. Most of them took off eventually for the marshes on the flat parts of the Turkish coast, but some headed for the distant Danube delta, on the same course the sailboards would soon take.

More quickly than Bolan hoped for, the dinghy was carried toward the rig. How long did he dare to wait? How close could he get before he risked a shouted question, the beam of a searchlight probing the gloom?

The platform's riding lights gleamed more brightly as the darkness thickened. Bars of illumination streamed from the windows and doors of the mess hall and living quarters on the upper deck. A jangle of folk music from a radio or tape deck drifted over the water, together with the hum of male voices and an occasional laugh. Up above, the wavering flame that topped the stack licked the dark sky.

When the distance had shortened to a quarter of a mile, Bolan reckoned he had ridden the good-luck horse far enough; it was time to dismount. He nudged Levski. They clipped the sealed packages of Semtex explosive to their military webbing and strapped the assault rifles to their backs. Levski checked his detonators while the warrior opened the flat-bottomed dinghy's cocks. The sea welled up inside the hull until the small craft was waterlogged, with its gunwales awash. Bolan spoke softly into his mike. "Team One, submerging. Curtain up." He waited until his earplug receiver relayed Stojkov's gruff "Team Two. Accepted. Operative," and the Team Three acknowledgement spoken from somewhere over the horizon by O'Riley. Then he tapped the partisan's shoulder, and the two of them tipped backward into the swell and turned toward the rig.

For the first two hundred yards they swam on the surface, making scarcely a ripple as the flippers thrust them effortlessly forward. Then, fearful that a stray shaft of light could strike a reflection from the goggle glass, Bolan gave the signal as they submerged. There was a tiny low-power penlight with a red lens, strapped to the Executioner's ankle, that Levski could follow through the underwater darkness.

A mile away to the east, to the southeast, to the north, Stojkov and his nine-man fleet were afloat, each soldier upright and manhandling his sail as the sailboarders converged in broad sweeps on the rig.

Westward, O'Riley turned into the wind and coaxed the cruiser up to its full forty knots. On the line behind, Botev, encumbered by the heavy, modified hang glider on his back, went under three times before he could get up on his ski. But once the breeze got under the triangular sail, lift-off was almost immediate, and he soared into the sky, climbing with each updraft until he was one thousand feet above the sea and the twin white brush-strokes of the cruiser's bow wave only a pale smudge on the blackness below. He unbuckled the ski and let it fall, then spoke quietly into his mike: "Team Three, A. Calling B, C and D. Are you aloft and receiving me?"

"Aloft and receiving," the responses came at once from the guerrillas B and D. Then, a little later, "Yes. Climbing," from C.

Bolan and Levski were past the ring of mine cables, swimming at a depth of forty feet. Ahead of them the blackness gradually thinned until the water paled to a translucent pearl color. After his last visit, Bolan guessed, the storm-wave gap under the derricks on the lower deck must have been more brightly lit as a precaution. Shoals of small fish darted past him, and once he saw the shadowy bulk of a huge sturgeon against the faint trelliswork of the rig's substructure.

At first he thought the hand on his ankle was Levski's, and he turned his head, wondering whether the Bulgarian was in difficulties. But Levski's arms were wrapped around another black rubber shape, the two of them windmilling together in slow motion as the current carried them back into the darkness, away from the rig. The sentry grabbing Bolan's leg was feeling for a nerve grip, the fingers crawling like an iron spider toward the knee, finding it, to send a jolt of agony searing through his body as he rolled, somersaulting, towing the attacker slowly after him while he drew his knife from his belt.

Close combat under water has an unreal, almost dreamlike quality. A fighter's only purchase is against the body of his opponent, the flippers rule out kicking, and blows are slowed down so much by the resistance of the element that they become meaningless.

Bolan brought up his other knee, inserted the flipper heel under his assailant's chin and pushed him far enough away to break the grip. They floated apart, drifted together and for an instant remained face-to-face, the sentry's hostile brown eyes staring balefully through the faceplate of his mask into Bolan's cold blue ones.

Then the guy's left hand eeled forward through the water, the point of a knife slashing for the Executioner's breathing tube. Bolan arched his back, turning aside his head and catching the killer's wrist so that the blade missed the tube and grazed the facepiece. At the same time his own knife hand circled in to stab in his assailant's belly.

Twisting, the man escaped with a ripped wet suit and a scratch. His free hand arched in from nowhere and snatched away Bolan's mask.

Black skeins of blood marbled the water between them as Bolan felt the gush of salt water against his eyes and nose, biting hard on the breathing tube mouthpiece to roll again, kick upward and drag the man with him.

They grappled, struggling for advantage like dancers in some ritual aquatic ballet while the tide moved them westward.

The Bulgarian jackknifed, diving for Bolan's belly and groin. That was his mistake—the last he made. The warrior kicked backward, out of range, so that the killer passed beneath him. His knife hand swept around in a murderous sweep, encountered resistance, insisted and jerked free, having sliced through the attacker's breathing tube between the scuba tank and the nape of his neck.

A storm of air bubbles gurgled upward. Bolan sank, wrapping his arms around the stricken man's lower legs, holding him there until the jerking and twitching ceased and he could allow the drowned body to plane down to the seabed.

He swam back to the rig. On the way he saw a flippered black figure emerge from a dense cloud of blood. He stiffened, letting his feet sink downward, his hand on the knife hilt. But there was a weapon strapped to the diver's back, and he carried sealed packages strung around his waist. It was Levski, victorious after a battle with the second guard.

He gave Bolan the thumbs-up sign, and together they headed for the illuminated sector beneath the platform. Eight minutes later they surfaced by the iron ladder climbing one of the pontoon legs. Bolan sent out the signal at once: "Team One, surfacing. Come in Three and then Two."

He listened for the replies, then shrugged out of the scuba harness, handed his plastic explosive packages to Levski and rested on the lowest rung of the ladder, feeding back energy dissipated during the underwater fight and the swim subsequent without a mask.

The active part of the operation was about to start.

**22**

Aleksandar Botev soared alone in a world of silence broken only by an occasional flutter from the sail's trailing edge as the hang glider neared stalling speed when it turned back into the wind to maintain height. The offshore rig was a cluster of jeweled lights a thousand feet below him.

When Botev got the order to go in, he muttered a brief acknowledgement, working the control bar beneath the hang glider's A-frame to drop the nose and approach the platform in a long shallow spiral. Bar and harness had been specially modified to allow handling of the RPG-7, and Botev had used his armorer's skill to add further improvements, but it was still hellishly tricky maneuvering the fifteen-pound, three-foot-three-inch firing tube into position with one hand.

Wind sang past the sail as the speed increased, numbing the partisan's face and drying the tears blown back from the corners of his eyes. He shifted his position, lowering his legs with bent knees so that he could sight through the eyepiece of the grenade launcher canted forward over his right shoulder. The upper deck of the rig, spiny with cranes and winch gear and the dully gleaming barrels of the naval guns, grew large in the optical sight.

Sawing the control bar one-handed, Botev banked, dropped the wing's nose more steeply and swooped toward his target. The RPG-7's effective range was three hundred to five hundred yards. Given the lack of stability and a shifting firing position, Botev reckoned it would be smart to wait until the distance shorted to two hundred fifty. When the gun platforms with their raked-back shields filled most of the lens, he tightened his hold on the pistol grip and fired.

The launcher's ignition roar was stunning. Flame spit from the tube's open rear-end; the five-pound, pineapple-shaped grenade leaped from the muzzle and streaked for the rig, towing a fiery tail as the rocket motor blew open the stabilizing fins and powered the missile on its hellburst way.

The HEAT warhead struck the underside of one of the gun platforms with a vivid flash. The thunderclap of the explosion rolled across the sea. At once a second launcher, higher up on the far side of the rig, daubed a crimson streak across the dark sky. The second grenade burst between two gun barrels, buckling the shields, distorting breeches and destroying the turntable mechanism of one platform.

Not all of the glidermen were so fortunate. The guerrilla identified by the letter *C* never got his wing higher than eighty feet and came down in the sea halfway between the rig and the receding cruiser. The fourth man, acting too hastily, mishandled the tube and fired when it was pointing down. The backblast burned away half the fabric of the sail, and the glider, losing buoyancy, plunged into the sea. The guerrilla, with most of his bones broken, was trapped beneath the fabric that remained on the floating A-frame and drowned.

Deflected by the swell, the grenade bounced into the sky and self-destructed half a mile to the south.

On the rig there was pandemonium. Botev, wheeling on an updraft created by the platform itself, was reminded of an anthill stirred by a stick. Men poured out of every door and scurried in all directions. The warning Klaxon blared. He could hear a babble of voices, orders shouted through a bullhorn. And then, from the tiny plug in his own ear, the frantic voice of his remaining wingman: *"Team Three, B to A. Alert! The chopper . . . the chopper!"*

Botev swore. Banking again, he looked over his shoulder. The outrigged helipad on the far side of the rig was floodlit. The rotor blades above the bird had begun to re-volve. The men milling around on the upper deck were ready to fight, but they didn't know who they were fighting or where they were. The chopper with its searchlight would find out for them.

Wingman B was flying in the wrong direction—and once the helicopter was airborne, no hang glider was going to outmaneuver it. The responsibility was Botev's.

Wrestling the spare grenade, once he had unhitched it from his webbing, into position at the front of the tube was a bastard. He needed both hands. He let go of the bar. The wing yawed sickeningly, lost height, dropping toward the sea.

At last! Sweating, he left the warhead in place and yanked at the bar, pulling up the kite's nose. He was already lower than the pilot flame topping the flare stack. He craned his head, squinting through the optical sight. The image of the chopper zoomed in as the delta wing gained speed. The turbo whine climbed the scale; the machine was already lifting off. Botev fired the grenade.

A streak of flame. The dull shell-burst thump of a direct hit. The flash of the explosion eclipsed by a dazzling fire-ball that boiled up and spewed burning debris over the rig. Then the blazing wreck falling into the sea.

Botev swooped through the column of steam that marked the chopper's grave, leveled out on a perfect approach and unbuckled his harness to drop into the water fifty feet from the storm-wave gap. He swam quickly for the pool of light.

Here, too, there was frenzied activity, but it was more or-derly than the panic above—Bolan and his men knew where they were going and what they had to do.

For as soon as the first grenade exploded, Stojkov and his team flitted in from the dark, skimming the surface of the swell, skating under the platform from all directions. Step-ping off the sailboards, they swarmed up the iron ladders, unslinging the caseless assault rifles as they climbed. Stojkov himself was the first up, following close behind the Executioner, because it was vital to cross the lower deck and make it up the central core before the defenders tumbled to the fact that the real assault was from below.

They raced between the louvered turbines, past the powerboats in their davits, and on to the upper deck. At the stairhead they dropped down behind a cast-iron generator housing and readied their G-11s for short-burst firing.

The defenders, most of whom had crowded to the perimeter catwalk when the first grenade exploded, were now dashing back toward the center of the rig. At least two of the sailboards had been spotted as they swung in from the dark, and there had been several bursts of automatic fire before the officer with the bullhorn ordered the regrouping.

Bolan and the partisan opened fire at once, shooting down an alley between the fake drilling rig and a line of cabins used as living quarters. One man at least was hit and fell; the others ducked back out of the line of fire. A long volley sent slugs screaming off the iron casing that protected the invaders.

The sailboarders were now scrambling up from the ladder. Bolan located them in a rough circle around the stairhead with orders to fire only when they were sure of making a hit. The bullhorn bellowed. "He's ordering them to split into three groups and circle around behind us," Stojkov said.

At that moment there was a shout from beyond the central control cabin. Someone had seen the last hang glider silhouetted against the stars as it turned to tune in with the wingman's second grenade. SMGs and some heavier, large-bore automatic opened fire. A flash of light and a fiery arrow charted the course of the rocket grenade as it homed once more on the gun emplacements. The whole platform shook when the missile erupted.

Bolan spoke quickly into his mike. "Team One to cruiser. You can come in now. Naval guns neutralized."

"Willco," O'Riley's cheerful voice acknowledged.

The bullhorn bellowed again. "He's telling some of them to climb the cranes so they can fire down on us," Stojkov reported.

"We have to break out of here," Bolan said. "We're in a defensive position and we should be on the attack. Deploy your guys under covering fire, Vasil, while I take out the big-mouth."

Botev, his wet suit still cascading water, appeared at the top of the ladder. "They caught the last two surfers in," he told the partisan chief. "Simonov was killed. He's floating with the sail fifty yards out. Danski has a bullet in the left arm. He's with Levski down below."

"Right," Stojkov said. "Take three of these guys and flush anyone out from the false storage tanks. Watch where you shoot, because that's where the gas missiles are. I'll take two more and circle the rig, bringing any of the bastards down from the cranes. You two—" he turned to the remaining guerrillas "—stay here and cover us while we go. Stop anyone going below. Levski needs time to work on the explosives."

"And report every move on the intercom," Bolan said. "Stalking our own guys we can do without."

Botev saw two shadowy figures at the far end of the alley and blasted off two thunderous shots from his Desert Eagle, then, while the defenders dropped out of sight, he led his three men at a run to the far side of the drilling rig. They vanished around the corner of the control cabin in the direction of the catwalk.

The two men left by the generators hosed a stream of lead left and right as Stojkov and his companions crawled away toward the cranes. Bolan, on elbows and knees, wormed his way behind the mess hall.

On the far side he saw the man with the bullhorn. He was standing in a command post, a kind of crow's nest halfway up to the outrigged helipad. He occupied a shadowed position from which he could look down on most of the deck, and certainly on all the alleys and the perimeter catwalk.

Bolan might have missed him if he hadn't raised the loud-hailer and barked another order.

The order was followed by the longest exchange of automatic fire yet. Someone cursed. A man screamed and then choked into silence. Blue smoke drifted beneath the arcs lighting the control bunker. But that same illumination reflected a sudden bright gleam from the horn's metal handle as it was lowered...and the Executioner was on his feet with his Beretta unleathered and the barrel arrowing toward the pad.

The 4.7 mm slugs from the H&K assault rifle would have been just as deadly, but Bolan wanted the knockdown impact of the 9 mm pistol's skullbusters.

His choice paid off. The guy swung around and raised his own gun as Bolan fired, taking two of the Beretta's three rounds high up in the chest before he could squeeze his trigger. Flung backward by the lethal force of the bullets, he tipped over the hip-high guardrail surrounding the command post and fell. His body was caught among the stays and girders supporting the pad, but the bullhorn fell into the sea.

Now none of the defenders could take his place and coordinate.

Bolan dropped and rolled violently away as a hellfire cannonade spit his way from each side of the bunker. Huge splinters pricked up from the deck. The ironwork sang. He rose to his knees behind a winch and shot out both the arcs. With less light and no central command, the defenders would be at a disadvantage—the assault team could at least keep in contact by radio.

On his feet now and running, Bolan headed for the corner of the bunker from which the heaviest fire had come, spraying 4.7 mm death ahead of him. The Bulgarian gunners, seeing the tall black figure pounding their way with his sci-fi weapon flaming, broke and fled. Bolan blew away two of them, saw a third stumble, fall and then drag himself out of range behind a cabin. The G-11 bucked and shuddered in his hands, directing a deathstream toward another group creeping out of a pool of light from lamps still burning on the far side of the rig.

Then abruptly he held his fire. Several of Stojkov's men were racing down an aisle between stacks of machinery to attack the runaways hand to hand. Bolan had already dusted two of them. He turned his back on the swearing, shouting, struggling crowd and raced for the radio cabin.

It was above the control bunker. Access to the higher level was via an iron companionway. Bolan flattened himself to this and began inching upward. Over the sounds of battle and sporadic bursts of automatic fire he could hear the radio operator frenziedly gabbling. And closer, inside his ear, the voices of his own teams.

"Three. Wingman B. Have swum to rig. Am coming up."

"Team Two. E." That was Stojkov. "Cranes now free of snipers."

"Two. H and K. Two clients holed up northeast perimeter. Flushing them out." And then a burst of gunfire.

"Two. F. Still guarding central stairway but K hit in throat. Replacement needed if position is to be held."

Bolan breathed into his own mike: "Team One. Command to F. Wingman B mounting, will reinforce. Do you read me, B?"

"Loud and clear," the last of the hang glidermen replied. "Willco."

The Executioner was at the top of the companionway. Warily, he rose upright and peered through the glass paneling the top half of the door. There were cans clamped to the radio operators head, a mike sprouted from his chest, his face was livid in the greenish light cast by the dials on the transmitter. Otherwise the cabin was in darkness.

The man was facing the door across the top of the transmitter.

Bolan dropped out of sight . . . but not quickly enough. The guy was on the ball. And he was fast. He had snatched a small automatic from the table and fired while Bolan was still a silhouette. The window erupted, drowning the sharp crack of the gun in the smashing of glass. Razored shards showered Bolan's head and shoulders as he crouched, ripping the wet suit and slashing his cheek.

The automatic fired again, half a dozen rapid shots that drilled the door and let faint green shafts of light probe the darkness.

Bolan slid down the ladder. There was no way he could bust in there and win, not with the guy positioned as he was. He sighed, reaching for the frag grenades clipped to his webbing. Hefting one in his right hand, he dropped the safety spoon and lobbed the grenade through the broken window.

The operator was ready for it, too. Bolan wasn't surprised, since he knew the man was fast. The grenade was scooped up and flung through the far window almost before it hit the floor. There was a bright orange flash over the sea and a cracking detonation that left the Executioner's ears ringing.

What the operator wasn't ready for was the second grenade that was tossed in half a second after the first. This time the explosion was louder, more stunning; the flash printed the windows of the radio cabin against the night. There was no further transmission to Perestrek 32.

"Team One Command. Radio out," Bolan reported. He dropped off the ladder and ran toward a fusillade of shots from different caliber weapons centered on the area between the central stairway and the drilling rig. Several bodies were sprawled on the wooden decking in front of the generator sheltering the partisans F and B.

In the distance, a man dropped from the roof of a cabin and sprinted toward the two guerrillas holding the stairhead. Bolan wasted him with a long burst. He whirled around, hearing Stojkov shout. The partisan chief was reloading his Desert Eagle... and immediately above him, clinging to one of the derrick arms, a hardman in combat fatigues was drawing a bead with a long-barreled Mauser pistol. Bolan snatched his Beretta from the quick-draw rig and loosed off two bursts in 3-shot mode as his hand flashed from his left shoulder to the full stretch of his arm. One at least scored, for the gunman uttered a high, keening cry and tumbled to the deck. The shot from the Mauser plowed into the floor.

Stojkov's eyes were blazing above the unruly beard. He jumped to the mouth of an alley and blasted two rounds from the .44-caliber cannon. In the darkness something stumbled and fell.

Bolan saw movement on the other side of the flare stack. He raised the G-11—it was a long shot—and ripped out a volley that punctured the stack and blew out from behind it a guy in a long-peaked fatigue cap who had been about to throw a grenade. The killer fell on the small bomb. Bolan winced at the muffled blast. In the light of one of the remaining lamps he saw on the pale wall of the refectory a splash of blood that resembled the five fingers of a gigantic hand.

Two more explosions near the far catwalk shuddered the framework of the rig, and then the warrior saw out of the corner of his eye a shadow move that shouldn't have moved. Once more he swung into a combat crouch. The movement came from in front of the generator. One of the men sprawled there had raised himself on one elbow, drawn a Stechkin automatic from beneath his body and aimed it at Botev, who had appeared with one of his team from between the fake storage tanks. The Russian gun belched fire before Bolan could bring his assault rifle to bear on the assassin. Botev fell with a bullet through his heart.

Stojkov swung around with a roar of rage, but Bolan had already nailed the killer. A quick burst had pulverized the top of his head, leaving a fan of brain tissue gleaming on the deck.

The two big men, the partisan and the Executioner, stared at each other across the littered floor of the rig. Smoke wreathed slowly in the lamplight. The acrid stench of cordite stung their nostrils. And suddenly they realized the platform was totally silent.

It was over. There were no more fences to jump.

The Bulgarian released a great gust of laughter and clapped Bolan on the shoulder. "Now is the time for the big cleanup!" he cried.

The partisans had been merciless: they had taken no prisoners and there were no wounded—every one of the thirty-odd members of the garrison was dead. The attackers had lost heavily, too. Botev was dead, the man shot through the throat had died, one of the wingmen was drowned and another lost at sea, a sailboarder had been wasted. And in addition to the surfer shot in the arm, there was another walking wounded on the upper deck.

This left Stojkov, Levski and six able-bodied guerrillas to help Bolan destroy the rig.

They had to work fast. If the Perestrek bosses were sending choppers to check out the score, they might have a couple hours, but there could be gunboats or other naval units within one hour's sailing time.

One of Stojkov's men had found an infantryman's portable flamethrower. With the reservoir strapped to his back, he burned off all the insignia tagging the jeeps, the M-548 carrier and the launchers as U.S. material. Boots and uniforms were piled on the helipad and sent up in smoke. The GI helmets were dropped into the sea. "We'll leave the TOW antitankers in place," Bolan said. "They'll help the blast when she goes up."

After that they started in on the heavy stuff. The twelve Sarin warheads in their safety case had to be transported with immense care to one of the cranes, from which, once O'Riley showed, they would be lowered to the cruiser. The four KrisKraft were incinerated in their davits by the flamethrower. The vehicles were pushed over the catwalk and into the sea. The Lance propulsion units were left with the TOW missiles.

The cruiser nosed in beneath the storm-wave gap when they were halfway through, and tied up to one of the pontoon legs. Loading the warheads brought beads of sweat to Bolan's upper lip. By the time the crate was safely stowed in the cruiser's cockpit, O'Riley's hands were shaking.

"We couldn't just bury the damned things here?" Stojkov asked.

Bolan shook his head. "According to the charts, it's only fifty meters here. They could get rolled by the tide, or heavy seas could break up the crate—anything could happen. But five miles to the north the seabed plummets to more than seven thousand feet. We'll sink them separately out there . . . and hope to hell there isn't an earthquake."

The Bulgarians were taking a launch moored below the rig to sail home, and Bolan was going with O'Riley to the Turkish coast. "What you have done for the honor of my country," Stojkov said, shaking hands before they embarked, "will not be forgotten, my friend."

"For the honor of all decent men," Bolan said.

"Perhaps we shall meet again? If so, I should be happy."

"It's always possible," the Executioner said. "There's still a hell of a lot of Methyl Phosphonyl Difluoride unaccounted for!"

And the fight against the kind of people who would use it, he might have added, never ends.

Levski had distributed the Semtex skillfully, each package designed to destroy a load-bearing girder or stay. "But I've left us enough time to stand off at least a mile," he said, "because when she does blow it's going to create a minor tidal wave."

The blowing was deceptive. It started with tongues of fire shooting skyward from beneath the flat-topped, spiny silhouette of the rig in a series of small explosions, continued with the ruddy flickering of light on the underside of scudding clouds that had blown up from the east, included a few seconds later the rumble of multiple detonations rolling across the swell . . . and then suddenly turned dramatic.

The darkness split open in a gigantic holocaust of flame. Blazing fireballs arrowed away to right and left and shot up to pierce the clouds. The thunderclap of sound, when it reached them, cracked their ears.

"Liquid fuel propellant always helps," Bolan commented, lifting field glasses to his eyes. The night-vision lenses showed him the entire superstructure, no longer supported by the buckling pontoon legs, tilting slowly over toward the sea. And then, when the huge gas cylinder fueling the flare pilot exploded, the rig plunged beneath the surface in a hellish cauldron of white water and steam.

When the waves racing outward from the catastrophe at last subsided, all that remained of the offshore rig were four mangled steel uprights projecting through an island of floating debris.

"There's no time like show time," said O'Riley. "What's our encore?"

"Writing a press release to explain to the world what happened," Bolan said. "Including an explanation of the bullet-riddled bodies. But maybe we should leave that to Department C.4."

When they had buried the Sarin warheads to the Executioner's satisfaction, O'Riley put about and set a course for the Turkish coast—passing a long way to the west of the drowned rig, where four helicopters and a couple of floatplanes were now circling like angry flies. Once they were safely out of the area, at O'Riley's suggestion, Bolan turned in.

He awoke, lying on one of the bunks in the saloon, with sunlight slanting through a porthole. The cruiser was rocking gently on the swell. The diesels were silent. The only sound was the lapping of waves against the hull.

Bolan flung back the covers and sprang to his feet. He went into the cabin. It was empty. So was the head. There was nobody in the cockpit. O'Riley wasn't on the bridge.

The enigmatic Australian had vanished.

So had the inflatable rubber dinghy normally stored in back of the cockpit. The Turkish coast was two miles away.

Bolan returned to the saloon. His camera case was there, along with his weapons, his accreditations, his ID documents. Propped up on the table was a card bearing Shamus O'Riley's name and an address in Beirut. There was no telephone number.

Beside the card was a gift-wrapped package. On the back of the card the Australian had written: *To freshen you up when you wake.*

Bolan unwrapped the package. Inside was a squat fifteen-fluid-ounce after-shave bottle from Lenthéric of Paris. The label proclaimed the trademark "Tweed."

He removed the stopper with its square teak top, and sniffed. The flask was filled with Scotch whiskey.

**DICK STIVERS**

Action writhes in the reader's own streets as Able Team's Carl ''Ironman'' Lyons, Pol Blancanales and Gadgets Schwarz make triple trouble in blazing war. Join Dick Stivers's Able Team—the country's finest tactical neutralization squad in an era of urban terror and unbridled crime.

''Able Team will go anywhere, do anything, in order to complete their mission. Plenty of action! Recommended!''
—*West Coast Review of Books*

Able Team titles are available wherever paperbacks are sold.

GOLD EAGLE

AT-1R-A

# Do you know a real hero?

At Gold Eagle Books we know that heroes are not just fictional. Everyday someone somewhere is performing a selfless task, risking his or her own life without expectation of reward.

Gold Eagle would like to recognize America's local heroes by publishing their stories. If you know a true to life hero (that person might even be you) we'd like to hear about him or her. In 150-200 words tell us about a heroic deed you witnessed or experienced. Once a month, we'll select a local hero and award him or her with national recognition by printing his or her story on the inside back cover of THE EXECUTIONER series, and the ABLE TEAM, PHOENIX FORCE and/or VIETNAM: GROUND ZERO series.

Send your name, address, zip or postal code, along with your story of 150-200 words (and a photograph of the hero if possible), and mail to:

LOCAL HEROES AWARD
Gold Eagle Books
225 Duncan Mill Road
Don Mills, Ontario
M3B 3K9
Canada